JACOB I LOVED

JACOB I LOVED

A NOVEL OF THE MYSTERY OF ELECTION

BY RON DURHAM

Higley

Publishing Corporation, Inc.
Jacksonville, Florida
800–842–1093

ISBN: 1-886763-03-8

Printed in the U.S.A.
by

Eerdmans Printing Company, Inc.
231 Jefferson Avenue, S.E.
Grand Rapids, Michigan 49503

DEDICATION

To my wife Faye, whose name—and life—mean "faith."

PROLOGUE

Onesimus, slave of Philemon, to my master:

You ask me of the ways of God, my lord? How He may choose the base of the world to exalt, the unworthy to receive honor and those despised of men to love and to be the bearers of His love?

I can only tell you a tale.

And why, my lord Philemon, do I begin with a story instead of a treatise on philosophy? Because my lord has asked of me something too high for the mind to reach without the stepping stone of the heart. And it is in the stories of the faith we share that God has knit together the heart and the mind.

Else I had as well try to tell the origin of the east wind, or how to enter the storehouse of the snows, or the way of a man with a maid! Indeed, what can I, who first learned of the one true God through you, my master, tell you of His ways? And even though I knew, what right have I to teach my teacher, from whom I fled those years ago?

You ask, I know, because of my devotion to the books, and because I am teacher over my lord's household. And I must make some reply out of gratitude for being reinstated in your house, and for the intercession of our beloved brother Paul.

I would not blaspheme the Name by pretending to explain His ways with the wisdom of Plato or Aristotle. Yet, in the stories, there is a way of knowing that is beyond the understanding. And these, my lord, I delight to retell, in the fashion I have received them in the Holy Scriptures, in the other writings and in the tales handed down from the memories of the ancients. In the telling of the tales, it may be that, as we better see a target at night by looking a little aside instead of staring at it full face, God's ways are also better seen in telling stories to the heart than in expounding philosophies to the mind.

The desert queen Rebekah, still beautiful despite the crown of silver hair framing the face under her veil, edged discreetly to the flap of the tent to look in on the all-male banquet. Her husband, Isaac, was at the center of the low table, ensconced on fleecy pillows and enjoying himself immensely.

"More venison" he shouted, although the voice that would have been a roar a few years ago now cracked from age and the desert's inexorable parching. After all, Isaac had been a part of the arid landscape for a century and a half. His white hair had thinned to a wispy halo, and his skin was hardly more supple than a badly-tanned wineskin.

"More venison!" echoed Esau, Isaac's firstborn, grinning with satisfaction—for the deer had been brought down by his own bow. Ruddy and robust, with curly, auburn hair cascading richly over the sweaty face of an outdoorsman, Esau had turned many a Semite girl's head.

Reaching over two large cousins, Esau seized a rump roast by the leg bone still extending from it, and handed the whole ham to his father. The seams in Isaac's dark face deepened into fissures as he laughed aloud, black eyes still able to flash their pleasure. The dozen men reclining around the low table roared their own delight, apparently sensing in the old man's virile joy some promise of their own longevity.

The laughter of one man at the table was more forced. Jacob, Esau's twin, but by a few minutes the second son of Isaac and Rebekah, tried valiantly to join in the merriment. As he had been second in birth, he was also second to Esau in build—slighter, decidedly more delicate and sensitive in both body and mind, though darkly handsome and well formed. Whereas Esau's eyes were hazel, as befitted his ruddy complexion, Jacob's eyes smoldered dark and beautiful in their own way, but he had never been as attractive to young women as Esau because of his natural shyness.

"Here, father," Jacob said eagerly. "Oil the red meat with the green olive!" He handed Isaac a bowl laden with fat, oil-rich olives as large as the end of his thumb, the fruit of trees Jacob managed to cultivate near the spring the clan used as a base from which to graze their herds.

"Yes, yes—the olives, my son," Isaac said. "But it is this red meat from the hand of your brother—this is the real *lechem*, the solid food that keeps a man's juices as potent as the young!" Again the men around the table burst into raucous laughter at old Isaac's joke on himself.

The olives sat untouched.

Peeking around the opening of the tent, Rebekah alone saw that Jacob reddened, even under his sunbrowned and naturally swarthy skin. Although Jacob had always been a distant second in his father Isaac's favor, he was Rebekah's favorite. So close were they that at his blushing she could feel her own face flush, too, and she sucked in her breath in involuntary identification with his pain.

It had ever been so. As an infant, it had been Esau whom Isaac would pick up and nestle in his arms in the evening, after coming in from overseeing his shepherds. He would actually coo to the child with a tenderness that was uncharacteristic of these rough, nomadic men.

As a boy, it was Esau whom Isaac entrusted with errands to the men in the fields. He was a boisterous lad, reaching puberty prematurely and boasting more hair on his chest and arms as a teenager than many men had at forty.

Jacob, on the other hand, was quiet and sensitive. On the one hand he would rather stay in and around his mother's cook tent than chase about the fields in the blistering Palestinian sun. On the other, he looked with longing at the camaraderie between his father and brother. Theirs was a small club in which he was tacitly forbidden membership.

Suddenly Jacob arose from the table, whirled on his heel and strode from the tent, head down to hide his hurt—and almost ran over his mother.

"Jacob, my son," she began.

"Leave me, Mother!" Jacob snapped.

"But Jacob—." Rebekah put her hand to her mouth to stifle a gasp, half of hurt and half of sympathy. She would wait. After his rage subsided, she would have a story to tell her son. It was time for him to hear the story of his birth. But for now, Jacob stormed into the darkness that impinged on the camp. Rebekah covered her face with her veil and slipped away to her sleeping tent to lie awake and worry, and to wonder.

CHAPTER 1

And why, my lord Philemon, do I begin with the story of Jacob? It would be easier to tell of one who enjoys the favor of men—easy enough then to see why he is favored of God. It would be impossible to look into this mystery through the glass of Job, for being graced with the election to suffer is a matter yet more hidden than that of being chosen for glory.

I will therefore tell my lord the story of Jacob, third patriarch from Abraham. Jacob the supplanter, the deceiver, Jacob the devious and the cunning; yet Jacob beloved of God, chosen to head the family of Him who cannot deceive. For in the story of Jacob are hidden the jewels of wisdom my lord seeks. It is the story of one who was skilled in the cunning and trickery of men, yet was chosen to bear witness to the guileless Truth of God.

It is this Jacob who wrested the birthright from his brother, yet was chosen to bear the birthright of the Promised Land to the Twelve Tribes of Israel. It is Jacob who wrestled with God, yet was elected to so submit to His will that he would be the channel of blessing for the nations. He whose soul was once in darkness was selected to father the people who would bring light to the nations.

My lord surely understands that I cannot fathom all this. But I can tell the stories as they were told to me, in faith that gazing at the deeds of God is better than boasting of understanding His ways.

Two thousand years after the creation of the earth, as the Hebrews reckon the years, all the lands of the earth were in turmoil. Earthquakes in the Great Sea had brought the sea-trading Minoans to their knees, and their Mother Goddess could not lift them up. The rulers of the 13th Dynasty in Misrayim, which is Egypt, or the Two Lands, were shaken by revolution in the Lower Kingdom; and neither the god Amon nor Osiris could steady their tempest-tossed ships of state.

In the land of Babel, it was near the time of the great king Hammurabi, who had struggled to enforce his new law in the land of Mesopotamia; but neither Marduk nor Ba'al could give the people a heart to submit to the law.

Our father Abraham was dead, and his son Isaac would soon breathe his last. Add to all this: Isaac's son Jacob was seen early to be lacking in scruples. But the Master of the Universe is greater than all the gods of the nations. In Him there was no turmoil nor shadow of turning. He saw in this one, this Jacob, more than the eye of man could see; and He loved him. This is Jacob's story; and by God's grace, though I am the chief of sinners, it may also be mine.

The sand was cold as Jacob threw himself to his knees behind a dune, but in his agony of soul he did not notice. More than kneeling before any god, he pled his destiny to the black sky. If the gods cared, or if the High God of whom Isaac so often spoke really saw, would they not already have intervened? So instead of a prayer, there came from Jacob a deep groaning that began with a rumble from the hollowness of his heart and ended in an anguished but inarticulate cry. Black-bearded face lifted to the skies, Jacob simply bellowed.

Yet there was a language behind the unformed words. Is it my fate always to be pushed aside by my father? By what right does my brother, who is only slightly my elder, insinuate his way into father's favor? What have I done that I cannot please him, or neglected to do that I might win his regard? Is there no feat of bravery or skill or even cookery with which to win a smile of approval from the old man?

Finally the words came, but in the form of curses. He called on El Shaddai, the mighty God of power, and also on Orion in the heavens and Amon in the south. He directed his helpless rage to whatever ba'als might be in the Canaanite desert, and to Marduk to the north, to the gods of the mountains and of the Great sea—all the deities Jacob knew he named, not in a plea for them to intervene, but in anger and bitterness shouting down curses on themselves by their own names until he fell face down on the cold sand, hoarse and exhausted, finally weeping huge, dry, heaving sobs into the unanswering desert night.

Rebekah loved this place, Beer-sheba, "well of the oath," so named by Isaac in a peace treaty with the king of nearby Gerar. Here at the north of the desert Negeb, the well's pure, cold artesian waters colored the campsite a rich green in deep contrast with the dry ochres of the surrounding plain—although even there enough grass and hardy shrubs provided grazing for herds.

The place was rich with *ruach* and *shekinah*, the mysterious presence of divinities. Isaac's father had settled here for a time; and it was here that he had distinguished again the voice of El Shaddai, the High God who had called him when he lived in faraway Ur, from among the myriad lesser gods that populated the place.

But such history and mystery were far from Rebekah's thoughts as she drew the cheeses from the cold depths of the *beer*, or well. It would be a simple, cold breakfast. The men were sleeping off their overindulgence in the night's revelry; Rebekah had not slept at all. She was removing bread from its close wrapping of soft lamb's skin when Jacob came up to warm by the fires.

He had slept fitfully, the night's anguish still showing in the dark rings under his eyes and in his downward gaze. Although he was in his mid-30s, Jacob still had a dependent son's need to be with his mother frequently. And he was anxious this morning to make amends for his rudeness last night. Rebekah eased his awkwardness by speaking first.

"You slept, my son?"

"Some, yes. Mother—I spoke so…well, last night I was—I was so—."

"Hush, my son. Say no more. I know well what boils up in your heart when your father—." She stopped, not wanting to grant validity to Isaac's favoritism by putting it into words. Perhaps she also knew instinctively that speaking of it would indict herself for her own preference for Jacob over Esau.

Rebekah handed her son a piece of hard bread left over from the banquet, and a chunk of goat's cheese. "We bake later today," she said apologetically.

"This will do," said Jacob. "I am not hungry."

"I would speak to you about a matter," his mother began. "It is something I have never told you because I felt it would only make matters worse with your brother and your father. But last night—seeing you—." She again caught her breath, recalling Jacob's rejection.

"It's all right, Mother," Jacob said. What good would it do to speak of it? He crunched the hard bread disconsolately.

"No," Rebekah said firmly. "I must speak of it. It may be that El can console you with what I will tell you, even when you can find no consolation from your father."

El, Jacob's mind echoed. What power did He have that Jacob had not cut himself off from in his tirade against the gods last night?

"There was a sign from El at your birth," Rebekah continued. She straightened up from tending to the fire, arching backward to stretch tired muscles.

"A sign?" Jacob repeated, warming to the story with the natural fascination of one hearing about his childhood, the stories sounding vaguely familiar in part, but also as though they were about someone else, perhaps a cousin or a friend.

"You know that Esau is the firstborn," Rebekah said, avoiding Jacob's searching eyes. "But there is more to the story—there was more to the birthing."

"What more could there be?" Jacob asked innocently. Esau was born, then I was born. The gods either had it planned or they cared not."

Rebekah always winced at the way her sons continued to speak as though the gods were as real as the great God, Elohim. But she would not be distracted from her story.

"Yes, Esau was born first. And believe me I was glad for either of you to see the light of day. I despaired for my life, carrying the two of you."

"For my part, I am sorry," he said, half jesting, hoping to break his mother's heavy mood.

Unsmiling, Rebekah again refused to follow another path in the conversation. "The two of you did not wait to be born to start fighting," she continued." There was warfare in my womb. In my pain and desperation I sought the High God El."

"And?" asked Jacob.

"And I received a strange answer to my supplication."

Jacob looked at the ground again. He never knew what to make of it when people claimed to hear an invisible god. His mother went on.

"The God El said to me: 'Two nations are in your womb, and two peoples born of you shall be divided; the one shall be stronger than the other...'"

"Cease!" Jacob interrupted, bolting to his feet and throwing the crust of bread violently into the fire. "It is bad enough that I live in my brother's shadow, he the strong one and I supposedly the weak. Would you worsen my anguish by telling me it is the will of El?"

"Wait, my son!" Rebekah protested, looking anxiously full into her son's face. "There is more. The word of El was also"—she paused for effect—"'The elder shall serve the younger'!"

At first Jacob did not catch the significance of what she said, so angry was he at the direction the oracle had at first taken.

"What are you saying?" he asked.

"I am saying that your brother Esau, he who is the firstborn of my twins, is destined to serve his younger brother." Rebekah's words tumbled over in a rush of emotion that overwhelmed careful speech. "I am saying that you are 'the stronger' in the eyes of El Shaddai—the very God of your father Isaac and his father Abraham. I am saying that no matter how your father may favor your brother, our Father El favors you!"

Jacob's jaw went slack as he looked uncomprehendingly at his mother. He simply had no mental container adequate to carry this new piece of information.

"What—how can this be?" he finally stammered.

"How?" Rebekah repeated. "What is *how* when we speak of the ways of Yahweh?* Who knows how or why? All I know is what the Voice said...and what I saw."

Author's note: Yahweh and its shortened form, Yah, are generally considered to be God's personal name, in contrast to the more generic El and Elohim—terms that are often used interchangeably with Yahweh, even though they may also refer to the gods worshiped by pagan peoples. Exodus 6:3 indicates that the divine name Yahweh was first revealed to Moses, who lived some 400 years after the time of Jacob. Yet the name not only appears regularly in the biblical material about Jacob, but as early as Genesis 2:4, and in non-biblical sources that may be much older. Perhaps the Exodus passage means that the real significance of the name was not made known until Moses' day. The narrative here assumes, with the text of Genesis, that the bare name, if not its deepest meaning, was known by the patriarchs.

Now here was something Jacob could perhaps grasp. "You not only heard all this...it was confirmed with a sign—something you could see?" he asked.

"A true sign," his mother nodded solemnly. "It is true enough that your brother was born first. But a strange thing happened as he was being delivered. A tiny little hand—your hand, my son—was holding tightly to Esau's heel. It was as though you were saying, 'Wait for me, wait for me, my brother! You are to serve me, by the will of God. Let me be first!'" Rebekah's eyes were moist as the emotion of the event, so long ago, reasserted itself in her heart.

Oddly, Jacob laughed. "So that is the sign!" he shouted, throwing back his head. "Hanging on for dear life, was I?"

Rebekah's own mood lightened, but she still said firmly, "You were giving notice that you would take Esau's place as the first-born."

"But that—." The dawn of understanding broke over Jacob's face. "That is the source of my name! Y'qov—'He who takes by the heel'!"

"You might have guessed," his mother replied with a smile. "Why else would we have so named you?"

"I supposed it was—I don't know," said Jacob, shrugging his shoulders and pacing up and down before the fire. "I never gave it that much thought. Some names are just names. But—hmmm—Jacob," he said slowly, with new awareness. "He who grabs by the heel. He who takes the place of. He who supplants. I like it, Mother!"

He took Rachel by her gnarled hand and put his lips to it gently. "You know the pain I have always felt...how I have never been able to win Father's approval. You told me this to ease the pain, didn't you?"

"That is a part of it, my son," Rebekah said tenderly. "For the pain, and for the sake of the man you are yet to be, by the grace of God."

She stood back, hands on broad hips and head cocked, looking at Jacob as though looking at a god. "I wanted you to know that there is more to you than your father can see. I did not want you to despair of being more than that. I wanted you to hear what I heard from Yahweh Himself. That you have been—what shall I say? That you are a chosen one, and that because you have been looked on with favor, you have a high road to travel, and great deeds to do, and—." She stopped, unaccustomed to such long speeches.

As for Jacob, he walked away from the fires that morning looking again at the sky, as he had the night before, but seeing this time its height and depth instead of its blackness, and offering up to it a lilting shepherd's tune hummed gently instead of curses shouted hoarsely.

But underneath the tune were rustlings of unrest. *If I am "the Supplanter" by the will of El,* Jacob thought, *what shall I do to assert His will and assume what is rightfully mine?*

CHAPTER 2

Esau, restless and impatient after only two days at his father's camp, struck out across the rocky desert before daylight. His five-foot bow was slung over his back and his throwing stick tucked under a broad, leather girdle. A goatskin flask of water and a bag of bread and cheese were slung over his other shoulder. For warmth in the early morning desert air he had thrust his huge arms into the slits of a sheepskin mantle—although in the dim, pre-dawn light an observer would have been hard pressed to tell where the man's hairy arms ended and the sheepskin began. Loose at the bottom, the garment flowed freely behind Esau as he strode strongly across the flinty hillsides, glad to be alone and in the wilderness.

While he reveled in the deference his father Isaac paid him on his infrequent visits to camp, it could not long allay Esau's discomfort at being around so many people. Better, for him, the wild hills and the hunt. Something untamed deep within his soul clamored for release, and it could be satisfied only when his arrow pierced an antelope or boar, or his throwing stick crushed the skull of a badger or hare. His kills were not only for food; often he was driven to conquer the wildness within by violently striking an equally wild creature without.

By the time the sun was a half-hour above the horizon it was warm enough for Esau to shrug his arms out of the woolly cape and thrust it through the belts and straps of the supplies girdling his shoulders. Already he had walked what would have been a half-day's journey for ordinary men, yet his pace was quickening instead of slackening: he was returning to his element. Whatever would he do, he wondered, when his father died and he, Esau, was expected, as firstborn son, to assume responsibility for the family? His ruddy brow furrowed as he contemplated the awful fate of tending to his mother and brother and cousins and the rest of the growing clan.

Even less could Esau imagine being the semi-nomadic band's spiritual leader. As firstborn, he would also be in charge of the family rituals that were to ensure fertile wombs for the sheep and goats, and enough rainfall for pasturage. Oddly, he was more familiar with the routine as practiced by the Philistines and other Canaanites he encountered on his hunting expeditions. Their gods were usable, and locatable. A figurine of a ba'al packed in a food sack could be transported wherever the hunt led, and had been known to yield fat kills. But this Yahweh whom his father Isaac revered—how could one use a god he could not see? And how could one live comfortably serving a god who claimed to be able to see and judge men's thoughts as well as their deeds? Esau shuddered involuntarily.

But the wealth—now there was a benefit of being firstborn that was not to be considered lightly. As he had winced at the thought of serving an unseen god, Esau now shuddered with a little wave of delight. With twice the amount of inheritance his brother would receive, he could advance a scheme that had long intrigued him. His hunting forays were invariably limited by small settlements of Philistines scattered throughout the land. Esau had long dreamed of marshalling a force of mercenaries to drive the Philistine and other, smaller Canaanite peoples from the land. His bronze face broke into a grin as the idea grew within. Perhaps it would not be long until his father, weakened with age, rewarded him not merely with the status of favorite son, but with the ultimate gift of death, with its resulting benefits to the firstborn.

Suddenly Esau's fantasy was interrupted by a faint odor on the desert air, a scent that was growing increasingly heavy and hot. He instinctively crouched, nostrils flaring in an effort to identify the smell and locate its origin. Wood smoke. A Philistine war party? Another hunter? His keen eyes squinted as he spotted a thin wisp of blue smoke curl from a ravine not thirty strides ahead. Crouching even lower, Esau crept silently toward a little knoll in order to spy on whoever had built the cookfire. He pressed his food-bag, waterskin and bow and arrows close, to silence their clatter.

His stealth was rewarded with more than he could have bargained for. From his sly perch on the little hill he could see a maiden—Philistine, he guessed—sitting by a small fire. She was only half-dressed, looking at her reflection in a tiny pool of rainwater and dew and combing her long, black tresses. Although it was virtually unheard-of for a woman to wander off on her own, Esau's huntsman's eyes noted the bronze dagger and the staff, heavy enough for an effective weapon, both within the girl's easy reach. Quickly he scanned the horizon for signs of her companions. Seeing nothing, he stood up boldly and gazed frankly on the woman from the safety of his vantage point.

Esau stood there openly for two or three minutes before the woman, sensing that she was not alone, looked up. Surprisingly, she did not start with fear or reach for her weapons.

"Ho, Philistine maid," Esau finally said calmly, speaking in a Philistine dialect. The arrogant half-smile of one in total control flickered across his face.

The woman did not reply, but stood up slowly, covering herself unhurriedly with the top of the garment she had lowered while grooming her hair.

"Do you not speak the language of Ashdod or Gath?" Esau asked.

Returning his gaze with equal arrogance, the woman finally spoke. "I speak all the languages of the Philistines," she said, "except to those with whom I do not choose to speak at all."

Intrigued by her pluck, Esau advanced slowly down the little incline to the bottom of the ravine and drew to within an arm's length of the woman. He stood at least a man's head above her, yet she faced him with chin upturned and with no move either to cover her face with her shawl or to reach for the knife or the staff. She was unafraid.

"Do you not fear to be here alone in the desert?" Esau asked, civilly enough.

"I fear no one," the woman returned. "I am in the desert because I choose to be."

Knowing this to be a lie, Esau smiled. "You mean rather that your people choose for you not to stay with them," he said. "You have been cast out of a camp—perhaps for lying with the wrong man, or with too many men?" His charge softened to a question.

It was then that the woman reached for the staff leaning against the red sandstone boulder—but Esau's hairy arm shot out and grabbed her by the wrist. "Do not fear," he said in a soft sneer. "Perhaps you have found the right man to lie with."

An unholy mixture of lust and scheming was forming a dim plan in Esau's mind. Sexual relations were strictly forbidden between the heirs of Abraham and the Canaanites, but Esau had often ignored the niceties of tribal custom to satisfy his needs. It mattered little to him that old Isaac kept prattling about the need to keep the "chosen" tribe set apart and "holy" from others in the land. Besides, the encounter he anticipated with this wench might lead to a liaison he could exploit later, after Isaac's death endowed him with the resources required to rid his hunting territory of Philistines. Setting up such an attachment would require something other than forcing the woman; he would need to use more finesse than was his nature in such situations.

So it was after just such calculated niceties that Esau arose a half-hour later from the *wadi*. The subdued woman watched him depart with a look not of loathing or protest, but with the lowered eyelids and half smile of a clear invitation for him to come upon her again in the desert, as chance or design might have it.

I had almost said, my lord Philemon, that "as luck would have it, Jacob was grazing a flock of goats in the same region in which Esau had shamed his clan's calling." I pause to weigh my words more carefully. For who can know whether events occur by chance or by prior arrangement? And if by prior arrangement, by good or evil Fates? My own kinsmen speak of Moros—Dark Fate—as controlling even the deeds of the high god Zeus. We who are followers of the Christ like to speak of His "providence"—as though providence itself is a deity, with a will of its own. My own view is that these things must remain a mystery until long after the events occur; it is only from the vantage point of the future that we can judge the cause of the past. But I stray too far into speculation and hasten now to return to the story.

Searching for pasturage for their flocks, Jacob and his band of herdsmen had pushed farther into the arid wilderness than they had intended. The land regularly received scant rainfall, and this year it had been almost nonexistent. Furthermore, centuries of grazing sheep and goats, whose teeth rudely rip clumps of grass up by their roots, had depleted the land's capacity. The herdsmen guided their goats into the shade of a few dwarf tamarisk trees in the bottom of a *wadi*, there to rest during the hottest hours of the afternoon. The herd fell silent, dozing in the heat. Droning flies spun dizzily over small piles of dung, singing the shepherds to sleep as well.

The dryness and the heat had been equally unkind to Esau and his hunt. Shortly before the sun reached its zenith in a brassy-hot sky, he had scared up a small, thin hare, only to see it skitter down a hole a finger's breadth in advance of his throwing stick. There were not even any dwarf trees for shade in this remote section. Esau slumped down heavily on a rock at the foot of a small cliff, seeking its scant shade. He wiped his brow with the back of a hairy wrist and drained the last drop of water from his wineskin. No matter; he would fill it at a spring he knew about at a tiny oasis an hour away.

After a few minutes' rest, he arose wearily and set off for the spring; but it was dry. Instead of a patch of green, Esau found the grass parched and brittle, the trees barren of leaf because of the drought, and only a damp spot in the whitened, alkaline soil where the spring had bubbled forth in better years.

He threw himself face down on the slightly dampened earth, licking the clay and trying to absorb through his body any available moisture. For the first time in years, he felt anxious about his survival. What good was it to know the countryside, to have in mind its every resource, when it withheld them as though by its own perverse will? A field mouse peeked at him from his tiny den in the protective shade of a rock, but Esau was too weary even to heave his stick or a rock. He must find water. And much more meat than the mouse would have provided.

But where? Straining to get his feet under him again, Esau shaded his brow with a trembling hand and squinted toward the southwest. He knew of a low-lying plain another two or three hours away—perhaps dew or run-off had collected there. At least there were tamarisk trees, small ones, whose shade would shelter him until evening cooled this great, flat furnace of a desert that lay paralyzed by heat, where the only motion was heat waves shimmering up from the sand. He dropped his fleecy cape carelessly to the ground; it was impossible to imagine the desert ever being cool enough for him to need it again. He stumbled on. Food …water…he knew he would have only enough strength to reach the tamarisk trees. Then…but he lacked the strength and the will to imagine his fate.

An hour before sundown, Jacob led the donkey packed with provisions up a small hill. He had sent the other shepherds by an alternate route toward a meeting point an hour away, hoping that their separate paths might turn up more than one patch of grass. From his vantage point on the little hill he surveyed the terrain. Suddenly he spied what seemed to be the form of a man sprawled in the dirt at the foot of the hill. Jacob scrambled down the incline, almost pulling the pack animal to its knees in his haste.

The body was lying face down, his mouth pressed to the earth as though trying to nurse some bit of moisture from her. Thinking that he had stumbled over a Philistine corpse, Jacob turned the body over with a tentative toe and not a great deal of interest. But even though it was encrusted with alkali and dust, the hide of the body seemed unusually ruddy. Then it dawned on Jacob— *it was his own brother!*

"Esau!" he gasped. He stooped quickly over the body and placed an ear on his chest. "He breathes!" he said to himself. Kneeling beside the massive form, Jacob poured a little precious water through Esau's cracked lips and into a gullet choked shut with dust. Esau sputtered and stirred.

"Stay," cautioned Jacob. "You are weak. But you are safe. It is I, your brother Jacob."

Esau's eyes opened barely enough to recognize Jacob; but even in his weakened state, he was chagrined at being in a position of weakness before his more delicate brother. He half turned his head to avoid Jacob's eyes.

"We will make camp here," Jacob said. "We will find the others in the morning." Immediately he wondered why he felt obliged to explain his life-saving tactics to his brother. Jacob hooked Esau's arm around his neck and, straining under the larger man's weight, half dragged him over to some boulders at the foot of a knoll and deposited him heavily in the lengthening shade. The donkey followed obediently, glad to anticipate stopping at last for the night.

By now the sun's rays were oblique enough for the desert to begin its quick, nightly cooling. Jacob slipped quietly but quickly to the herd of goats he had herded into a huge V in the rocky hillside. He caught a gentle she-goat, milked her with a few strong strokes and brought the warm liquid to Esau. Fresh and warm though it was, it was cooler than the nearly-unconscious man's roasted lips. Jacob kept the soothing milk on his brother's lips until the ruddy, rumpled head could be held up on its own strength. The milk refreshed, but was not sufficient to revive.

"Meat," Esau croaked. "Have you no meat?" His eyes were sun-burned and bloodshot, bleary and half-hidden under lids too heavy to hold wide open.

"I had just trapped a few quail and gathered a batch of lentils when I came upon you," Jacob replied. "You would choke on them in your condition—but stay! I will make them into a stew. It will at least keep us alive." Hastily building a small fire, Jacob took a small clay pot from the ass's pack. He boiled small chunks of the tiny birds together with the dry, red, bean-like lentils, musing on the irony of the situation as he stirred the rough but nourishing stew. If it pained his brother to find himself helpless before Jacob and requiring his ministrations, Jacob found the situation no less irksome. He stifled a bitter chuckle at the irony of having to save the life of one he envied so, and who in fact hated him.

"You spoke?" Esau asked hoarsely.

"No, I—," Jacob began. Then, on an impulse to break the awkwardness with gallows humor, he added, "I was just wondering what you might trade me for this good stew."

"Trade you?" Esau echoed, rousing to an elbow.

"Why not?" Jacob continued. "What would a man not give for his life?" He was ashamed to find himself warming to his joke.

Esau was quiet for a moment. What was his brother up to? His brain was still too addled from sunstroke to think further. "Ah, yes. I might have known. You have always been jealous of me. You have always resented my father's love. Of course I will trade you something—the very thing you covet. *I will trade you my very birthright.*"

Jacob, squatting at the fire, stopped agitating the boiling stew in mid-stir and looked quizzically over his shoulder at Esau. His brother was serious! Such a thing was not done. Could he take advantage of Esau's sunburned mind? At least he would press the game further.

"Done!" he said, hiding a grim smile as he turned back toward the pot.

"Done!" said Esau, falling heavily back to the ground. Although the exertion was almost too much for his famished state, he was not too exhaused to think: *I would promise anything to get out of this situation alive. It is an illegal transaction anyway. Father will annul it.*

Thinking no more about the words the two had bandied about, Jacob brought the bowl of stew over to his brother. He lifted the great auburn-crowned head again and poured revivifying red stew into the parched mouth until it protested, "Enough!" Esau lapsed into heavy sleep, and Jacob stared the fire's coals into ashes. Then he rolled himself up in his long outer garment and drifted off into a dreamless sleep.

When he awoke at dawn's first light, Esau was gone.

CHAPTER 3

Jacob and his herdsmen grazed their flocks of sheep and goats back toward Beer-sheba at a pace that gave him more than enough time to think about his brother's rash agreement. A part of him relished the episode with dark and lustful imaginings of the position the birthright would give him. He also allowed himself to wonder if it would, finally, win him more favor with old Isaac. Another part of his tender soul felt guilty about having taken advantage of Esau when he was in such a desperate state.

Still another set of thoughts included a mental image of a tiny hand grasping for all it could find from his mother's womb, settling on the heel of his barely older brother. Surely there could be nothing devious about an infant's unconscious response to the will of El. And surely the birth omen was to be acted on. Yet, was the transaction legal? Could Esau complain before Isaac's tribal court that he had been defrauded? The thoughts droned 'round in Jacob's head over and over again, first accusing then congratulating him, eventually as monotonous as the relentless heat of the Palestinian sun. And he could no more stop their parade into the projected destiny in his mind than he could call on the sun to restrain its rays. The entourage picked its way across the flat, grey stones of the northern Negev, the animals murmuring crossly at the heat and pausing here and there to nip at dry shoots of grass with little more color than the rock from whose crevices they straggled. The sun and sand worked as artisans here, creating shimmering images on the horizon, mirages that danced to the abrasive, high-pitched hum of hidden locusts, the whole scene etching a monotonous tableau in the mind. It would be good to get back to the oasis with its friendly ghosts of Grandfather Abraham and promises past.

I must pause here, my lord, to comment on the faith of Abraham and how it had become imbedded in the soul of his grandson Jacob. Humanly speaking the promise of Yahweh to Abraham was a promise unkept. That is, our father Abraham, though chosen for grace, died before realizing the fulfillment of the promise —before seeing his seed become like the stars of the heavens and the sands of the seashore. I insert this into our story here to remind my lord that the grace of being chosen of God is not always to be seen except with the eye of faith, nor savored save with the ear of hope. And how Abraham could have died in hope, while realizing the impossibility of inheriting or seeing his seed inherit the promise, is as hidden a mystery as the choosing itself. But I hasten to return to the story.

"They come," a servant girl reported, shading her eyes with her hand and squinting toward the south.

"Good," Rebekah said. Straightening up from her cooking pot, she brushed an unruly silver lock from her forehead and looked where the maiden was pointing. Aged though Rebekah was, she had been going about her chores at camp with a new energy that made the servants wonder. Telling Jacob of the circumstances of his birth, and of the omen that had won him his name, seemed to refresh and lighten her spirit. Every mother has dreams for her sons, but telling Jacob that the great God El apparently had also singled him out for a special destiny seemed to free Rebekah to act on the promise. Not for her the uncertainty and doubt that preyed on Jacob; Rebekah felt her commission with the clarity of an angel sent from the court of El to do His express bidding. The tune of an ancient lullaby in a minor key welled up spontaneously as she bustled about, giving orders for the preparation of the evening meal. But her thoughts were on the work before her—

the ways and means of assisting El in establishing Jacob as the true Supplanter, the rightful heir of the birthright.

After all, had not Father Abraham's wife, Sarah, also acted to fulfill the promise of El by giving her servant Hagar to Abraham for wife to make up the deficit of her own barrenness? El was a high God, but how could He carry out His will without the willing hands of His followers? At the moment she had no idea what she would do to assist Him but sharing the omen with Jacob had closed the chapter on all previous anxiety and sadness at the sight of Isaac's favoritism for Esau. Although her heart sang, Rebekah's firm mouth was set in a determined, straight line as she busied herself at directing her maidens' work about the camp. Tonight she and Jacob would talk, and plan.

For his part, Jacob lost little time in seeking out his mother after reaching the camp. He must tell her of the transaction in the desert and seek her advice, although he was aware of discomfort in his belly as he wondered whether she would approve of the bargain he had exacted from Esau. Instructing the shepherds to bed down the flocks and herds, Jacob walked into the ring of cooking fires and put his hand on Rebekah's shoulder. She turned, and their eyes linked in the tender closeness of mother and grown son.

"My son!" Rebekah said in greeting, grasping both his hands. "The herds pastured well?"

"Hardly well, mother, but well enough," Jacob replied. "The drought is long and the grass is short, and scarce. But we lost none—in fact, we gained."

"Gained?" his mother echoed. It was long past the season for ewes and does to throw offspring. "Surely you did not take animals from the herds of the shepherds of Gerar?"

"And why not?" her son teased. "If their flocks be heartier than ours, why not?"

"You use me for sport!" Rebekah scoffed, playfully pushing Jacob away. "How is it, really, that you speak of gain?" Jacob's dark eyes grew serious as they darted around the circle of cookfires to be sure none of the others were within earshot. "I gained in a trade with my brother."

"Your brother was with you in the field?"

"Not at first. I came upon him. He had run out of food and

water and had fallen. I found him almost dead. It grieved us both, I think, that it was I who had to revive him."

"He is well, then?" For a brief moment, Rebekah had a thought beneath her dignity: What if Esau died, and the birthright reverted to Jacob naturally?

"He is well," Jacob assured her. "But he is not as rich as he was a fortnight ago. He paid me handsomely for saving him."

"And that is the gain you speak of?" Rebekah asked, turning again to her pots.

"That is the gain. But he did not pay me in gold."

"Of course not," Rebekah said. "He would have had no gold with him in the field."

"No," Jacob agreed. "But he had with him something of far more worth than money."

"What, then?" asked his mother, growing weary of the guessing game her son was playing. "What could your brother have had that is more valuable than money?"

Jacob lowered his head, his brows low over eyes that sought his mother's for their first reaction to what he would say. "My brother traded me his birthright for my stew, he said quietly."

Rebekah paused at her pot for only a moment, but she involuntarily drew in her breath sharply. "He what? He couldn't!" she said, without turning around.

"I wonder," Jacob returned. "It was all on a moment. I had no such idea in my mind, but there it was on my tongue. I have said it was awkward. I did not ask to be put in the position of saving my rival. But if I must do so, I naturally thought of what he would give for my services. And there it was, as it were, on the table of treaty before us—his birthright for my stew."

"He bargained his birthright away?" It was both a question and an exclamation. Turning around now, Rebekah straightened up and gripped her son with a steady stare, not accusing or judging, only inquiring of facts that she already sensed might be fit into her previous musings about assisting El. Jacob had already taken steps to do so!

"He did that. And since then, on our way back to camp, I have been wondering about it, asking about it in my mind. Can such a thing be done?"

Rebekah turned again to her pots, not answering for a moment.

Then she said quietly: "It can be done. It is sometimes the way of the Canaanites, and since El has promised us their land perhaps their law goes with it." She paused, stirring her pot vigorously as though to stimulate her thoughts. "But it is not that simple."

"Then you are not angry?" Jacob asked. "It is done?"

"Angry? No, my son! It is the will of El. But no—it is not yet done."

"But what more—what is not simple about it?"

"The head of the tribe—your father Isaac—he must confirm such a transaction. The birthright is not Esau's alone to trade away. It is still in the power of your father to set the seal of his blessing on whomever." Rebekah stopped, a cloud crossing her face. *But your brother despised what his father would give him,* she thought. Then, fairly spitting out the words, she hissed, "Esau deserves no part of the heritage of the firstborn!"

Neither spoke for awhile. Both were lost in speculation about what might happen, each knowing how unlikely it would be for old Isaac to approve. He would be angry at Esau's having traded away his family privilege, but even angrier at Jacob's having taken advantage of Esau's plight to drive such a bargain. *Would Isaac even cut me out of my heritage as second son?* Jacob wondered. Finally he spoke. "What is to be done, then?"

"El will show us," Rebekah said simply.

Not again, Jacob thought. His mother clung to the belief that every step should be directed by God. Still, he had no better idea. He shrugged his muscular shoulders. It was growing dark, and he turned to seek his tent. While many questions remained, at least the hasty transaction with Esau had not angered his mother.

Lying by his wife's side, Isaac was restless. He turned so often that the stack of bedskins beneath him slid askew. Sleep was even more remote for Rebekah. She arose and padded outside the tent to pluck from the smoldering ashes of the fire a stick with one end glowing. Returning to the tent with the ember, she lit a small oil lamp by which to see how to straighten Isaac's bedskins.

"You are not sleeping," she said, hoping that stating the obvious would encourage Isaac to talk. Never had he looked older or more frail than in the flickering lamplight. Suddenly Rebekah knew that he would not be with her much longer. She shuddered a little, not so much from sorrow, for the days were long passed when there was much tenderness between them. But Isaac was the son of promise, and she was his wife. He had declined to take another wife, risking the narrowing of the chain of inheritance. She would have been ungrateful had she not felt something at the thought of his passing. Neither Rebekah nor Isaac could know that the old man would actually live another twenty years and more.

Similar thoughts of the length of his days lay heavy on Isaac's own heart. He would not, of course, accept the invitation to talk at length with a woman. He only said, "I must speak with my son."

"Which son?" Rebekah asked. Although she knew Isaac would speak thus only of Esau, she always seized every opportunity to remind him that Jacob was also his son. "And at this hour?" she continued, not waiting for an answer. "He sleeps. He has been away for two days—probably with those Hittite women."
Although they were actually Esau's wives, Rebekah lost no opportunity to characterize them as less than worthy of the clan of Abraham.

"He has before him years to sleep, and who knows the days remaining for me?" Isaac said wearily. He moaned and grunted and sighed his way to his feet with great effort, and made his way to the door of the tent with short, unsteady steps. He faltered, and Rebekah sprang to his side, ignoring the stiffness in her own bones.

"Stay," she said softly. "Lie down again. I will fetch your son Esau."

Isaac waved a hand in resignation, but as his wife stole off into the darkness the old man found his staff and stood outside the tent to wait. He raised bleary, almost sightless eyes to the heavens. By now he could only imagine how brilliant and numerous the stars must be against the dark, clear Canaanite sky. He wondered: Have even the stars heard of such a plan as revealed to his father Abraham by the very Ruler of the universe? He lapsed into the philosophical musings of one whose time is short, surveying his life swiftly in order to fix its furniture in his mind before leaving the room.

In a way, he, Isaac, a mere man, had been chosen over the stars—it was he, not they, who was heir to the promise to Abraham. It would be his seed, not the stars', that would become more numerous among the nations than the stars themselves. The frail body shuddered involuntarily and the gnarled hands clutching the staff trembled both with the wonder of it all and the chill of the night air.

Rebekah soon returned with Esau, only half awake and grumbling at being disturbed. "My son?" Isaac asked.

"Who else?" Esau returned, grumpy with sleep.

"Hush!" Rebekah said, with uncharacteristic sharpness. "Your father would speak with you."

Ducking under the tent flap she returned to her bed, knowing that, her errand completed, she was now dismissed from the presence of the men. But she strained to catch every word of their conversation through the goatskin tent walls.

"My son," Isaac said again. "I am heavy with years. I do not know how many days El has planned for me."

"Are you ill, Father?" Esau asked uncomprehendingly.

"No, no, except from age. But my bones can feel the time approaching when . . . ." He stopped, his brittle voice cracking. "It is time for me to sign over the promise of El to you, my son. It is time to seal the birthright with the blessing."

The sound of the word *berakah*, blessing, echoed as an inward, unvoiced *Brrrr!* for Esau, bringing a chilling shudder of remembrance. He had put the incident with Jacob in the desert out of his mind, so rarely did he think about the birthright. But now, even in his sleep-befuddled state, he saw an opportunity to annul the bargain he had made in return for his life. If his father Isaac sealed the birthright to him with the customary formal blessing before Jacob could press his claim, perhaps nothing would come of it.

"In the morning," old Isaac continued, "or even before the dawn, take your weapons to the field and bring down the antelope or the deer El has prepared for the feast of the *berakah*." He put his hand on Esau's firm, strong shoulder, smiling weakly in the darkness. "We will feast—just you and I—we will seal the birthright with the blessing."

Esau clasped his father's outstretched arm. "It will be as you say, Father. I will bring just the sort of meat my father prizes most. I will be honored to have the blessing. I will cherish the birthright." It was not totally a lie; he had often thought of how the responsibilities of the birthright, part of which he dreaded, did not altogether outweigh its benefits.

"It will be good, my son," Isaac said, suddenly tired by the midnight exertion. "Sleep now; we will feast at the setting of the sun tomorrow." He turned abruptly to his tent. Settling this had relieved him of a certain load, and his steps were steadier as he made his way back to the bedskins and eased his body down heavily by Rebekah's side. His wife, of course, had heard all. But she said nothing as she covered her husband and sent him off to sleep. Her own mind teemed with ideas for intervening in the momentous plan she had overheard.

Rebekah had a herdsman enter Jacob's tent to awaken him before first light, the nomad's code not allowing even a mother in her adult son's sleeping tent. Jacob came out stretching, wondering what could be so important at this hour. "We must act, my son!" Rebekah said breathlessly.

"Act? When—what shall we do?" he replied, realizing only slowly that his mother must be taking up their previous conversation about the birthright.

"El has given us what we seek!" his mother continued. "He has arranged a way to seal the birthright to you. Last night I heard your father planning the feast of the *berakah* with your brother."

"So soon?" asked Jacob.

"Just so. Your father sees the end of his days. This is why he plans the feast of the blessing. And this is why we must act—*now*. Once the birthright is sealed with the blessing, there can be no changing it."

"But what can we do?"

"Listen! Even now your brother is in the field pursuing your father's favorite meat for the feast. The absence of the rains has driven the antelope and the deer afar, and it will be late before Esau returns. Your father will be expecting him; but he will be receiving *you*."

Jacob leaned away from his mother, head tilted quizzically. But he said nothing, knowing that she would explain.

"You must go to the herd and kill two young goats," she continued. "Prepare them in a savory sauce, spiced and seasoned just as your father loves the venison. You will act the part of your brother, and present the meat to your father at the feast. *You*, my son, will receive the blessing! You will be the sworn heir to the birthright of the firstborn son of the promise!"

Jacob was silent for a moment. Would the ruse work? Should it even be attempted? He had won the birthright by exploiting his brother's plight. Could he now add trickery and deceit to his store of ways and means? One obstacle was most obvious.

"You are forgetting one thing, Mother," Jacob said quietly. "Our skin. Father will know I am not Esau if he touches me, for Esau is so hairy." While Esau's hirsute hide was something of a badge of manliness now, he had been teased as a boy by playmates who called him "Goatman." Jacob shook his head skeptically. "It is too risky. If I were found out, Esau's blessing would be confirmed anyway, and my father would ordain me only with a curse."

"A curse? He has already cursed you!" Rebekah said, anger rising swiftly in her voice. "In his favoring your brother Esau he has already defied the will of God. And in any case—let any curse rest on me. I will intercede if your father finds you out."

Jacob was silent. It was true that his mother could usually win her way with old Isaac.

"Enough of this!" said Rebekah. "Slay for me two kids from the herd. I will soak the meat in goat's milk and prepare it so it tastes like venison. And you will prepare the skin so it feels like Esau's. Quickly, now! We must act before your brother returns!"

Jacob started to protest that he did not understand how the goats' hides would transform him into Esau, who was hardly *that* hairy. But he knew his mother's moods well, and her tone of determination now meant that he had only to follow her instructions in order to be on the winning side of any contest they entered. Although still with grave doubts, he left obediently for the nearby herd. He knew of a pair of black and white spotted goats, twins no more than two months old. They would do nicely.

While Jacob was gone, Rebekah marched purposefully across the encampment to the tent of her son Esau. A boy, an undershepherd, lounged outside. He scrambled to his feet in respect as the matriarch approached. "*Shalom*, my son," she said kindly.

"My la—*shalom* to my lady," he returned, unaccustomed to speaking to women of royalty.

"You know of the feast our lord Isaac has set with his son Esau?" Rebekah asked.

"Yes, lady," the youth replied, "I have my lord Esau's festal garments laid out inside the tent. He was anxious to prove his efficiency as a valet.

"Very good!" Rebekah said warmly. "I am planning a fine surprise for him. I am making him a set of new garments for the feast of the blessing. Would you be so kind as to fetch me the garments you have prepared, so I may take their measure?"

"Certainly, my lady," said the youth. "My lord Esau will be glad."

Rebekah smiled knowingly. "At least he will be surprised," she said. Then she walked swiftly back to her own tents with the garments.

Jacob had just returned with the twin goats, already slaughtered and disembowelled. Rebekah summoned a maiden to help her skin and dismember them. While the meat soaked in rancid milk, the two women went to work dressing the hides. First they scraped the undersides with sharp flint knives until all remnants of flesh were scoured away. Then they pounded the hairy side, stone upon stone, beating it into even greater suppleness. Finally Rebekah took a flint knife to the hairy side, thinning the coarse hair to a fraction of its natural thickness. She shook out the loose hairs and repeated the process. When she was finished she had the maid fetch Jacob again. Then she dismissed her helper and led Jacob to the back of her tent where they were hidden from the view of the rest of the camp.

"Sit here, my son," she commanded, motioning to Jacob to sit on the ground before a boulder on which she enthroned herself for the fitting. The hands that had cut and sewn countless goatskin garments deftly trimmed one of the hides into a kind of cape. She draped it over Jacob's shoulders and tucked it under his loosefitting woven garment and up under his flowing hair. She pulled the two ends of the cape snug under his chin and fastened them tight with two slivers of bone. Only a small patch of the hair cape could be seen under Jacob's chin, and mere glimpses showed now and again at the nape of his neck when he would turn his head and swing his locks of rich, dark hair.

"Now the arms," said Rebekah. Jacob stretched out first his

right arm and then his left as his mother fashioned and fit two long sleeves from the other hide. Stretching the scraped hides tight around his arms, she secured them with rawhide lacing from the underside, pulling the seams tight so that even a sighted person would have to search to find them. The tops of the goat sleeves extended up under the shorter sleeves of Esau's outer tunic, which Jacob had donned.

Finally, Rebekah stepped back to evaluate her work. "Behold!" she said. "Now you are your brother Esau!"

Jacob looked down at his now hairy arms, and felt the mane on the back of his neck with some embarrassment. "But will *Father* think so?" he asked. "That is the test." Rebekah only nodded, but her brow did not betray the slightest doubt.

While her maiden roasted the marinated goat meat, Rebekah gave Jacob a voice lesson. "If you are Esau, speak like Esau," she gently challenged.

"What shall I say?" Jacob asked, suddenly self-conscious and fearful. "I feel foolish, Mother."

"Only because I am not Isaac," his mother replied reassuringly. "Speak as to Isaac, with your brother's voice."

"Er—Father?" Jacob said tentatively.

"Lower—the voice should be lower," Rebekah coached.

"*Father?*" Jacob said with more confidence, lowering his voice and making it more husky. He was warming to the charade now.

"How is that?"

"Good," his mother said. "But keep practicing."

In half an hour, the maid returned with a half dozen savory, boneless pieces of goat meat on a wooden platter bordered with leeks and wild tubers, Isaac's favorite vegetables. Rebekah again dismissed her aide, gave the laden platter to Jacob, and kissed him on both cheeks.

"Go now, my son!" she said, her eyes glistening with emotion and excitement. "And may God go with you. Do not linger at meal, lest your brother Esau return and find you in his place. Do not fear; it is the will of El that you supplant him."

Almost trembling, Jacob could find no words, but only bowed to his mother with affection.

Isaac sat alone in the meal tent waiting for the hour appointed for the feast of the blessing. Although he could tell it was not yet dark, he had come early to stare into the night of his own blind eyes. As he contemplated the task before him, he began to rock slightly back and forth, a soft, barely audible moan escaping his tightly drawn lips at each forward motion of his body. Despite the joyous occasion, he found himself filled with anxiety, and not a little sadness. Esau, his beloved, had not lived up to all of Isaac's expectations for the firstborn son. Rumors were continually reaching the old patriarch that Esau was not too careful about the women with whom he made his bed. Isaac had admonished him frequently about the impropriety of lying with the *'am ha-aretz*, the people of the land. And more than once Isaac had had to pacify a Philistine nobleman whose acknowledged hunting grounds Esau had raided. He was too eager to possess the land of promise.

A sigh welled up from the depths of Isaac's aged and burdened heart, then his body shrank as he exhaled heavily, as though he were expelling such anxiety. Perhaps the simple ceremony of the blessing would draw out Esau's true potential. Perhaps the man would grow into being equal to the grave responsibilities looming before him.

It was then that Jacob entered with the simple but rich meal. *"Father?"* he said in his practiced voice.

"Yes—yes, my son," Isaac responded, turning to the light source he could vaguely identify. "Is it you, my son Esau?"

"It is I," Jacob lied. "I have returned with the savory meal for the feast of the blessing, just as I promised."

"So soon?" Isaac asked. "It is not yet dark."

"God was with me. The doe stood in a little thicket only three hours away. It is a good sign. We must eat while the meal is fresh."

Something wasn't quite right, Isaac thought. Certainly El could arrange for the deer to be wherever He wished, but he assumed that the drought had driven most of the wildlife far to the northwest.

"Is it really you, my firstborn son?" he asked again. "Come near! My eyes cannot—come and let me see you with my hands." Jacob's resolve melted. He had hoped to avoid his father's touch. Cold drops of perspiration stood out on his forehead and made his hands clammy. He could feel his legs going weak, and he feared he would faint.

Suddenly a glow of light behind him, as though the tent flap had been opened again, made Jacob start and turn to see who had entered behind him. But the tent flap had not been disturbed. There was only a softly glowing light inside the tent. His mouth agape, Jacob turned to his father. But Isaac sat as though petrified, his eyes on the ground before him. He seemed paralyzed, and certainly could not see the glow.

Jacob began to tremble. Immediately he was aware of a voice that seemed to emanate from the light, yet well up from within his mind, as though another soul was speaking to his soul without the benefit of voice.

"Fear not, Jacob, the Lord is with you!" he heard—or sensed. Then, to his even greater astonishment, the light separated in two, one part joining Jacob at his left and the other at his right.

"Wh—who are you?" Jacob somehow stammered, although he was certain that his lips did not move.

"I am the angel Gabriel," said a voice at his right.

"And I am Michael the archangel," the glow at his left seemed to say. Then Jacob was aware of something solid supporting his arms on both sides. A rising tide of warmth and inner peace and calm welled up in his soul. He felt strong and tall—somehow even taller than the tent. It was as though he stood both within and without the shelter, a part of the drama, but somehow also looming over it and even directing it with the authority of a divine playmaster.

"We have come from El to be with you in the feast of the blessing," the glow on the left said.

Jacob looked again at his father Isaac, but the old man still sat like a stone, apparently oblivious to the supernatural visitation Jacob was experiencing.

"But I—surely you know that the blessing and the birthright actually belong . . ." Jacob began, not knowing whether to look to the right or the left. Suddenly he felt foolish about presuming to fill in gaps of knowledge for such obviously divine beings.

"It is not necessary to speak to us about it," said the voice from his right. "Speak to your father Isaac." And with that, the lights retreated, rejoined themselves into one glow, and disappeared. Jacob was left alone again with Isaac. But now his brow was dry and his legs strong.

Suddenly old Isaac emerged from his suspended moment. "Come," he said again. "Come near, my son." Jacob stepped resolutely up to his father. The old man caressed his son's head gently, allowing his gnarled hand to descend to the left sleeve, by which he pulled Jacob's arm to his chest. He would not appear overly suspicious; the bony fingers of his other hand traced the back of Jacob's hand only lightly and fleetingly. He was satisfied. "The voice is as the voice of Jacob, but the skin is that of my firstborn, Esau," he said; but he was smiling. "My sons are as one," he finished. "Let us join our hearts together in the feast of the *berakah!*"

It was a solemn meal, and brief. Jacob was certainly not anxious to be overly talkative, and Isaac was reticent from heaviness of heart. Just as Jacob had passed the test, so did the goat meat. Rebekah's art had seasoned it into venison. The food washed down with heavy, red wine, it was time for the blessing.

"Kiss me, my son," Isaac intoned. The formal kiss consisted of both men kissing each other on both cheeks. The clothes Rebekah had borrowed from Esau placed the final seal on the deception.

"Ah," said Isaac, "who but my son Esau has the smell of the field watered with heaven's dew?"

Lifting his blind eyes and raising his hand, Isaac prayed: "May the Lord our God also water your seed and the seed of your fields! May the earth bring forth its abundance, making you grow strong. And seeing your strength, may many nations bow down to you, and may you be lord even over your brothers, who will serve you. And may you carry the promise given to my father Abraham: those who curse you will be cursed, and those who bless you will be blessed. Amen!"

It was done. The birthright Jacob had bought with a single bowl of stew was now sealed with the blessing. There would be no undoing the double transaction. The strange omen at the birth of the Supplanter, whose tiny hand had grasped the heel of his firstborn brother, had blossomed into reality.

Jacob kissed his father again, hurriedly. Without waiting for servants, he gathered up the remains of the simple meal, bowed his way out of the tent, and collapsed with relief in his own quarters.

CHAPTER 4

Mercifully, the rays of the sun were beating more obliquely on Esau by the time he neared the camp with his kill. It had been a hard hunt, with the drought, but he had been rewarded with a doe that had taken refuge at a spring—and hence lush grass—for at least the last two months, he guessed. She was so fat that Esau was glad he had taken along a servant to help carry home the carcass on a pole between them.

While field-dressing the doe, Esau had noted with satisfaction the firm, red flesh. Good meat was a good omen, and his heart was light as the pair approached camp. He would have to hurry to have the venison prepared in time for the feast of blessing that awaited him. No matter; his father would wait for his favored son.

Esau had little long-range concept of what the blessing would mean. His was not the mind that took flight to the future, creating dreams of nation-making, much less dwelling on how possessing the birthright might put him in a position to lead the sorely needed reforms in Canaan, where slaves were often treated worse than cattle, and children were sacrificed to blood-lusty gods. For Esau, it was enough that he stood above Jacob in his father's eyes, and that he would inherit a double portion of his wealth.

And in the back of his mind was the thought that perhaps the blessing that awaited him would cancel the sale of his birthright. Back at camp, Esau gruffly commanded two servants to prepare the venison. Deftly skinning the doe, they quartered it and skewered it on a spit to roast over an open fire. Meanwhile they prepared chard and lentil soup to accompany Isaac's favorite food.

Lingering in the meal tent after feasting with Jacob in the guise of Esau, Isaac's brooding returned. He sat staring in the darkness of his blindness, wondering how El would transform the son of blessing from a willful, devil-may-care hunter into the responsible head of a clan. It had been a good meal-of-the-blessing, and that, at least, was a start; yet the old man could not shake the mood of pessimism about the future.

Finally he bestirred himself, hoisting his tired old body to his feet with the aid of a stout staff. He tottered to the doorway of the tent, noting when he lifted the flap that there was no hint of light, which his film-covered eyes would still have been able to vaguely discern. Darkness had fallen.

Suddenly Esau rounded the tent rope and ran head-on into his father. Esau's arms were laden with platters containing the venison turned out in a meal as fine as that which Isaac and Jacob had just finished. With an outdoorsman's agility, Esau first juggled, then balanced, the platters of food.

"You were about to give up waiting, my father?" Esau asked reprovingly.

"Who is there?" Isaac demanded.

"Your son Esau."

"It cannot be so!" Although Isaac recognized that the voice was different from the one Jacob had feigned, his mind would not at first allow him to concede the awful truth that would shortly dawn on him. "It cannot be!" he repeated. Esau just left me!" he protested.

"No, my father," Esau replied. "Esau has just arrived. Let us feast as we had planned."

"But no—we—that is—we have already feasted!" old Isaac said.

"We who?" Esau asked, now fearing for his father's sanity. "I have only now returned from the field, and we have yet to eat."

"Then who was just here, with the game? Who did I just honor with the firstborn's blessing?" Isaac stopped, looking around with wild stares as though, with enough effort, he could penetrate this mystery with sightful eyes.

Then the deception came clear to the eyes of his mind. Isaac's great, grey head sagged to his chest, and he muttered a single name in answer to his own question: *"Jacob!"*

"Jacob?" Esau echoed innocently.

"I have just sworn the blessing of the firstborn to your brother!" Isaac fairly shouted.

"Not the blessing!" Esau cried desperately. "What are you saying, my father?"

Old Isaac's voice arose in a quavering wail. "He deceived me! The hair on his arms—Jacob came in your stead, pretending—we feasted, and I gave..."

Esau staggered and fell to his knees as though struck with one of his own arrows. "Jacob!" he spat out the name with an oath, his voice rising. "Has he then supplanted me again? It was not enough that he won from me the birthright, he has..."

"He won the birthright? What do you mean?" Isaac asked.

Before Esau could stop himself he had blurted out the story of the transaction in the desert. Had he been a more cautious and prudent man he would have withheld, hoping to regain the blessing by pressing his claim to the birthright. But all possibility of cool, legal maneuvering was consumed by the burning flash of his anger.

For a moment, old Isaac's anger rose at his favored son's careless bartering away of the treasured spiritual heirloom. But his displeasure soon faded to stunned questioning. "Then Jacob has both the birthright *and* the blessing?" he marveled, groping unsteadily to find a low, rawhide stool he knew was by the entrance to the tent. Esau was too devastated, too focused on his own plight, to assist him.

"But you can still bless me, Father!" he implored. Still on his knees, he grabbed old Isaac's hands and drew them to his lips. "My brother must not win both the birthright and the blessing!" By now, the rough outdoorsman was uncharacteristically in tears.

"He has both—by whatever means," Isaac said stonily. "The birthright is sealed by the blessing. I can only give you a second blessing."

"Bless me, Father, by any means!" Esau cried in anguish. Suddenly, that which had never claimed his fervent interest appeared essential to life itself, now that it was being taken from him.

"Yes, yes," Isaac said in weary resignation, trying to summon what comfort he could for his favored son. "I cannot rescind the blessing of the firstborn. It is done; it is sealed. Yet, we shall see...you shall have your blessing." He turned from Esau, lifted his blind eyes toward the heavens and stood in a half-trance for a long moment. Then he spoke:

> "Thus says the Lord our God:
> 'Yahweh sends His vouchsafed word,
> That you shall live by your strong sword.
> And as befits preordained plan,
> Will live in dewless, desert lands
> And serve him who stole your right
> For a time and times 'til by your might
> You rebel at a place you will elect
> To throw his yoke from off your neck.'"

Thus saying, the old man slumped in emotional and spiritual exhaustion. Esau, still on his knees, leaned toward his father on the leather stool. The two embraced, Isaac beyond emotion, and Esau heaving tearless, wrenching sobs into the night.

Esau's sorrow and searing disappointment soon hardened into rage. "I will slay him!" he muttered, pacing in his tent. "He did not know, but when he bargained for the birthright he bought also my swift sword. Tomorrow—tomorrow this thief shall surely die!" He threw himself on his bedskins, biting his lower lip and commanding his sobbing to cease.

A maid whom Rebekah had secretly posted outside Esau's tent cocked her head thoughtfully. This must be why her mistress had asked her to station herself where she could hear and observe Master Esau. She stole away silently and reported Esau's words to her mistress.

"It is as I feared it would be," said Rebekah. Her confidence had worn thin now. Despite her loyalty to Jacob, she found herself pitying Esau's raging helplessness. Had she only spawned a clan war by her efforts on behalf of her favorite son?

Only one solution seemed to present itself: Jacob must go into temporary exile. Perhaps if he waited until Isaac died to return, the removal of the patriarch as a visible reminder of the birthright would enable Esau's anger to subside.

Rebekah comandeered a servant to guide her to the nearby plain where Jacob was overseeing the separation of weaning lambs from their dams.

"My son?" she called. At her summons, Jacob slapped the thick, ochre dust from his rough shepherd's garments and retreated to her side. "I have a hard word," Rebekah said grimly. "Your brother Esau seeks your life."

Jacob looked at the ground. "I am not surprised. I have expected as much, and I am ready for him."

"Nonsense!" Rebekah said. "Of what use is the birthright if you die at his hand?"

"And you are sure it is I who would die?" Jacob said, looking up quickly and fixing his mother in the stare of one who expects more affirmation than he could ever transform into self-confidence.

"No matter. Either you or he or both—this has become a tiresome business. You must flee for a time."

"I have also thought of that," Jacob said quietly. "But I am not a coward." The fact is that while such a serious breach in the two brothers' relationship may well have caused Jacob to flee only months ago, his new possession had given him some bravado, however poorly founded. "If I am indeed the one chosen to receive the Promise, will not Yah defend me against the wrath of Esau? Is not he the real usurper? Besides, I am not a coward!" he repeated.

"No, of course you are not a coward," his mother said in a tone calculated to passify and reassure. "And certainly Yah is with you. But there is no need to allow this thing to erupt into a clan war. Go away for a while, I beg you. You will return. It will only be for a few months," she lied, "until the matter is not so fresh and painful for your brother."

Jacob looked down thoughtfully. If he could avoid bloodshed, he should do so. "Where would I go?" he asked.

"I have thought of that, too," Rebekah said. "You will go to my brother Laban, your uncle, in the land of Paddan-aram, which is Haran. It is time for you to be thinking of taking a wife, anyway—and where else to find a wife than in the home where your father Isaac found me?"

Jacob's resistance melted before the symmetry of the plan and the sentiment with which his mother sketched it. Like father, like son—it would be a journey in the footsteps of the servant of him whose favor he still yearned for. Besides, he knew well the Semitic maxim, "He who courts danger will be overcome by it; he who avoids danger will overcome it."

"Then my uncle would welcome me?" he asked.

"Laban is a stern man, and you would have to earn your place there," Rebekah said candidly. "But the Aramean blood is a bond. He would welcome you. *And,*" Rebekah added coyly, her chin tucked to the side and her eyelids fluttering flirtatiously, "your uncle Laban has daughters. Come—we shall discuss it with your father."

Taking Jacob by the hand, Rebekah bustled back to the camp. Isaac was yawning sleepily after an afternoon nap.

"My lord?" she began, virtually shoving Jacob in front of Isaac. "We would speak to you."

"Speak, then," Isaac said, still in the ill humor of first awakening from sleep induced by eating too much. "It is your son Jacob and I," his wife said, accommodating his blindness. "We have a plan to strengthen the bond between our families, yours and mine. Pray let us send Jacob to my brother Laban in Haran to take a wife. If he stays here, he will surely marry the daughters of the Hittites, who will plague us with their gods and their pagan ways."

Old Isaac's head rose abruptly as he tried to locate his deceitful son. "Jacob!" he hissed. "Truly you have proved to be the supplanter! What kind of love for your brother . . . ." His remonstrance broke off as he was convulsed in a fit of coughing—a providential attack, Jacob was sure.

Recovering, the old man lost his train of thought amid his wife's suggestion. He wanted to avoid tribal warfare as much as anyone. And the Hittites. Rebekah had chosen her words well. The son of the promise must not marry with the pagans.

"Haran, eh?" Isaac said, finally. Vague and distant memories of Rebekah's family, and his ties with them, flooded warmly if indistinctly into his thoughts, and he lingered with them so long that Rebekah had to nudge him gently.

"Eh? Oh!" Isaac said, returning to the scene at hand. "Yes, yes, of course." He looked up, unseeing, toward the spot where he sensed Jacob stood. "It is good, what your mother says, my son. Go at once to Paddan-aram, the Way of the Arameans, to Laban, your uncle. Choose there a wife. These Hittite women and their gods—they will not be useful to our task of bearing the Promise."

Jacob knelt before his father. He was surprised to find tears welling up in his eyes. The thought of leaving his family—especially his mother, but also Isaac—was suddenly overwhelming. "Bless me, my father!" he said, his voice breaking. Before the prospect of leaving his family, the formal blessing was not enough. He needed the warmth of a personal blessing from a father, not just the institutional commission of the head of a clan.

"A double blessing?" Isaac began. "The blessing of the birthright, *and*—but yes. Already you are blessed of God, and you should also be blessed by your father.

"May El Shaddai, the Almighty God, protect you in your going," Isaac began, his voice lapsing into the semi-chant of a formal blessing. "May He cause you and your wives to bear seed and be fruitful."

Enjoying his intonations, he allowed his voice to soar to a higher pitch as he continued. "May El Elyon, the Most High God, bless you in your coming again to this land that God promised to my father Abraham, so that you may take possession of this land where we now live as aliens."

Jacob's heart was encouraged by hearing the words of the Promise. It all put a more pleasant cast to his taking leave of his family, and to the long journey that lay before him. He arose, and kissed Isaac and Rebekah on both cheeks.

By dawn of the very next day, he was gone.

CHAPTER 5

I once watched two Macedonians wrestling, my lord Philemon. One was much lighter than the other, but more agile. They wrestled outdoors, the only bounds established by a ring of men cheering the one and jeering the other. The lightweight man teased and tormented his heavier opponent, working him up to a rage. Then, just as it seemed the heavier man would catch and crush him, his more agile opponent sprang up, caught a tree limb and left the larger man clawing the air and bellowing like a mad bear. Truly there is no rage greater than having one's opponent disappear, leaving no place for wrath save within the heart, where it does its work of ravenous rotting. Thus was the rage of Esau, when he found that Jacob, the object of his wrath, had fled.

Oh—the heavy wrestler was felled like a stone when the man with the "upper" hand dropped from the branch and caught his maddened opponent in the jaw with a well-aimed heel.

With embarrassment and anger turning his already florid face purple, Esau's reaction to enraged helplessness was a tragicomic scene around the Hebrew encampment for two days. At first he went about loudly proclaiming how he had been cheated. "Was ever there a more devious man than my brother?" he cried, like an actor appealing for applause. And there was much nodding of heads and grumbling in sympathy among his relatives and underlings. Everyone knew the law of the firstborn birthright: double portion of the inheritance, head of the clan, chief of any city-state they might form, priest and interpreter of the gods. Esau would have been able to raise a vigilante force, both from among his kinsmen and his subjects eastward in Edom, to wreak vengeance on Jacob the outlaw had he been present.

But sympathy for one who is placed in the shadow of another soon turns to a mild despising, as though it is felt that fate, after all, knew their relative worth and rendered a decree that time would prove just and fair despite all present appearances. Besides, the wrath of others who are not directly affected by one's own anguish is difficult to maintain. Toward the end of the second day Esau found that the little groups that had at first gathered to hear his complaint and share his anger grew smaller and dispersed earlier.

Mounting his favorite riding camel, Esau whipped the beast to a bone-jarring trot into the desert. He would take his still-seething spirit to his Hittite wives, there to be mended by their charms. Despite their pagan ways, Esau's two wives were not banned from the Hebrews' camp. After all, the Abrahamic clan had always included a variety of ethnic samples from the great cradle of civilization. But Esau preferred that they camp apart, within an hour or two of the main Hebrew camp. Even though he was not Rebekah's favorite, she favored his choice of wives even less, with the disdain of any mother who believes that few women are worthy to replace her own love for her son. And Isaac's preference for Esau had not extended to his wives, for their ways and worship were odious to him as a follower of the One God. Ironically, the Hittite women's gods were a part of their appeal to Esau. He found their devotion to Kal, god of the hunt, useful. So he had taken to wife Judith and Basemath, daughters of Beeri and Elon, respectively—two Hittite warlords to the far north who had stopped at the Hebrew encampment on their way from a treaty-making mission to Egypt.

"Esau, my lord!" his wives chirped in unison as he approached, each scurrying to embrace him first and perhaps win his affection for the night.

"Hmmph!" was his only response as he ordered his camel to

kneel and slid from atop the beast's sweating back. Hot and sweaty from his ride, he ordered water as he flung himself down heavily in the meager shade of a tamarisk tree growing by the spring near the two tents.

"Your time at the camp of your people did not go well," Basemath noted. Darker than Judith, and more plump, she wore a loose fitting, pale blue woolen robe. The dozen bracelets on each arm jingled pleasantly in Esau's ears.

"I have been robbed," he said. Both wives gathered closer, anxious to hear the tale.

"Who would have dared, my lord?" said Judith.

"My own brother, Jacob!" Esau fairly spat out the name. "He robbed me of my birthright and my blessing, and then fled like a coward to our kinsmen in Mesopotamia." The wives looked at each other in dismay. They obviously had a stake in the double portion of the firstborn son's inheritance.

"But how could this be?" asked Basemath.

"Never mind—it is done. The matter is closed, unless one of your Hittite gods can bring recourse. My gods—including the high God El my father loves so much—do not care."

Again Judith and Basemath looked at each other. Judith's black eyes snapped like coals burning in her pale face. Her slender body's shapeliness was scarcely hidden by a filmy brown garment with a light leather girdle encircling her high waist and criscrossed between modestly sized breasts.

"Perhaps Hannahanna can be summoned," she speculated. "The grandmother goddess has been known to rescue such situations."

The cool water and rest, along with his wives' interest in providing succor, soon enabled Esau to relax in the shade of the twisted tamarisk. "Shall we divine the will of this Hannahanna, and feast tonight on a kid from the herd?" he asked.

Instantly his wives were on their feet. Judith built a fire in the cook pit while Basemath selected a white, six-month-old kid from the little band secured nearby in a rough pen of thorny brush. She expertly slit its throat. Holding it by ears and tail while the blood drained into the sand, she lifted her swarthy face to the darkening sky in a silent incantation.

The Hittite woman brought the kid to Esau, whose practiced

knife disemboweled the little animal in swift strokes that guided
the entrails to a heap on the ground a little way from the tents.
Judith ran over to them and the three sat solemnly staring at the
position of the liver.

"It is almost completely covered by the rest," said Basemath.
Judith put her hand to her mouth. "It is not a good omen," she
said. "There is no recourse." Slowly she raised apologetic eyes to
her husband's. "It is fate, my lord. I am sorry..."

"Fate?" Esau exploded. "Is this the best your gods can do—to
put their own seal of approval on my treacherous brother's deed?"
"Not approval, my lord," Basemath said quietly. "It is only that it
is something even the gods cannot change. It is often thus."

"Often thus?" Esau echoed. "It is not often thus with Kal, when
I order him to find venison. Where is the power in saying only 'It
is fate' and 'It cannot be changed'?"

The Hittite women looked at each other, then down at the
ground. They were hardly theologians. They could only convey
what *Hatti* priests had handed down for generations.

Rising quickly from the divination, Judith went into her tent.
Moments later she emerged with an object wrapped in coarse
cloth, and two small, clay tablets inscribed with cuneiform writing. Although Esau could not read the script, he knew that they
were sacred texts.

"Think you that the books can challenge this fate that has paralyzed your gods?" he asked insolently.

Judith did not reply. She sat down in the sand before her tent
and unwrapped a carved image some eight inches high. It was of
a rather crudely carved nude goddess riding atop two lions. Perfectly balanced, the figure held aloft both hands, one grasping a
raven and the other a serpent.

"And who is this?" Esau asked skeptically.

"This is the Great Mother," Basemath said by way of introduction. "There is none higher among the gods."

"I will ask the Great Mother if some lesser god has forsaken
his duties and allowed your brother to despoil your inheritance,"
Judith explained. "Perhaps she will require him to restore your
fortunes—even against unseeing Fate."

Basemath joined her on the ground, with Cybele, the Mother
goddess, before them. Esau also sat. The two women began to

chant the incantation written on the tablets. As they finished the words on the first tablet, Judith lifted her eyes to the heavens and cried, in the Hittite tongue:

"I adjure you, Mother Cybele, to pursue whatever god has neglected his duties to protect the family fortunes of my husband." Then she lifted the image and made it to travel in sweeping arcs above her head, north to south and east to west—the path she willed for Cybele to follow in search of a delinquent god. Back and forth she waved the image, faster and faster until her slight body almost tumbled to the side.

Basemath opened her eyes and said quietly, "It is useless." And turning to Esau, as Judith brought the airborne image to rest heavily before her: "It is useless, my lord. The spell does nothing."

"The law of fate stands," Judith added wearily. Slowly she returned the image to its wrappings.

The three sat silently for a time. Finally Esau announced, "I will sleep while you prepare the kid." His wives went about their work preparing the evening meal with the heaviness of disappointment. It was not, of course, the first time their prayers had failed, but they had hoped for better results—both for the sake of their husband and their own financial future.

As he drifted toward sleep, Esau pondered the attempt to enlist the Hittite gods in his cause. Which is better, he wondered—a God like El, who apparently had the power to set a man's fate, but might later be persuaded by a thief like Jacob to change His mind; or the Hittite gods who were impotent before a force such as fate. Was fate, then, a higher god? And if so, did this lend credence to father Abraham's claim that there was really only *one* God?

It was too far-fetched a claim, and at any rate Esau was not given to such speculation. He put it all out of his head with a single, deep sigh, and was instantly asleep.

It was a week before Esau came again to his parents' tents at Beer-sheba. His anger having subsided to surliness, he sought out his father Isaac, prepared to heap on him scorn and ridicule for so lightly handing the blessing over to the wrong man. If Jacob was unavailable, he would vent his complaint on his father. He began, however, on a meek note.

"What has happened between us, my father?"

Isaac was braiding a tether from the hairs of an ass's tail, one of the tasks his blindness did not forbid. Gnarled as his fingers were, they intertwined the material this way and that with swift precision. A round rope the diameter of his little finger was taking shape between him and the stake in the ground to which the other end was fixed. At Esau's abrupt voice Isaac looked up as though he could see him.

"You have been gone long, my son."

"It is not pleasant to be where I am not wanted."

"You speak of something between us, and of being unwanted …It is the matter of the blessing," Isaac surmised.

"It is. We—you and I—we lived as though your blessing was upon me. It is strange that you blessed another," Esau said heavily.

Isaac made a half-dozen deft twists of the strands of hair before answering. "I was deceived. You know of the matter. It could not be rescinded. It is not our way." His voice was firm but not gruff. The rims of his eyelids grew red and moist. "Truly my blessing is upon you, my son. But God chooses whom He wills."

Esau was waiting for that point to be made and he seized upon its faulty logic. *"You would blame El for my brother's deceit?"* he hissed viciously.

The weariness in the old man's voice betrayed his having spent long hours covering this ground. "It is not mine to blame or excuse. What your brother did was deceitful. And he took advantage of you in bargaining for the birthright in the wilderness. But somehow, El is with him."

"Then I curse your God, El!" Esau exclaimed. "I will not honor a God of deceit."

Isaac's hands paused on the hair rope, but only for a moment. He wondered how far to go with his son on this topic. Should he confess that Esau's ways had more than once shaken his father's confidence in him as being of the stuff of the firstborn rights?

"Perhaps El knew you would curse Him, and thus sought one who would not," he said quietly, without remonstrance.

Baffled by such illogic, Esau made two or three false starts before he could get a sentence together. "But He did not know I would have cause to curse him until I was already robbed of my rightful due!" he said with no little exasperation.

Isaac himself was ill-prepared to defend or explain the ways of El in heated debate; he only knew He was God the Almighty One, and he was seeking a way to put into words what he could but sense. "The world is in two halves, an upper and a lower," he finally ventured, remembering a conversation he had had with two traveling philosophers from Achaia only the month before.

"What?" asked Esau, even less prepared for such a digression.

"It is true—the world is like two halves of a coconut —there is an upper half in which dwells God and His hosts; and there is the lower half, in which we dwell. But the two halves are one whole, and El Shaddai governs them both. What He ordains from the upper realm matches what occurs in the lower, for it is all one world."

"Ah, then," Esau replied, rising to the challenge out of his recent experience with the Hittite gods. "Then your God rules our world as well as His, and being all powerful He chooses whom He wills and determines our fate?"

Isaac was silent a moment. "It is at least partly true that—."

"Then the god Fate rules us!" Esau snapped, sensing superior logic in his argument.

"No, my son. In some way, He both elects whom He will, and grants them the power to elect whether to be chosen. The willing in the heavens somehow is a match with the doing on the earth. The two halves match. There is one world, and one God."

"Doubletalk!" Esau exploded.

The two sat silently for a time. The drone of the flies provided background music for the faint swish of the hairs as Issac worked on with his hands. Their minds had taken the matter as far as they could push them for the moment. Isaac had called on the analogy of the Achaians for good reason; the Hebrews were neither theologians nor philosophers. They were more proficient in doing the will of the God they claimed spoke to them than in explaining His ways.

Still, an example came to Isaac. "Take your grandfather Abraham," he said, choosing his words carefully. "You know our story. It was not because father Abraham was a great man that El revealed Himself to him and gave him the Promise. But in the revealing, in the choosing, father Abraham showed himself to be a good choice. Can we not believe that God chooses those whom He foresees will act as His chosen?"

Esau turned that one over carefully in his mind before replying. He could see the implication of the statement for himself. "So you are saying that I did not prove myself worthy to be chosen as bearer of what was rightfully mine—right even by the laws of your God," he said, the sentence starting slowly and softly, but ending with vehemence.

Old Isaac had not meant for the conversation to turn into an accusation; and indeed the broad way in which Esau stated the case was not precisely what he meant. But not knowing how to soften what Esau had taken to be an indictment, he decided simply to say no more. He worked harder at his plaiting.

But if Isaac had concluded his part of the dialogue, Esau had not. "Say it, then! I am simply worth less in El's sight than is Jacob—and somehow El *knew* that this would be the case. Which means, if He is El Shaddai, the Almighty One, He not only determined beforehand that I *would* not be as worthy as my brother, He also determined that I *may* not!"

Again, while this was not at all what Isaac was arguing, he could not immediately fashion a reply without simply restating what he had said. And he sensed that Esau would not be able to hear it even if he could find a way to present his case more eloquently. Wiping his eyes with a skein of hair, he concentrated on keeping his fingers moving over the fast-lengthening rope. If such talk did not clarify the ways of God, at least it lent itself well to rope-making.

Something in the old man's sudden reticence disquieted Esau. While he felt he had the better of the argument, he had glimpsed a certain elegance of balance and wholeness in Isaac's picture of the world. But it would not do to seem to soften by telling Isaac so. Esau arose abruptly, not honoring his father with a word of closure or farewell, and stalked away to tend to business with the shepherds. With Jacob gone, he bore most of the supervisory work himself. There would be little time for hunting, he thought bitterly.

Chapter 6

It was not without some embarrassment that Esau took up again his everyday work with the shepherds. They were among those to whom he had complained so loudly, and although they had taken his side, the birthright business did not concern them directly—especially those hangers-on who were not Abrahamites and caught up with the matter of the "Promise." They were late with the shearing, and they were more interested in getting on with their work than in remaining embroiled in such affairs.

Esau threw himself into details of the work before them, working out places and dates for shearing that would not involve driving the flock too far in the heat. For two days he visited nearby sheep-camps, occupying himself with the work so intensely that he did not dwell on his loss. But on the evening of the third day, as he was returning to the base camp, he saw his mother retrieving a day's washing that had been spread on rocks to dry—and the bitterness returned.

"Mother," he acknowledged in a low voice, hardly more than a mutter as he passed by, intending to march on to his tent without stopping.

"My son. Stay awhile. You have been away."

"You noticed? Yet not as far away as your son Jacob."

Rebekah lowered her eyes. "You, too, are my son."

Esau softened. He was not interested in pressing the point of his mother's favoritism for Jacob, for he knew well how he had formerly traded on his father's regard. But, unable yet to put the matter of the birthright and blessing behind him, he could not resist saying, "Your brother Laban will soon be enjoying the visit of the next patriarch of our tribe." Had he known of Rebekah's involvement in the ruse, including her expert work sewing up the goatskin for Jacob, he would have said far more.

"Esau," Rebekah said evenly, meeting his gaze. "There is *the* blessing, and there are other blessings. Do not think that you have no favor in God's sight." Now that the blessing of the firstborn was safely where she was sure it had been intended, her motherly instincts could allow her to be concerned about Esau. But it was a futile gesture.

"Ah, yes—let us salt the remaining meat now that the best portion is spoiled," he said. Not a bad analogy, he told himself, to have come to mind without forethought. He would not give his mother the benefit of comforting him. His voice rose with his returning anger. "I have no need to hear of your God's concern for me. Nor do I need a birthright or blessing from Him. I have spoken with my father about His ways, and they are hardly befitting a good man, let alone a god. I have my own ways, and my own wives, with their gods." He used the latter weapon with the vindictive purpose of reminding his mother that his Hittite women had replaced his need for Rebekah's love, and that their gods were more reliable than El.

"My son," Rebekah pleaded. "Do not—."

"And as for your son Jacob," Esau interrupted, gratified to see that his barbed words had found their target, "It is a pity to be so ashamed of one's deeds, and so afraid of one's own brother, as to have to take flight."

Rebekah did not want Jacob branded a coward. "I sent him to Haran," she said. "It is time for him to think of marrying, and if he stayed here, there are only these Canaanites, women of the uncircumcised—." She stopped, realizing she was only making matters worse by tacitly berating Esau for having married his Hittite women. Esau was quick to catch the inference.

"Ah, yes—reminding me of my sins against the heralded pure

line," he said. "I need no more of this." With that, he turned on his heel, packed his riding camel and rode off toward the tents of his wives. His small achievement in creating painful repartee with Rebekah had opened a floodgate of revived anger, which he wore like a fine plume in a sultan's turban as his beast lurched into the desert.

By the time Esau had traveled half the distance to his wives' camp, his anger had heated up a bitter meal for his parents. If it displeased them to have Canaanite wives in the family, why not supply them with even more, in return for their sorry allegiance to his rights? He grinned grimly at the prospect, even in his anger. Why not? He was growing restless with only two wives anyway. Suddenly he pulled up the camel with a jerk, as his anger gave birth to a sudden plan.

Of course—his uncle Ishmael's daughter, Mahalath! At the mere thought, Esau pulled the head of his grumbling beast to the west. Mahalath the voluptuous, a cousin with whom Esau had more than once sported. Her charms were untidily packaged, to be sure, and she carried too much weight for a long journey, but it was Jacob, not Esau, who was on the move! She was a perfect choice—the daughter of Isaac's half-brother, with whom there was already tension. And he would see to it that the inter-clan marriage did not smooth over the differences, but added to them instead.

Whipping his beast to a faster gait, Esau rode far into the night before stopping. He was up before daybreak, coaxing his groaning camel to its feet and pressing on across the treeless plain toward the tents of Ishmael. Three days later he arrived, dirty and exhausted, but still congratulating himself on his plan.

"Ho, brothers!" he greeted two other nephews of Ishmael who came out from the camp with staves at the ready, not knowing who approached. "I come in peace—it is I, Esau, son of Isaac." He bowed as low as he could from atop his camel, and touched his forehead in greeting.

"Is it you, Esau?" one of the men answered. "You are welcome to our camp!"

Dismounting, Esau turned his weary beast over to the second cousin and walked with his arm around the other toward the tents of Ishmael.

The old man emerged from his sleeping tent even as the two

approached. Even before greeting him, Esau became aware of the twittering and giggling of female voices to his right. But he kept his eyes on Ishmael as he said, "Shalom, my lord Ishmael! Greetings from your brother Isaac and his kinsmen!"

"Who is this that brings greetings from the favored child of my father?" growled Ishmael. Older even than Isaac, Ishmael was a short, squatty man, totally covered with badger skins even in the heat. He had the swarthy skin of an Egyptian, the race of his mother, a slave girl whom Abraham's wife Sarah had lent him to compensate for her own barrenness. Ishamel's hair and beard were now thin, but they retained enough sickly color, despite his age, to make his face appear always dirty. Perhaps it was, Esau thought, as he drew near enough to smell the old man.

"It is Isaac's unfavored son, Esau," he said, bowing and again touching his forehead.

"Hmph!" Ishmael muttered. "You need not come to me with such lies—I know you have always been my brother's favorite."

"*Have been*," said Esau. "My brother Jacob—." He stopped, his political sense for once issuing a warning. No need to prejudice the old man against giving his daughter to Esau in marriage by going into the misfortunes of the birthright. "As you say, my lord," he finished.

"What brings you across the desert to my home?" Ishmael asked, not one to waste time with small talk.

"Marriage, my lord." Esau cleared his throat. Seeing the women he had heard, now peering around the next tent, he raised his voice for their benefit. "I have come to ask the hand of your daughter, my cousin Mahalath."

The twittering of the women rose in pitch and intensity. As for Ishmael, this was good news, and an opportunity to be rid of a mouth to feed in return for the asset of a dowry. What a fine bargain! He forced a smile through his wispy moustache. "The hand of Mahalath, eh? What a fine—." He stopped himself before revealing his delight. Better to haggle from a position of hardship. "What a fine mess you would leave me in! You would carry away one of the best cooks in my camp?"

"My lord Ishmael has many other cooks," Esau replied evenly. He knew the old man's game well. It was a ruse as old as the land, and one that must be played out even though all parties knew precisely what was in the other's mind, and the difference between that and their words.

"Ah, but this one, this Mahalath—she could fatten a stick," Ishmael said. Spying the woman in question among the eavesdropping females, he said with authority, "You there—Mahalath-Basemath, the cook—come here!" A heavy-set, raven-haired woman with a broad face and nose waddled over to the men, lifting her veil as she came and covering her face up to her dark, red-rimmed eyes. Esau noted how different she was from his Hittite wife Basemath, whose name she shared.

"Mahalath," Esau acknowledged, rather flatly. She had matured from plumply attractive to more shapelessly heavy since he had seen her.

"My lord Esau," she said, eyes down, attempting a coy voice. She bowed before both men.

"See, my son," said Ishmael, expansively including Esau in his family. "She is all here!" he said, laughing too loudly. "Let us go into the meal tent and discuss this, ah, delicate matter."

An hour later Esau and Ishmael emerged, both rather unsteadily. There had been much lifting of cups and loud smacking over the dregs of the heavy, red wine. The trade had been arranged, and a date a fortnight hence set for the marriage feast. Seeking out Mahalath to take his leave, Esau found her with her companions again—and noticed that they were foreign women. They giggled nervously, veils upraised, as Mahalath did the introductions.

"You are Hittite?" Esau asked, with slurred speech, of the one called Adah. He could tell from the way her ears were pierced, and from the bangles across her forehead with the god Kal engraved upon them. A light-skinned, slender beauty, Adah leveled grey eyes at him frankly.

"Yes, my lord. But I follow these Ishmaelites."

"And you?" Esau asked, turning to the third woman, a short woman with unusual auburn hair, dyed or natural he could not tell.

"I am Hivite," answered Oholibamah.

"I am favored to be chosen to wed my lord," Mahalath-Basemath said. "But it will be hard to leave my companions here. They are as sisters to me."

The wine had robbed Esau of caution and replaced it with vulnerability. On impulse, he blurted out, "Why leave them, my dear?" He dropped his shaggy head and leered up at the women from bloodshot eyes.

"My lord? Surely you do not mean *you* would join *our* band?" his bride-to-be said anxiously. She had been only too glad to hear talk of a marriage that would take her away from her tiresome family.

"No, no," Esau reassured her. "I only mean—*I shall take all three of you to wife!*" Even as the words rolled out sluggishly over a slowed tongue, Esau again congratulated himself. He would pay no dowry for these foreign women, who had freed themselves from their families. And that grey-eyed wench that looked as though she could not be embarrassed—she would no doubt be able to please a man in all sorts of Canaanite ways.

Amid even more giggling and twittering the three women danced excitedly at the prospect of what seemed to offer a new adventure—and all together. How quickly their fortunes had changed.

And as Esau rode slowly away the next morning, he, too, was thinking of fortunes. He had just obtained three wives for the price of one.

CHAPTER 7

Traveling light in his haste to flee Esau's wrath, Jacob set out for Haran with only two servants. Shinab was a diminutive, wiry man who would not need much food or drink in the trek across the desert. Sabteca was a tall, thin pagan who was nonetheless more trustworthy than some of the believing servants in Isaac's household.

His servants alternately rode and led two pack asses, while Jacob was astride a camel. They headed due north, even though they could have gone a little south, circled the southern end of the Dead Sea, then turned north on a well-traveled caravan route. But that way would have taken Jacob through some settlements that Esau had established on several of his wide-ranging hunting expeditions.

Jacob knew that Esau himself might be in the area, his ruddy hair and florid complexion blending in with the red sandstone of the land he called Edom, or the Redlands. There he had organized a few scattered tribes into a small nation, establishing his hegemony with bribes and a brief show of force on the part of his armed servants. While the inhabitants had little love for their lord Esau, they had no reason to think any more of his brother Jacob. Better that they stay west of the Dead Sea, Jacob decided. They would make their way generally up the Great Rift, the crease in the earth that extends even into Egypt and provides a bed for the Nile. They would turn northeast after making their way through Canaan, picking up from there the ancient road that led to the land of Haran, in northern Mesopotamia.

They journeyed in the day, despite the heat, to prevent their noise from attracting bandits who could slip up on them under cover of darkness. The land gradually grew more hospitable as the miles slipped away to the south. On the third day, about noon, they passed the ancient city of Salem on their left. Here had lived the storied king Melchizedek, so great a king that father Abraham had actually tithed to him a part of the spoils taken in the defeat of the captors of his nephew Lot.

Even this city, mused Jacob, is a part of the land of the Promise. And shall I then inherit the city of Melchizedek? It was a thought born more of gratitude than arrogance. And unnoticed by Jacob (for who among us can always know the workings of our soul of souls?), this acknowledgment of his chosenness as a gift began a work in his heart that was the first of many small changes that would one day make Jacob unrecognizable as the Supplanting child of deceit that tricked the birthright from his brother.

The land gave way to pleasant vineyards, and to tall poplars lining cultivated fields on gently sloping hillsides. It was dusk when the lead ass, herded by Shinab, reared and brayed noisily, startled by something up ahead. They could see the twinkling torch lights in the village of Luz, a hundred yards away; perhaps a shepherd or farmer was returning late from the fields. Jacob, who had been walking at the rear of the tiny caravan, hurried up to help his servant calm the animal.

"Ho, my little *athon*," he said soothingly, using the common name for donkey that implied a compliment for their endurance. "Steady there. What does it see?" He and the two servants peered into the gathering darkness.

"There, my lord!" said Shinab. "It is no one; but there is a light."

A believer in El, the man thought he detected a presence in the place. He shuddered slightly.

Sure enough, the ass had been startled by a soft, blue-white glow just off the trail and not 30 steps ahead.

"It is only a white stone, made to glow by the moon's light," said Sabteca. He was a realistic pagan, and had little room in his view of reality for anything like a "presence."

The travelers drew closer, tugging heavily at the donkeys' lead ropes to overcome their protests. As they neared, it proved to be just as Sabteca said—a stone the length of a man's forearm, half as wide, and a hand-span thick. Apparently it was a piece of chalky limestone, although what had seemed to be a glow subsided to a more natural look now that they were in its presence.

"We will camp here," Jacob said. The two servants pulled the asses on around the edge of a little hill before unpacking them, according Jacob the distance of his dignity as master. They did not build a fire, but shared dried figs and hard, crusty bread for their supper, washing it down with rainwater and dew that had collected in a hollowed out rock. Weary from their travels, they talked only a few minutes before settling down for the night.

Jacob folded a rough woolen blanket into a square, placed it on the strange rock for a pillow, and spread out his pallet. Lying on his back, his mind began the eternal musing of a man sleeping outdoors: How far away are the stars? Is there a God behind their cold glitter, a Being who knows my name and feels kindly toward me, tiny speck that I am?

He picked out the Great Bear, then the Lesser. He knew their stately course through the seasons. According to some seers, human destiny was attached to the steady predictability of the stars. Jacob wondered if his own fate were somehow written up there in the deep blackness. And if so, could Yah intervene, changing His mind and commanding a corresponding change in the stars? Or, once He set their cosmic orbit, was he, too, bound by the very regularity of creation?

Jacob drifted off to sleep with the Promise on his mind: *If you can count the stars in the heavens, so can you count the number of your descendants.* It was at once humbling and a point of pride: for what Aramean wife would not rejoice to be married to a man who bore such a promise from the Ruler of the universe?

My lord Philemon: I pause before recounting the story of the stairway or ladder. In some of the books it is recounted as a dream; in others a vision. For my part, I hold it was a vision, such as God from time to time conveys to His servants, rather than a dream, which can be not from God but from the churning of the belly, the result of a mean meal such as that of which Jacob had partaken. The ancients, as you know, put very great significance on such experiences, when sleep drives away distractions of the day and the sounds of the night become the very whispering of God.

Four or five hours after Jacob rested his head on the rock, he thought he felt it vibrate ever so slightly. The earth moves! he thought—an event not unknown to the area—and he sprang to his feet looking wildly about for a place of refuge. Or did he? In a way he seemed still to be asleep, and only dreaming that he arose. Before he could decide whether he was awake or sleeping he saw a shaft of light beginning at the blue-white stone and extending beyond his vision into the cloudy overcast that had formed since the little party camped.

Jacob tried to call out to his servants, but it was as though the words lodged in his throat. He was dumb, and his gaze was fixed to the pale light as by a magnet. He shut his eyes tightly to drive away his mistaken impressions or else clarify what could be a dream. But, strangely, the sight was no less obvious even with his eyes closed, as though he beheld it with the eyes of his mind. So pervasive was the vision that Jacob soon stopped struggling to avoid it and tried to penetrate its meaning. As his eyes bore into the shaft of light it began to come alive with huge figures scrambling up and down a stairway that extended upward from the stone. He could tell—though how, he knew not—that they were angels of the nations. He had heard of such—as well as demons appointed over certain lands. That one was the angel of Babylon, this one of Greece, and another—dressed appropriately in a rusty-red garment—of Edom.

The superhuman figures hurled themselves up and down the staircase faster and faster, until their forms began to blur into each other, the colors of their garments tinting the shaft of light with all the hues of the rainbow. Suddenly it became a gigantic prism in which Jacob saw scenes from each of the nations represented by their angels. Some of the scenes he recognized from the tales shared around tribal campfires for as long as he could remember—events from the past. There was the ark of Noah riding high on the crest of the Great Flood ...Babel, tower of insolence, with its builders being scattered throughout the nations ...Abraham (known then as Abram) responding to the call of the high God El when he lived in ancient Ur...Abraham about to offer up Jacob's father Isaac as a lad atop the Mount of Moriah...Isaac preceding him to the land of Haran where he, too, took a wife.

More amazingly, he was apparently being treated also to events that were yet to be—though how he knew they were in the future he knew not. There were scenes involving people he somehow felt he should know, but whom he could recall in no lore or tale by which to recognize them: a figure bearing some resemblance to Jacob himself, but on a throne carved with images he recognized to be Egyptian...a tumultuous scene of a rag-tag band of shabbily dressed people being pursued through walls of water by soldiers whose dress identified them as Egyptians...battles, apparently between Hebrews and Philistines...a giant looming over a young man who defiantly felled him with—of all things—a slingshot...a glorious Temple built on hills he recognized as those of Salem, so recently passed on his journey.

The swirling images occasionally were swept up into what seemed a higher dimension—or was it more distant? In one scene the Temple whose glory had awed Jacob lay under seige. In sickening detail he saw starving men and women with distended bellies boiling something that Jacob somehow sensed was the flesh of their own children. Then a boulder as though hurled from heaven crashed down upon the scene, scattering people to the four winds of the earth. They stood on farflung shores in forlorn knots of humanity looking back wistfully to what had been their homeland.

Suddenly, grim-faced, pallid soldiers in grey garb that appeared to Jacob like underpants, and wearing no robes, surrounded the little bands of Hebrews and herded them into crowded camps. Horrible scenes of rape and theft and mutilation gave way to a vision of huge vaults, like metal caves, into which people were forcibly thrust—Jacob himself at the forefront. Then he was outside the vision again, watching as the doors to the caves clanged shut and a mist arose from them accompanied by the death-cries of those within...and the stench of rotting flesh.

In another series of episodes, Jacob saw himself and his brother Esau facing each other in anger, each waving toward the hills and valleys of Canaan and pounding their chests as though to assert their right to the land. Suddenly a deep cleft in the earth opened between them, and multitudes of what seemed to be their tribes and kinsmen drew up at the brink on either side, in full battle array.

At one end of the rift, men from Esau's hordes began to throw up an earthen embankment as a bridge across the rift. It was completed in the flick of an eyelid, and screaming soldiers mounted on swift horses and wielding strange, curved swords attacked the followers of Jacob. In turn, Jacob's forces, dressed in other-worldly garments of olive green and mounted on some sort of monstrous, metal camel or other beast, counter-attacked.

In a flowing change of imagery, the soldiers' spears and swords seem to enlarge before Jacob's dreaming eyes, and to be transformed into huge metal cylinders aimed at the opposing troops. Fire belched from the noses of these barrels, and explosions like the volcanos of which Jacob had heard erupted across the battlefield. As the smoke of these unearthly blasts cleared, Jacob's heart broke to see countless women holding their mangled dead, rocking back and forth, moaning the universal cry of those who must give up their loved ones in futile and bloody battles over which they have no control.

Even in his trance, Jacob was aware of anguish so deep it seemed to penetrate his mind and extend into his very bones. He shut his eyes against the rivers of blood that flowed out of the battlefield and overflowed the chasm that still separated him from his brother. As he raised his pain-ravaged face to the sky, an involuntary gasp wracked his body and formed itself into a prayer:

"Enough! Enough! Great El, what have I done in wresting the birthright from my brother? Even though it were to carry the right of possession to all this land, can it be worth this carnage? I cannot bear the burden of bearing the birthright! It is a birth-*blight*! Return, I pray You—return this horrible sign of Your favor to my brother!"

Opening his eyes in his vision, Jacob was at the point of fainting, not just from the light and motion but from the dizzy feeling that time had collapsed about him, allowing past and present and future to meld into a single swirling mass that both swept Jacob up in its stream and stood him on the edge of the cosmos in sickening vertigo.

He was about to try to flee the monumental and stunning scene, when all at once the pulsating lights ceased their play, melting into one calm, continuous stream of indescribable beauty. The battling armies faded into a mist, and unseen voices—angels', Jacob supposed—began to blend in thunderous but harmonious praise to Yah, whom Jacob instinctively realized was the High God El.

Finally, at the top of the cosmic stairway, and coming into view at the crest of a swelling chorus, stood a figure that could only be El Himself.

The books are silent, my lord, as to the appearance of our God. As you know, our ancestors by faith, the Jews, do not allow artistic renderings of Him, having more humility than my own countrymen who do not blush to carve supposed images of the divine on everything from trees to tombs. The word of mouth descriptions of Him whom Jacob saw are various. Some say He appeared only as a glorious light, others as a pyramid, like those of Egypt, and still others as a giant human, as though He who is un-image-able donned for a moment the form of a man in order to be recognized by a man. Of more importance than the form El took is the burden of the blessing He extended to Jacob, portrayed in the vision of the stairway.

And before Jacob could flee, or even bow, a Voice of infinite power, yet filling the poor man with reassurance, spoke these words:

> "Fear not, Jacob, son of Isaac, son of Abraham. I am the Lord, the God of your fathers, Ruler of the universe and of the land on which you lie—the land which I give to you and to your offspring, which shall be as numberless as the dust of the earth. And as the angels you have seen fill the space between earth and heaven, so your seed will spread east and west and north and south, for a blessing to all the families of the earth! Henceforth you must not fear the burden of bearing my favor; for others, even the sons of Esau, may share the birthright—both for glory and for suffering—if they will live as chosen people.

> "And fear not that you are a fugitive from your father and mother. Fear not the wrath of your brother Esau, and fear not that the land I will give you will not also be his land. For I am with you to bless all nations, as I will be with you on the way to your kinsmen in Haran. I will bless you there, and bring you again to this land which I give you, in order to accomplish my word according to the promise to your father and your father's father."

At this the angelic chorus, which had subsided while their Captain was speaking, burst into praise so mighty that Jacob started. Heavenly musicians appeared in the shaft of light, accompanying the chorus with trumpets and lyres, transforming even the light into some kind of tangible music that filled the eyes and heart as well as the ears.

Jacob threw himself on his face before the onslaught of sound and sight and emotion, and as he did so the vision faded into the night.

Jacob opened his eyes to the quiet of the hillside near Luz. He had no sense of time, no way of discerning how long he had slept before the vision or how long it had lasted. He lay there trembling for a time until he could calm his soul. As dawn began to wash the eastern sky with pale light, he knew what he must do.

He sprang from his rude bed and noticed that the strange stone was glowing even more in the growing light of dawn than it had in the dark of night. "How fearful is this place, and how full of the presence of El!" he said aloud.

At that moment Shinab appeared, rubbing his eyes open. "What is it, master?" he inquired anxiously. "Are you well? Are you yet dreaming?"

"No, no, I am not dreaming; and I am very well. This place is none other than Beth-El, the house of God. Fetch me the oil from the lead ass's left wallet." Relieved, but hardly understanding, the servant stumbled off to retrieve the olive oil.

"It is El who guided our feet to this place," Jacob said as Shinab returned, accompanied now by his fellow-servant. "And this stone is none other than a stone from the precious stones in the throne of the unseen God in the farthest heaven, fallen to the earth as a sign that He is with me, and will not forsake me." Jacob set the stone upright and poured a little oil on it. "This place shall no more be called Luz, but Beth-El, the House of God," he intoned, "and this stone I anoint as the dwelling place of God and the very gate of heaven."

So saying, Jacob and his men broke camp, packed their beasts, and wound their way down the hillside to the little village below. There they enjoyed fresh fruit for a simple breakfast as the market opened for the day, replenished their supplies, then made their way north, toward Haran, toward Jacob's uncle, Laban, and—Jacob prayed—a wife.

CHAPTER 8

The routine of a long journey had established itself by now. The three travelers, Jacob and his servants Shinab and Sabteca, plodded steadily north, toward the sea of Kinnereth, intent on going as far as they could each night. To the west, toward the Great Sea, lay a ridge of mountains, and a lower range of hills separated their route from the River Jordan.

My lord Philemon—I must stop a moment and remark how the feet of Jacob the Chosen were now treading the land where our Lord and Savior, the Christ, would walk many years later. The mind wonders whether the sense of destiny growing in Jacob, and the strange promise that this land where he walked would belong to his descendants, made the land holy to him, as it would become holy to those who follow Jesus, seed of Jacob.

Did Jacob sense that he was building a people when he walked so near the spot where our Lord would later build yokes in his father's shop in Nazareth? And when the three laid eyes on Kinnereth, the sea that would one day be called Galilee, did Jacob marvel at its beauty as we who are his spiritual seed marvel at the beauty of Him who walked on its waters?

But I digress by my musings...

The travelers made more than a night's stay of their visit to the village of Hamath *(said by some, as my lord may know, to be the present city of Tiberius, named after the Roman emperor)*. Lying on the shore of Kinnereth, with Mt. Tabor at its back, Hamath was a welcome sight. They would rest here for two days and replenish their supplies, for when they left Kinnereth and veered northeast toward Damascus, they would leave also the verdant setting of their travels thus far. They must prepare for the desert.

From the north shore of Kinnereth the little party pointed toward "the pearl of the East," the storied city of Damascus, chief city of the Syrians. They soon saw the snows of Mt. Hermon to their left and journeyed on, mile after wearying mile, until finally the gleaming, white walls of Damascus came into view. Nestling in oasis-like greenery, it was like a bit of carved jade, with the surrounding desert a complementary setting. "Apum," or "canebrakes," the Egyptians called it, after the lush canefields that lay to the east of the city.

The weary travelers stopped at the first inn they came to on the outskirts of the city. Upon learning that the place had a stable for their beasts, they secured rooms, bathed at the public baths, and went into the tavern for their evening meal.

The place was already noisy with travelers and native Damascenes eating and drinking and gaming. The game tables especially caught Jacob's eye. He had been known among his father's herdsmen as a crafty opponent who always won more than he lost—by means that most agreed were illegitimate, but that they could not prove.

The three ordered wine and sat down near a table where a game was breaking up. A richly dressed man, perhaps ten years older than Jacob, stood up to leave, then paused as he noticed the interest with which the three travelers were watching.

"Ah, my friend, I take it from your dress that you are traveling through our fair city?" the man said suavely, twirling the ends of his jet-black moustache. By saying thus, he identified himself as a native—and, Jacob guessed, a man of the world who preyed on travelers unschooled in the sophistications of the city. He decided to play it that way.

"My lord has sharp eyes," he said ingratiatingly. "We are from the south, beyond Canaan, simple shepherds making our way to my kinsmen in the north." Shinab and Sabteca nodded politely at the stranger, but settled back on a bench to allow their master Jacob to make what he would of the situation.

"Welcome, my good man," the Damascene boomed. "I noticed that you watched our little game closely. Are you a sporting man?"

"Hardly, I am afraid, my lord. There is not much opportunity to learn of such among my father's sheep." In a single sentence, Jacob had managed to type himself as both an ignorant country bumpkin and a youngish man not yet ready to venture far from his father's protective arm. "But I have always thought I would like to learn," he added eagerly.

This was too good, thought the Damascene. He both lived *for* such opportunities and *from* them; and he proceeded to ply his trade on this untaught rustic.

"Sit, sit, my friend," he said, motioning to a stool like a gracious host. "I am called Dalmanutha. I will gladly teach you."

On the game table lay some three or four dozen small, white disks or pellets carved from bone, and a single ivory cube. "We have many games here, but this one is simple to learn," the Damascene said condescendingly. Sabteca looked at Shinab and winked. This would be highly entertaining.

Dalmanutha explained the game. "We simply make a wager before the game—say two pieces of silver—and the other either matches it or raises it. We then take turns throwing the die. Whatever number falls face-up, that's the number of disks we are allowed to retrieve from the pile in the center. When they are all gone, the player with the most disks wins the joint wager. What could be simpler?"

Nothing, Jacob thought. But to reinforce his ruse he said, "I am sorry, my lord. It does seem simple, but I—would you mind repeating the rules?"

"Not at all, not at all," Dalmanutha gushed. "And don't be embarrassed if it seems complicated at first. All will come clear with a few plays."

Well, Jacob thought—let's hope that *all* doesn't become clear, because I would be very glad to take this man's money on to Haran with me.

The Damascene made the first wager, and Jacob modestly matched it. The die came up three, and Dalmanutha skillfully and smoothly slid three disks from the pile over to his side of the table.

It was Jacob's turn. "Three pieces of silver," he said.

"Good, good," said the teacher. "Shows courage."

Jacob's roll of the die came up with a two on top. As he reached to the center of the table to select his disks, only Shinab and Sabteca, watching closely, saw Jacob's lean, sensitive forefinger give an extra twitch as they touched the pile of disks. And only they knew that as Jacob drew back his arm, the long, full sleeve of his tunic would contain at least one extra disk, perhaps two.

"Sorry," said the Damascene.

Jacob looked up quickly. "Excuse me?" Surely he had not already been caught.

"Sorry that you rolled only a two, to my three," said the teacher. "But your luck may improve. Let us continue."

Continue they did, with the pile of bone disks shrinking while those of the players increased. The game was over in twenty minutes.

"Now what?" asked Jacob innocently.

"Why, now we make an accounting of our disks. And the one with the most disks wins a bonus of five pieces of silver."

Jacob had five more disks than Dalmanutha.

"Well, well," my young friend," he said, a bit too loudly. "You see? You learn quickly. Soon you will be teaching the master."

Without asking about another game, the Damascene assumed it, and pulled the disks back to the center. It was Jacob's turn to put up the first wager. Dalmanutha doubled it. The second game was on.

Again the student won; and this time the teacher was not so gracious. His face reddened. "Another," he growled.

And another they played. This time Jacob allowed Dalmanutha to win, to avoid suspicion.

By the end of the fourth game, Jacob had won three months' wages for a shepherd. The Damascene was in a fine rage, but endeavoring to hide it. Jacob was in his element, with all his considerable feints and pretensions in their sharpest display. His winnings were so remarkable that the pair had attracted a crowd of other local gamesters, marveling at the "beginner's luck" of this stranger who was no doubt visiting the city for the first time.

But something was wrong. Instead of enjoying the sport, Jacob sensed a growing uneasiness in his heart. He looked up at the rapt faces of his audience. What so enthralled them? Only the tricks of a cheat. It had never bothered him before. Why could he not enjoy this sport as he once did?

Suddenly it dawned on him that the whole scene was reminding him of his deception in stealing the birthright. But there was something else, now. His mother's words echoed from deep within his soul:

> You are a chosen one...
> You have been looked on with favor...
> You have a high road to travel...
> I tell you this for the sake of the man you are yet to be...

The echo grew into a roar so loud and insistent that Jacob sprang up from his stool, hands over his ears, his eyes shut against the judgment he had pronounced on himself. He would have to do something to relieve this anguish of soul. He would confess to Dalmanutha, and before these onlookers, that he had been cheating. And he would return all the Damascene's money.

But before Jacob could open his mouth, Dalmanutha leaped to his own feet at the sudden move of his opponent. As he did so, two stray bones from his own sleeves spilled to the floor. Of course! As Jacob suspected, the Damascene lived by the very means of which Jacob was so ashamed.

The crowd gave a collective gasp. Most knew that Dalmanutha lived by ill-gotten gains, but they were not prepared for the evidence to fall so brazenly from his sleeves.

As for Jacob, he could at first only stare at the richly garbed Dalmanutha, whose face was now red with embarrassment instead of rage. "I—well, well," the Syrian said lamely. "Imagine this. It seems that accidentally these disks crept—."

"No," Jacob said quietly. "It was no accident."

"Why, surely you don't think that I—."

"I think that you have cheated me, as I have cheated you," Jacob said evenly.

"Wha—what do you mean?"

"I mean, my lord Dalmanutha, that we are both frauds."

The Damascene was not ready to concede that he had been found out—especially now that he had opportunity to take the offensive and draw attention to this intruder.

"Fraud?" he roared. "I swear to you my young friend —these disks found their way to my person quite by accident. But *you*— you are confessing that you have cheated me?"

Jacob had no idea now where the situation would lead. He had been brought face to face with the cold reality that he, the Chosen, he who was to inherit Yah's Promise, was no better than this professional swindler. His chagrin and shame was almost more than he could bear.

Meanwhile, the crowd of Damascenes moved in to support their local representative. Menacing hands moved toward daggers.

"The traveler cheats!" said one.

"He confesses!" added another.

Dalmanutha looked from one to the other, appealing with his eyes for such continued support. "Get him!" he cried.

Suddenly it was Jacob whose hand was filled with a great, shining blade. *Thunk!* went the heavy knife as he brought it down squarely in the center of the table with such force that it split one of the bone disks neatly in two.

"*No!*" he cried. Sabteca and Shinab were on their feet at their master's side, their own knives drawn for action.

The crowd drew back. The authority in Jacob's voice and his aggressiveness, in place of the defensiveness or flight they expected, momentarily checked their advance. Their murmurings subsided as Jacob spoke.

"In the name of Yah let us not make a poor state of affairs worse!" he went on. His Hebrew tongue provided just enough difference from the local dialect to make his speech seem supernaturally anointed.

"I have come to you as one chosen by the most High God, traveling through your city, enjoying the food and drink of this inn— and I have disgraced both God and myself by cheating this, my unsuspecting opponent, of his money."

The crowd was utterly quiet now, stunned at such self-deprecating language. Jacob continued.

"But you—you are no better. Do you greet all strangers by cheating them? Is this the way the great city of Damascus has achieved its reputation?"

A few of the men looked at each other with wide eyes. Others looked down at the stone floor. Some began to turn away. The blood they had smelled suddenly lost its appeal. They were not at all sure what had happened; the appeal to universal morality Jacob was making was lost on them, but it somehow made a riot or a murder seem out of place.

Jacob jerked his knife from the table and replaced it in the sheath at his sash. He and his servants backed away slowly from the table, back toward the entrance to the inn, and finally out into the night.

Shinab and Sabteca were almost as shocked as the Damascenes at what they had heard. Was this the same Jacob they had known around the campfires at home, where he gladly took money from his fellow herdsmen? Whatever their questions, Jacob's tone of voice had warned them that too much was going on inside him to make questions appropriate just then.

And for all his bravado inside the inn, Jacob himself suddenly felt weak and limp. He knew little more than his servants the source or the reach of the changes he sensed were taking place in the depths of his soul.

The third day out of Damascus, in the juniper- and oak- clad hills of Gilead, the three travelers came upon a caravan coming from the northeast. Two guards came riding to meet them, mounted on lean, swift-looking horses with sweat lathering off their bellies and from under the harnesses about their rumps.

"Ho, travelers," the guards hailed them boldly. Although the caravan was in no danger from these three, the guards still wanted to know their business. "Have you come from afar? And where are you bound?" asked the first guard.

"We have come from Canaan and beyond," Jacob answered. "We make our way to my kinsman, Laban, son of Bethuel, in Haran, beyond the Euphrates."

"Laban the Aramean?" the second guard responded.

"The same."

"I have heard of him...a rich man, as I understand," said the guard.

"That may be," said Jacob. "Can you say whether we are on the right way, and how many days' journey it may be?"

"You are on the right way," the first guard answered, and you have perhaps four or five days' journey yet. But we passed some

71

of Laban's herds only the evening last. If you will veer from these hills to the plain there, to the east, you will come upon Laban's own herdsmen—perhaps even his sons. They may be only a half-day's ride from here."

Jacob sat up taller, refreshed by the mere word that the land and the people he sought were actually real enough to be known by these fellow-travelers.

"We are in your debt," he said. Then, not wanting everyone, even the caravaners, to know their every move, he added, "but it may be that we will go on directly to Haran, since my kinsman Laban may not be with his herds."

"As you wish," said the first guard, and the two rode back swiftly to rejoin the caravan.

Jacob had no intention of staying on the road to Haran. The road had been long, and the words "Laban and my kinsmen" were in danger of becoming as unsubstantial as a desert mirage. He was eager to locate any kinsmen as soon as possible.

"Come as you and your beasts can," he said to his servants. "I will ride ahead."

With that he urged his complaining camel into a faster gait, lurching out of the hills and on to the sparsely-grassed plain in the direction the caravaners had indicated.

As a thirsty horse quickens its pace when it smells water, Jacob smelled his kinsmen up ahead.

CHAPTER 9

After half a day, Jacob topped a low knoll and spied a cloud of dust across a sweeping plain toward the northeastern horizon. Sheep, he suspected, although they could be goats here where forage was even scarcer than in the grasslands of Jacob's long experience to the south. The pillar of dust rose in a column from a confined area; apparently the animals were being herded together, perhaps to be watered. Had the scene been played out in Jacob's own territory, it may have been shearing time; but this far north Jacob suspected it was too early for shearing.

As he surveyed the scene and imagined the reason for the little assembly, Jacob felt a kinship even at this distance, both from the sense of the shared lore and common trade shared by sheepmen all over the world, and the anticipation that these very herdsmen might be his blood kin.

Raising himself to his knees atop the camel saddle, Jacob now spied a second, smaller column of dust, to the north of the larger band of sheep. The second flock was moving slowly toward the first; some kind of rendezvous seemed anticipated. Looking behind, Jacob saw that Shinab and Sabteca were catching up with the pack asses.

"We have found them!" Jacob shouted, sweeping an arm in

the direction of the dust clouds. "Our journey has almost ended."

"How does my lord know those herdsmen are those whom you seek?" Sabteca asked. "Haran is yet another several days' journey."

"The caravan—the overseer back at the oasis told me that at about this distance we would begin to come across flocks from Haran," Jacob explained. "And besides—would I not sense my own people?"

Sabteca shrugged. *He* certainly would not; he would leave the intuiting to his master Jacob. "Nevertheless," Sabteca responded, "let us approach with care."

Ignoring the caution, Jacob wheeled his camel about and urged the reluctant beast at a fast walk down the rocky hill, clattering hoofs and scattering gravel creating their own dust cloud. Sabteca and Shinab followed more slowly, leading the pack animals.

Protesting Jacob's haste though it did, the riding camel soon settled into a long-strided gait that swept it and its rider across the plain like a swift desert wind. Jacob would lose sight of the dust clouds he pursued when they descended into shallow *wadis* and hollows, then would renavigate according to their position when his ground-covering steed topped out on higher ground.

In a half-hour they had closed the gap enough for Jacob to see that three herdsmen were tending the larger herd. And it was indeed a flock of sheep, not goats, perhaps several flocks gathered together. The smaller dust cloud indicating a fourth flock was still some distance away; Jacob could tell that he would reach the main flock before it would.

By now the herdsmen had caught sight of Jacob hurrying his beast toward them. They walked around to the front of the band of dirty beige sheep to confront the oncoming stranger. Although he seemed to be alone—Sabteca and Shinab were not yet in view— they wanted to be prepared for anything.

Smelling the flocks ahead, and the water they gathered for, Jacob's camel voluntarily stepped up his pace. As they drew nearer the herd, Jacob saw the shepherds shift their heavy staves to both hands, at the ready.

"Shalom!" Jacob called as soon as he was in shouting distance. The men did not reply, preferring to let this stranger come close enough to reveal his intentions before extending friendly greetings.

"Shalom," Jacob repeated, as he pulled up his mount to a shifty-hoofed stop before the two shepherds. He wondered if these northerners understood his tongue.

"Peace be to you," the tallest shepherd finally replied. He spoke in Aramaic, but there were enough similarities to Jacob's Hebrew that he could understand most of what they said.

"What brings you to these pastures?" another asked, with more inquisitiveness than apprehension in his voice. Taking note of the heavy rime of sweat on Jacob's camel, and of his dust-encrusted garments, the shepherds knew their visitor had come from some distance. He was no bandit lurking in local *wadis* for convenient prey.

"I am Jacob, son of Isaac, son of Abraham, who dwells in the land toward Egypt. We have come from there seeking our ancestral home in Haran." Jacob motioned to the rear, where the dust from his servants and the pack animals was only now visible.

"We?" echoed a shorter herdsman. "How many souls are with you?" he asked, more wary now.

"Only my two servants," Jacob said reassuringly. "Are you from Haran? And is it far?"

"We are from Haran," said the first shepherd, "and it is two days' journey from here."

"It is well," said Jacob. "And in Haran, do you know my kinsman Laban? For he is my mother's brother."

"We know him well," said the herdsman, relaxing and lowering the position of his staff upon hearing the familiar name.

"And is he well?" Jacob persisted.

"He is well," the shorter shepherd said, and added with a sly grin, "and he is very rich. His flocks and those of our own lords graze these lands together, we three and Laban's herds sharing the little water we can find."

"Even now we await the flocks of Laban," the third herdsman offered, "to water them together with ours here at this well."

Following with his eyes the shepherd's outstretched arm, Jacob saw the reason for the gathering of the flocks. They stood at the point of a rocky ridge. Below, two *wadis* joined at a point that boasted the only green grass and bushes Jacob had seen on this treeless plain. The foliage spoke of a spring or a well that sent moisture seeping down both *wadis*, making two green fingers of a Y, with the spring at its base.

Jacob could see now that a modest amount of water welled up among the larger rocks toward the base of the hill. A little digging had made a mouth for the trickle, and the pool had then been enclosed with a crude wall of stones and covered with a great slab of yellowish sandstone. Apparently the spring lacked the force to run a stream when capped by the stone; it would well over into the *wadi* below only when it was removed.

"And even now, they come," the shepherd said. Turning the other direction, Jacob saw that the smaller flock he had seen from so far away was now only a few dozen furlongs away.

"Ah," said the second herdsman. "This will be Rachel, daughter of Laban himself, and her herdsman."

The very daughter of his uncle Laban! Jacob sized up the situation quickly. Something within told him that it was important for him to make a favorable impression on this, his cousin. Yet he would much rather speak to her alone than in the company of these strangers. Signalling his weary camel to kneel, he slipped stiffly to the ground.

"Well, now," he said to the shepherds. "I will help you water your sheep and you can be on your way," he offered.

"We must wait for the flocks of Laban," the tall shepherd said.

"But there is no need—it is not yet evening. There is still grazing time before you will bed your own flocks down for the night," Jacob insisted.

"The time is not the problem, friend, but the weight of the stone—the rock atop the well is too heavy for us to lift. We await Laban's shepherd so he can help us move the stone. Then we water the flocks together—Laban's down that way, and ours up the *wadi* from here."

Not wanting to press the point far enough for the shepherds to wonder about his motives, Jacob desisted. He could help them move the stone, but to insist further would be to invite them to question his own stake in making so much of their proceeding immediately to water their flocks. He would not risk their hostility.

Killing time, the three men spoke of the condition of the flocks in such dry weather, and of the weather itself. After a quarter hour they turned toward the hollow tinkling of neckbells on the lead sheep in Laban's flock. Finally the beasts stepped hesitantly into view, their gait light and cautious as they caught sight of the strange men, but their thirst impelling them closer.

The followers of the animals in the forefront pressed upon them from the rear, causing the sheep in the first flock to murmur restlessly. A young ram scaled the little ridge above the spring, and others followed, threatening to disperse the whole herd. The herdsman of Laban's flock had not yet come into view when a lithe, brown woman came around the bend of the *wadi*, not ten steps from where Jacob waited, crouched on his haunches in the universal stance taken by men of the field pausing at their work. She was a desert maiden of singular beauty. Jacob stood up slowly, his breath involuntarily catching at the young woman's comeliness and grace. She quickly lifted a mauve veil, modestly covering all but her darkly beautiful eyes in defense against this strange man's frankly admiring stare. Yet she faltered for only a moment in her steady pace toward the spring. Her strides were smooth, her flowing desert robes concealing with difficulty a well-formed body that somehow spoke of soft femininity not yet hardened by this desert work. Coils of naturally curly auburn hair escaped her headwrap, providing a monochrome setting for the burnished copper spangles cascading over her forehead after the fashion of unmarried women in Paddan-aram.

Jacob tried to disguise his nervousness with a cough. It had been exciting enough to anticipate finding relatives in this faraway place. It was overwhelming to discover that one of them was a woman of such charm. His gaze transfixed, he began backing toward the well, giving ground before this rustically regal creature. For her part, Rachel smiled under her veil at the way this fine specimen of a man seemed determined to make himself into an absolute boy.

"Shalom, lady." Jacob finally found his voice.

With fine desert decorum, Rachel acknowledged the stranger's greeting with only a nod, and modestly lowered her eyes.

Stumbling over a stone in his backward trek, Jacob recovered quickly and tried again. "The water, lady—the sheep—." It was hopeless to speak, since the thoughts and impulses coursing through his mind and body were racing much faster than his tongue could move. Instead, Jacob sprang into action. Before the three waiting herdsmen could protest or assist, he leaped to the mouth of the well. Never taking his eyes off his cousin he turned his back to the well, and crouched in order to place both shoulders beneath an overhanging lip of the great stone atop its mouth. Then he stood up abruptly. The sharp, upward thrust of his shoulders lifted the stone high enough for its weight to shift to the other side, allowing it to slide slowly and heavily to the ground. Clear, cold spring water gurgled from the depths of the well and began to form a forked brook, running merrily toward Rachel's thirsty sheep in one direction, and, in the other, toward the larger flock.

The feat, ordinarily performed by three or four men, was one that the athletic Jacob might have barely performed without the extra strength the sight of Rachel had excited. But with this added surge of energy, the stone would have had to be twice as heavy to resist.

Under her veil, Rachel's mouth dropped open; there was no way to hide her widened eyes. It was her turn to be tongue-tied. "Why, th—I thank you, my lord," she stammered.

Panting from the exertion, Jacob grinned. "It is little enough—for a kinswoman," he said, his voice courteously low.
Rachel turned and faced the stranger for the first time. "Pardon, my lord?"

"It is true. You are Rachel, daughter of Laban. And I am Jacob, son of Isaac, and of Rebekah, Laban's sister—and your aunt."
Rachel drew in a sharp breath. "But how—how can this be? Where did my lord—?"

"I am come from Beer-sheba, and Gerar, desert lands to the south, toward Egypt, where I live in tents and follow our herds. I am sent here to—" Jacob stopped. He was not anxious to mention either the deception that had caused him to flee the wrath of his brother, or his mother's eagerness for him to marry a woman of Paddan-aram. "We are weary of being separated from our kinsmen," he finished simply.

A broad and uninhibited smile spread slowly over Rachel's face, and for Jacob it was as though the desert had just bloomed. She had heard of her relatives to the south, and now to meet one who must certainly be their most handsome representative, and to discover the depths of his attachment to the clan...Before modesty could forbid, she flung her arms around Jacob's neck in perfect indifference to the reaction of the shepherds, who were still standing with slack jaws, amazed at the emotional display no less than the exhibition of the stranger's strength. They were kin, but still...

With equal abandon Jacob kissed Rachel on both cheeks, fighting desperately to contain his embrace to the greeting of a relative instead of giving rein to the passion her beauty excited in him.

They were still clasping each other and laughing when Shinab and Sabteca, leading the pack animals, came upon them. They stood awkwardly for a moment until Jacob, suddenly aware that there was someone in the world other than Rachel and himself, looked up.

"Ah," he said with only a little nervousness. "My men—that is, my cousin—my servants—this is my cousin Rachel!" Nodding in awesome recognition, the two servants had no doubt that, for Jacob, the long journey had been worth every step.

The two days' journey to Haran were a blur outside of time for both Jacob and Rachel. Leaving Shinab and Sabteca with Rachel's own shepherd-servant to tend the flock, the pair mounted Jacob's camel and pointed it toward the north, toward home.

"The river!" said Rachel, as the pair topped a knoll overlooking the legendary Euphrates. Its serpentine coils and the green swath it painted on the otherwise barren land gave Jacob a thrill as he imagined allowing its slow flow to take him down to the very land where, according to the ancients, God had first taken the *adam*, the dust of the earth, and fashioned it into Adam, the man of His creation.

But this was no time for history. Jacob and Rachel urged the camel down the gravelly embankment. They forded the Euphrates at a shallow point, pausing only at a sand bar at midstream to splash its refreshing water on each other, laughing and playing like children.

Along the way the cousins chatted incessantly of relatives and climes, of sheep and shepherds, of the mysterious sense of guidance among the members of the Beer-sheba part of the clan. They marveled at how they anticipated each other, so similar were their ways. Their thoughts, their dreams, their questions—with the same blood running through their veins they were not only discovering each other, but the family tree.

They did uncover one difference that gave Jacob some pause. Once, when speaking of his father coming to this same Haran to win the hand of Rebekah, Jacob made a reference to his having been guided there "by the hand of Yah."

"Who?" asked Rachel, sensing that her cousin had referred to a divinity but not being familiar with the name.

Jacob turned from his perch at the front of the camel saddle to look briefly at his dark-skinned cousin. He had not thought about the differences between the God of Abraham and Isaac, and the gods of Paddan-aram.

"Yah," he repeated, "the Most High God. He was the God who called our father Abraham even when he lived in Ur. He is the God of the Promise—." He stopped, realizing that he was only adding the unknown to the unfamiliar. Then, drawing a deep breath, he recounted as briefly as he could the story as it had been handed down from Abraham.

"Your god, then, has promised your family this land you speak of, the land of Canaan?" Rachel asked. "What of the Canaanites? We have often heard of kings who claim that the gods have given them territory inhabited by others—and it is never realized except by bloodshed and heartache."

Jacob was quiet for a moment. It was a question he, too, had tried to fathom. "It is different," he finally said, simply. "It is not 'the gods'—it is the God of gods, the High God, the Master of the Universe. All the lands of the earth are His, and He gives them to whom He wills."

Rachel did not answer immediately, either. She still did not understand, but there was something compelling about the simplicity with which her cousin spoke. "Will you then fight for the land?"

Jacob was surprised that this perfectly natural idea had never occurred to him. "Fight?" he repeated. "Why, no. It's just that El—that is, Yah (he did not want to confuse Rachel further by using various names)—has promised it to the seed of Abraham. It is a gift He will give in His own good time, I suppose. And it's not a matter of having to *control* all the land to prove it is ours. The Promise as we have received it is not that the land is ours to boast of, but to bless others with. Yah said to Father Abraham, 'in your seed shall the nations of the world be blessed'—it's supposed to be a blessing to others for us to inherit the land."

It was all too much for Rachel. She was aware of the power of the gods, especially of Inanna, goddess of love and war, and of Nanna, the moon god—for she had seen the results of paying homage to such gods in return for special favors. If such a high god wanted to do thus with the land of Canaan she would not argue the point. But she wondered—especially about a promise that was intended not to bless Yah's followers but those among whom they lived. There was something grand and selfless about this strange idea, but she was glad she was not a Canaanite, she decided. She would think more about it later; for now she would point the conversation elsewhere.

"I know that the gods formed the world, or the world was made from the gods—at least that we ourselves did not make it," she said, hoping to show that she could converse about such matters since Jacob was obviously interested in them. "Our father Laban has told us of Oannes, the god who was half fish and half man. He came ashore in Babylon and taught our ancestors writing and farming and law." She stopped to test Jacob's reaction. When he did not speak, she continued. "I think this must have been after the Great Flood, since Oannes came from the sea."

"We know well the story of the Flood," Jacob said. "But of Oannes I do not know. Our stories tell of Noah, a righteous man whom Yah spared in a great ship."

"Yes, yes!" Rachel said, glad to find that their heritage had some points of agreement. "The god Cronus sent the flood, and Xisuthros was a great hero, and the ship—."

"Cousin!" Jacob interrupted, throwing his shaggy head back and laughing. "In such a short time you would convert me to your gods? There is one God—is not this the faith of the house of Laban?"

Rachel was relieved that Jacob could laugh, so serious was he about all this talk of divine guidance. She laughed, too, although she could detect an underlying gravity in the whole matter. If Yah alone was God, then…They would be discussing this more, she was sure.

At last Jacob's laboring camel struggled to the top of a rocky hill from which a broad panorama spread out below. "There!" cried Rachel happily. "We are home!"

Jacob reined in their mount, which was only too ready to rest. He sat for a moment, taking in the scene and reflecting on the goodness of Yah. Gone, for a moment, were the recurring pangs of guilt at having deceived his brother. Gone certainly was the weariness of the journey and the endless, lonely miles that lay behind him. He took a great breath, exhaled slowly, and said quietly, "Blessed be the Lord God, the father of Abraham and Isaac!"

Rachel clasped her arms about Jabob's waist more firmly than was necessary simply to remain atop the camel and even leaned her cheek against his sinewy back, oblivious to its coat of dust and sweat. Whoever this god was of whom Jacob spoke, he had caused Jacob to be a man of more gracious sensitivities than the men she knew in Paddan-aram. She wondered to herself if she would be able to love him only as a cousin.

A little group began to assemble in front of the home of Laban, lord of these lands, as the two riders on a single camel approached an hour before sunset. It was a matter of curiosity and one that called for some vigilance when any visitor approached. And when a servant saw the sun glance off Rachel's copper-spangled crown, and shouted her name, everyone within earshot—including Laban and his wife—dropped what they were doing to run together, hands shading squinting eyes, ready to greet her—and whoever it was that was brazen enough to attempt to gain entrance to their manor by riding in with the master's daughter.

Jacob's eyes swept the little company as his camel sank heavily to its knees for the pair to dismount. The round-faced, middle-aged woman with broad bands of grey in her hair would be Rachel's mother. The big man with hands on hips and feet spread wide as though more ready to challenge the intruder than welcome Rachel—Laban, no doubt. As Jacob approached, he noted that Laban's facial features belied his bold way of standing. A too-wide mouth ran uncertainly across a sparse, grey beard, like an undependable *wadi* through a struggling grassland. Dark eyes crowded a sharp, thin nose as though shrewdly perceiving its need for support. The eyes shifted from Jacob to Rachel to his wife, only to make the little circle again. Eager as he was to meet—and to admire—these kinsmen, Jacob could not suppress the thought that there was an irresolute quality in this desert don. This was a relative who would bear watching.

Laban spoke first. "Rachel?" he began, in a tone more uncertain than welcoming. Jacob was surprised at how high-pitched and thin the voice was for a man of his size.

"Father! Mother! Leah!" Rachel replied, ignoring in her enthusiasm her father's tentativeness. At the last name, Jacob singled out a solidly-built young woman, her veil so discreetly high, the bangs of her hair so low, and her form so shapeless as to defy guessing her age; but he knew from what Rachel had said on the way that this would be Rachel's sister Leah, three years older. He could see enough of her hair to tell that it was precisely like Rachel's, glints of copper fire flashing in the lowering sun.

At Rachel's greeting, Laban, his wife Ishtarah, Leah, and five or six servants moved forward to embrace her. Jacob stood back, knowing that his favorable reception would depend in part on first allowing Rachel to be greeted in relative distinction from this stranger she had brought home. After kissing each of her relatives once on each cheek Rachel abruptly stood back, arm outstretched toward Jacob.

"You will all be glad to know this man," she announced with uncharacteristic formality. "This is our kinsman, Jacob, son of Isaac and Rebekah! He has come to us all the way from the land of Canaan—which," she added, "is south, toward Egypt." She gave a little nod of triumph at the geography she recalled from what Jacob had told her.

At the mention of Rebekah, Laban, who had been leaning forward intently, straightened suddenly in surprise. "Rebekah? My sister?" he asked incredulously, his eyes beginning to moisten. "Is it possible?" He bent forward again, wiping his eyes and peering at this man who must be his nephew.

Rachel clapped her hands together in delight. "The same!" she proclaimed victoriously. Jacob took the introduction as permission to step toward the little group. "I am indeed Jacob, Rebekah's son, my lord," he said rather formally. But his emotions were so near the surface that he fairly blurted out the rest: "Son of Isaac, son of Abraham, my lord Laban—and your servant." He knelt on one knee and bowed before his uncle.

"And *my* son, then, as well!" said Laban, dropping all reserve. He reached out to lift the younger man to his feet. For a moment the two stared into each other's faces, finding in each other's eyes the unmistakable bond of kinsmen. Laban's composure broke and he clasped the dusty traveler to him in a warm embrace. "My flesh and blood!" he said brokenly. "You are welcome here!"

Ishtarah and Leah greeted their relative with a little more reserve, but Jacob hardly noticed.

He felt that he, no less than Rachel, had returned home.

Chapter 10

In the week that followed, Jacob could not hear enough of his relatives' history. Laban, he discovered, enjoyed the status of royalty-once-removed. None other than the great Hammurabi had named one of Laban's own uncles-by-marriage governor of Haran. It was said that Bethuel, father of Laban and Rebekah, had once been granted an audience with Hammurabi himself.

Jacob's aunt, Ishtarah, bore the name of a Babylonian goddess, a fact that, while awe-inspiring, did nothing to reassure Jacob about the family's knowledge of Yah. The fact was, the family seemed little oriented to divine matters. Most of the talk was of relatives and land and flocks and herds—congenial enough, but always with an overtone elevating that which could be seen over the often unseen will of the gods.

Little matter, Jacob concluded—except in the case of Rachel. As he watched her move among her family and tend to her household duties, Jacob became aware that from his first glimpse of her at the spring in the desert he had settled on her as the object of his mission.

The Laban manor was spacious, almost elegant, speaking of prosperity. To the right of the main house's entrance, an alcove with lamps constantly burning in it caught Jacob's attention when he first entered, and he found himself returning to stare at it frequently. It was an altar, of sorts, with a wooden shelf on which were images of minor gods—*teraphim*, as Laban's family called them. Although Jacob never saw anyone going there to pray, they would frequently include the alcove in a brief detour on their way in or out of the house, reaching out in passing to touch one or another of the terra-cotta figurines. They were stained a dull, dark brown from the touch of many hands, both family members and servants stroking them, Jacob supposed, for good fortune.

One task of Laban's daughter Leah was to keep the lamps in the alcove burning. Once she came with a fresh supply of oil as Jacob reclined in the hallway on a sheepskin-covered pillow, gazing at the alcove, his thoughts roving over the difference between Yah, whom no one could see, and these very visible gods.

"My lord finds the *teraphim* of interest?" Leah asked. She no longer wore her veil in Jacob's presence, a recognition of his now-familiar status as one of the family. Her smile was not unattractive, and Jacob noticed again how the color of her hair was identical to Rachel's. But something about Leah's eyes gave her face a certain flatness. They were almost hazel, but with no highlights, making them merely a dull beige. Her perpetual squint told Jacob that she did not see well. It was as though her eyes were so light-colored they had been sunburned there in the desert.

"Yes, my sister," Jacob replied. "But I do not understand their place in this household."

"Place?" Leah repeated, looking at the crudely-shapen images. "Why, this is their place. What—?"

Seeing that her eyes were not the only dullness about her, Jacob hastened to elaborate. "Their place in your life, I mean. I never see you praying to them, or asking their blessing. Are they alive to you? I mean, do they represent actual—?" He stopped, sensing that his questions were missing the mark.

Leah waved her hand as though to dismiss his questions, since she did not understand them. "I never think of such things," she said indifferently. "The gods are the gods. If they smile on us, then the sheep bear abundantly. And if not, what's the good of praying to a piece of stone?"

"But do you ever wonder what the good *is*?" Jacob insisted.

"Oh, I leave that to Father. And he doesn't inquire of the *teraphim* for that kind of thing. Sometimes he goes behind the sheepfold and kills a kid and opens it to divine from its entrails...but if you ask me, it's a waste of livestock. I always try to catch him at it so we can at least dress the meat and get some good out of it."

Setting the cruse of lamp oil on the shelf, Leah made a show of adjusting her loose garment. It was a rather wanton gesture that revealed more of one breast than Jacob wanted to see. He blushed and turned away. Seeing his indifference, Leah busied herself at her task with some chagrin and impatience. Noticing the lack of reverence with which she filled the holy lamps, Jacob decided to drop the subject. They moved in different worlds; she had no taste for talk of anything without a sensual point of reference, and he was not interested in the intimacy she offered.

As for her sister, Rachel—after a month, Jacob's initial admiration grew into discomfort at being unable to express his feelings for her. He made himself go into the field with the herdsmen and assist the shearers to keep from being tormented with her untouchable presence. But at mealtime, and in the long evenings of family conversation, he found himself unable to keep his eyes off of her graceful form and burnished hair.

For Rachel's part, she was far too sensitive not to notice all this, but her natural shyness and sense of decorum made it difficult for her to interpret Jacob's behavior. He had finally told her that one reason for his journey was that his parents feared he would marry Hittite women if he stayed in Canaan. Yet his long absences in the field made it seem as though he had come to marry a career in his uncle's business. More than once she had caught him gazing at her with what she took to be stifled interest, only to find him retiring early from around the family fires as though to avoid being left in her presence.

Once, as Rachel was returning from gathering sticks for the fire, Jacob rounded a corner of the house on his way in from giving the sheep shed a final check for the night. It had just been busy-work, to give himself a respite from Rachel's tantalizing presence. Yet she was so transfixed in his mind that when they bumped rudely into each other it was as though the apparition in his wakeful dream merely merged into her full-fleshed form.

"Oh!" cried Rachel, genuinely startled.

"Sorry! No—it is my—," Jacob began. But when he clasped her to keep her from falling his mouth could form no more words. He would have let her go and stepped back in embarrassment had she not wilted in his arms.

"No, no?" Rachel protested. "Truly, it was my—." Now it was her turn to be speechless, and she was more in danger of falling from the emotion of being in Jacob's arms than from the slight jolt.

No matter, she thought swiftly. I have wanted such a moment. I will not flee it now.

Feeling Rachel relax in his arms, Jacob drew in his breath quickly. Incapable of any thought, swift or slow, he impulsively bent his shaggy head down, tenderly lifted Rachel's chin until he could stare her full in the face, and kissed her full on the mouth for a long, long moment.

Instead of protesting, Rachel willingly gave him her lips. When he finally released them, Jacob said softly, "You must have known how much I have dreamed of a moment like this."

Her modesty finally catching up with her feelings, Rachel tucked her head down demurely. "I—that is—I have wondered." Then she looked up again at him in defiance of custom and said, "I have dreamed of it, too. But you are gone so much. And even when you are here…"

"I have not been able to say how I felt," Jacob explained. "I have had to make myself be distanced. I have not been here long enough to…" His weak explanation trailed off into silence and he kissed her again, long and deep, with the longing of weeks— or was it centuries?—melting into the ecstasy of the moment.

Finally, Jacob said, "I must speak to your father."

"About what?" Rachel asked innocently.

"About marriage, of course."

Rachel looked up at him with a surprisingly level and knowing gaze. "Of course," she agreed.

Jacob was ecstatic. "You mean you—. But your father. Will he— would he?"

Rachel placed two fingers over his mouth. "My father will be as glad as I am," she said, with such enthusiastic volume that Jacob looked around nervously to see if anyone heard. "He thinks both his daughters have waited long enough to marry!" Rachel said playfully.

Then, softer and more soberly she added, "It's Leah we should be asking about."

"Leah?" Jacob repeated.

"She has told me she feels a great deal for you," Rachel answered. "And after all, she is the firstborn. But it's made me insane with jealousy. And you—?" she looked up at Jacob earnestly, searching for the deepest meaning she could find in his eyes. "How do you feel about Leah?"

Jacob would have laughed aloud had not Rachel been so serious. "I think she would make a fine sister-in-law!" Jacob said with a grin. He girdled Rachel's waist with his arm, more boldly this time, even with some possessiveness. "I can say this now," he whispered softly. "I have loved you since first I saw you in the field. I believe Yah has guided me to you. And I want more than anything for you to be my wife."

Certain she would faint, Rachel blended her body into Jacob's once more, reaching up to embed her hands in his full mane of hair, finding his mouth again with hers.

The fires inside the house died out and the others went off to their quarters wondering, for good reason, what had happened to Jacob and Rachel.

Early the next morning, Jacob sat on the ground outside the main house, waiting for his uncle to emerge to organize the servants for the day's work. In one hand he held a light, hair rope, and at the rope's end was a great cow, heavy with calf. The odd scene greeted Laban as he stepped off the low veranda.

"My lord, Laban," Jacob said nervously, rising to his feet.

"Jacob, my son?" Laban returned, cocking an eyebrow quizzically.

"I would speak to you about—that is—." Jacob was having difficulty.

"Yes, yes, my son," Laban said impatiently. "What is it? Is the cow ailing?"

"No, Uncle," said Jacob, embarrassed. "She is only about to calve. I purchased her from your servants. She is the first of a herd I am starting to gather with the wages my lord is paying me for my work with your flocks and herds."

"Well, then, what's the matter? Is she not sound?"

"She sounds very well—I mean, she is very sound, my lord," Jacob stammered foolishly. Clearing his throat he made himself continue in a firmer voice. "I wish to make a gift of her to my lord."

"A gift?" echoed Laban. "To me? But you have just purchased her from me."

"True, my lord. It is not a gift so much as the price I would pay—that is, my lord has something I long to—." Finally, abandoning attempts to follow protocol, Jacob hitched his shoulders high as he drew a deep breath and blurted out: "I would ask for the hand of my lord's daughter in marriage, and I offer this cow as *mohar*, the bride price!" His shoulders fell as he heaved a sigh of relief at having been able to speak his mind.

Laban drew himself up sharply, whether in anger or only surprise Jacob was unsure. "This is *mohar?*" he asked. This is the way of marriage in the West?"

Jacob colored. A cow was perhaps an average bride price among ordinary desert families in Beer-sheba and the Negev. He had not thought of how it might be received in a more well-to-do clan such as Laban's. "It is all I have, my lord," he answered lamely.

Laban screwed his already rambling lip line into a grimace of disdain. "A cow," he said dully, making the word describe the animal as a useless bauble.

"A cow great with calf," Jacob reminded.

Actually, Laban had both suspected and anticipated that this handsome westerner would ask for his daughters in marriage. His keen eyes had seen how Jacob looked at Rachel. Furthermore, his nephew was a good worker, and under the tradition of *erebu* marriage Jacob could be required to live and work for a time in Laban's own household instead of returning to his homeland, in return for marrying the daughter of such a nobleman. Laban would not be losing a daughter, as he had lost a sister when Isaac's servant had come on a similar mission to Haran. He would be gaining both a son and a valuable worker. But Laban felt bound to remain in character by bargaining for a greater bride-price.

Making a show of veiling his scorn, Laban glanced at the tethered animal. He motioned to Jacob to sit again, and squatted on the ground facing him, assuming the eternal bartering position in the Middle East.

"Jacob, my son," he began, his voice dripping with studied patience and condescension. "A cow—even a cow about to calve—what message would I give my people about how I value my daughter Leah if I let her go for such a *mohar*? I would be giving her a dowry of far greater value. It is not fitting."

"*Leah?*" Jacob responded. "No, my lord, no! I am asking for your daughter Rachel!"

Laban looked up quickly. "But it is Leah who is my firstborn. It is not fitting that her younger sister marry first."

Jacob fell silent. He knew the custom, although in his passion he had not faced it in his mind. But now his ardor also fed his hope that he could drive a good enough bargain that would entice Laban to ignore tradition and grant him the love of his life. But he knew it would take more than a pregnant cow.

"Work!" he said, looking up suddenly at the older man. "I could work out a more generous *mohar* for Rachel," he said, with rising excitement.

Laban scratched at the ground with a stick, as though calculating the merits of the offer. Actually, he could not have been more pleased with the way he had allowed Jacob himself to suggest an *erebu* contract. "Hmmm," he mused. Then, slowly and reflectively, "Working out the bride price... that is not totally impossible ..."

The two men sat silently for several moments. Jacob knew not to press the point, but to let Laban's shrewd mind go through whatever machinations he felt necessary.

Then, at what he judged to be the right moment, Jacob resumed the bargaining. "Five years' labor. I will serve you for five years in return for your daughter."

Laban sat silently. It was a very good bargain for him, but he dared not show it. Instead, he managed a frown.

"Five years," he said slowly. "It is very little time." Pausing to appear to be measuring the offer carefully, he then said abruptly: "Seven. Seven years."

Jacob was ready for a counter offer. "Done!" he said.

"Very well," Laban responded. "It is not the best bargain for me, but after all, you are my kinsman. Better to marry my daughter to one of our own than to strike a better bargain with a lesser man. It is done. We shall draw up a contract of *erebu*. You have struck a bargain in marriage." He reached out his right arm to Jacob, who grasped it heartily with a grin. Both men felt they had made the transaction of their lives.

The two strode immediately to a little anteroom adjacent to the sheep cote where Laban's bookkeeper Peleg labored over clay tablets containing records of the buying and selling of flocks and herds, the birthing of the young and the shearing of sheep. Bald and toothless, the old man looked up as Laban, then Jacob, entered the tiny room.

"My lords?" he acknowledged, forcing reluctant bones to stand. "Peleg, my good man," Laban said expansively. "We require a new tablet on which to cut a contract."

The stooped old man turned to a bin behind him. From beneath a dirty, moist towel he produced a soft, flat clay tablet, placed it on his rude desk, and selected a stylus from a clay pot. He sat down heavily and waited for Laban to dictate.

With fluency born of long practice, the lord of the desert manor dictated the terms of a standard marriage contract. Excited though he was, Jacob's shrewd business sense forced him to listen. It all seemed straightforward enough until Laban came to the phrase "seven years." "After which time," Laban continued, "the bride price being paid in full, the daughter of Laban will be given in marriage to the said Jacob, in accordance with…"

"Wait!" Jacob interrupted.

Laban turned to him impatiently. "Yes, yes—what is it?"

"*After* which time?" Jacob began. "I had assumed that—." Then the cunning of Laban's bargain descended on him. He must pay the bride-price *before* receiving the bride. It was a small detail in their previous conversation that, in his ardor, Jacob had not pursued. He noticed that the wandering line of Laban's mouth ended in a slight, sardonic smile and his eyelids half covered his shrewd eyes in the fashion of a man of the world who had been over such devious ground many times before.

Jacob knew he could do nothing but agree to the terms. He was determined not to show Laban his disappointment, so he returned the older man's half leer with a level gaze and a lying smile that said he knew very well the terms of the marriage contract and was satisfied with them. Certainly, Rachel was worth it.

What was seven years of work compared to her love? "Nothing—no, it is well," he said. "Please continue."

Jacob heard little else as Laban's voice droned on. Finally he was through. A shearer, another of Laban's nephews, was called in to witness the marriage contract. The bookkeeper finished the last impression in the soft clay and added it to several others on a shelf to dry. Laban and Jacob clasped arms again and the transaction was complete.

Jacob had to restrain himself from literally running to the main house to seek out Rachel. He described the seven-year *mohar* as though it was a part of his intention all along.

"Oh, Jacob!" was all Rachel could say. She flung her arms about him, her eyes moist both with joy at the thought of being united with her beloved, and with sorrow at the prospect of the seven-year waiting period.

Yet she determined to be content. She would be Jacob's bride, and that was enough.

By noon the next day, Jacob had worked off eight hours of his 61,152-hour contract.

CHAPTER 11

Jacob proved to be an expert livestock manager. His contract with Laban included a share of the profits from the flocks and herds in his charge, most of which he took in stock, building his own herds and pasturing them far away from Laban's.

Jacob's rich head of brown hair now sported a few streaks of grey. He was browned and hardened by life in the fields. He and Rachel had managed to keep their relationship chaste, although more than self-discipline was involved. Jacob simply stayed in the fields with the flocks for days at a time.

Finally the time came when Laban's household rang with loud and joyous wedding plans. They were so elaborate and the whole compound was so chaotic that Jacob almost wished he had swept up Rachel seven years ago, ignored his bargain, and fled with her to the desert or back to his parents. But he had worked so long in preparation for this moment that he could well tolerate the stressful intensity of wedding details and the protocol of greeting distant relatives to whom he would soon be more closely related. Besides, he sensed a momentous, almost cosmic, destiny in the event and was quite willing to invest it not only with seven years of labor but with all the considerable ceremony and ritual of the Semitic heritage.

"Rachel, my love," Jacob said one morning as he found her hemming a new veil, the copper highlights in her hair fairly gleaming in the early slanting rays of the sun.

"Oh, Jacob!" she cried, leaping up to greet him and throwing her arms about his neck. "It is here!" she whispered. "The time has come!" Locked in her embrace, Jacob could not remember the years that had intervened between his agreement with Laban and this joyous moment.

The wedding ceremony itself would be followed by a week of feasting and merry-making for which relatives began arriving three days before the festivities were to begin. Jacob could not begin to keep track of the new people that descended daily on the compound. So many tents were pitched around the main house that the place took on the character of a village. The smoke of twenty cook-fires joined that of the huge, main fire-pit, where, the day before the wedding, servants dutifully turned the seasoned carcasses of sheep and goats and calves, and filled and refilled casks of wine and smaller jugs of milk.

The talk around the fires was all of this new-found relative from Beer-sheba—he who had the good fortune to marry into Laban's family and become a potential heir to his wealth. Was it Rachel or Leah he was marrying? Little matter; many knew them only collectively as "Rachel-and-Leah," and probably could not distinguish them from each other—especially behind the veils which usually covered their faces.

A rude but colorful canopy was erected at the rear of the main house. Dyed animal skins were draped over rough poles supporting a dome of bent sticks covered with brilliant tapestries and representing the upside-down bowl of the heavens. The nuptials would be said beneath the canopy, symbolizing the fact that they were being said under the aegis of the gods of the air.

When at last the day of the wedding arrived, the servants became hard-pressed to keep the wine casks filled, long before noon. Finally, at sundown, a boisterous crowd of relatives trooped to the wedding canopy, bringing the bride with them. Dressed in a loose-fitting, light ecru garment of spun silk and artfully draped in filmy veils, she led a procession of twelve virgins to the entrance of the little covered hutch. An elaborate coiffure brought her copper-colored hair down below even the copper spangles dangling from her headdress, almost to the white veil covering her face. Behind the curls, her eyes were turned demurely to the ground. The twelve virgins, poised to welcome the groom with tambourines and smiles, arranged themselves on two sides of the path he would tread.

"He comes!" a half-drunken cry rang out. Jacob emerged from the main house robed in rich, gold brocade and sporting a pompous purple turban that made him look top-heavy.

The father of the bride officiated at the simple ceremony. His words committed the bride, but not the groom, to faithfulness. In accordance with the wedding contract, Jacob could divorce her, but the privilege was not reciprocal. Laban bestowed two rings upon his daughter—a circle of pounded brass for her finger, and a more highly polished gold ring for her nose, binding her to be led about by her husband as obediently as an ox.

Suddenly they were married.

Then the feast—the real ceremony for which all were waiting—began. Servants complained of the huge quantities of red meat and fruit, wine and cheeses they were required to prepare and serve for the rambunctious revelers. It was all very tiring for the bride and groom, and only a half-hour after the torch lights were lit they tried to excuse themselves quietly from the head table and retire to their quarters and their wedding night.

But the raucous crowd would not have it. Seeing the couple rise from their food and drink, five or six men, cousins, arose, unsteady and boisterous, their cups raised to honor the bride and groom with suggestive toasts that had all the banqueters roaring with laughter.

"Sleep well, my loves!" cried one.

"*Sleep?*" cried another. "Little chance of much sleep on this night!" The crowd laughed far louder than the lame comment merited.

Finally the bride and groom were allowed to leave the great banquet tent and make their way to the marital bed. They lit no torch lights in the room that had been prepared for them, preferring to grope their way in. They undressed silently, and with not a little embarrassment.

Jacob was barely able to note that the love-making was a trifle disappointing before he sank into a wine-enhanced sleep.

Always an early riser, Jacob awoke at first light. His head hurt mightily. Staggering to the door, he sympathized with the dawn's futile attempt to brighten the dismal refuse left from the night's revelry. Dinner rugs that had been spread for the guests to sit on at table under the banquet tent were strewn haphazardly over the entire area. The canopy lay on its side, the victim, Jacob guessed, of a brawl that must have broken out among relatives whose inhibitions had been lowered by lingering too long in their cups.

He would have shaken his head at the sight, but its first movement brought such a rush of pain that he clutched it with both hands and turned back into the room. He looked fondly at his new bride, wondering if she would—.

"Rachel?" he asked, half to himself. Something was wrong. The tousled hair was right, but the breadth of the shape under the hair blanket was unlike…*"Rachel?"* he asked again, more insistently, this time intending it for her. He lurched over to the bed of skins, bent down, and flung back the blanket. Now it was a shout: *"Rachel!* No, it is—it cannot be!"

Rachel's sister Leah rolled over on her back sleepily, stretched, and yawned a gaping yawn. "Mmmm, my lord," she mumbled. "It is yet early. Come back to bed." And with that she pulled up the blanket again and rolled over to go back to sleep as if Jacob's world were not crumbling about him.

Frantically, Jacob paced the room, the awful realization of the deception making him forget the pounding in his head. How could this have happened? It *couldn't* have happened, he decided, stooping again to the sleeping form at his feet and lifting a corner of the blanket to prove that he was delirious.

He was not delirious. It had happened.

Jacob's crazed mind raced back to the moment under the canopy when he had seen his bride for the first time that eventful day. The fact was he had *not* really seen her. The copper hair, the copper spangles, the veil positioned high on her nose, the loose-fitting dress, his own excitement—all had conspired to convey to him the image of the woman he had expected to see. But in fact he had actually married Leah. He had sat with her through the wedding banquet. He had lain with her on his wedding night.

But where was his beloved? By what trickery had—? Jacob

dashed madly out the door and ran toward the little room where, seven years earlier, the marriage contract had been engraved on the clay tablet. He flung open the door to the bookkeeper's shed so violently that one hinge came loose. Without stopping to see to it, Jacob attacked the shelf where rows of dusty tablets were stacked.

The ones on top—they would be too recent. Jacob flung them aside like a wild man, caring nothing for the way some shattered on the hard-packed clay floor. Two-thirds through the stack he slowed his frenzy enough to glance at the headings impressed in what had been soft clay. "Bill of Sale" read some, others "Lease Agreement," and still others "Siring Services" of rams and bulls.

Then his eyes stared as they finally settled on the tablet headed, "Contract of Marriage." Here it is! Now he would have the evidence he needed to expose his devious uncle's scheme and prove his case for Rachel. His fingers traced the somewhat crudely formed characters as he mumbled through the legal language. Louder and louder grew his ravings as he neared the end without finding what he sought.

"Aaiiee!" he cried, finally, in an anguished roar that awakened even the most drugged revelers in the camp. Jacob raised the tablet above his head, and slammed it down onto the hard wood of the writing table, shattering the clay into a hundred pieces.

The agreement had committed Laban only to give Jacob his "daughter" in marriage. Neither daughter's name was mentioned. Jacob had no evidence at all that his uncle had agreed to defy custom and give him Rachel.

Even in his rage and foggy mental state, Jacob's mind carried him back to a tent in faraway Beer-sheba where his aged father Isaac had sat at table. Jacob's own hair-covered arms loomed before the eyes of his memory. His shaggy head sank to his chest as he recalled the deception by which he had won the birthright from blind Isaac. Bitter, tearless sobs wracked his body.

After a long moment, the question recurred: *Where is—where was—Rachel?*

Jacob strode unsteadily from the bookkeeper's shed, stepping over the door that hung limply by one hinge. His steps became firmer as he made his way to the main house, and toward Rachel's room. As he neared the tapestry marking her doorway, he heard her sobbing softly. He brushed aside the drapery without ceremony and knelt by the pallet where she lay.

"Rachel!" he said hoarsely.

Immediately she sat up, seized him frantically and clung to him desperately. "Oh, Jacob!" she said. "I am so sorry! Can you ever forgive me?"

"Forgive you?" Jacob returned, incredulously. "Why? For what? I am the one who married— What happened?"

Forcing her sobbing to cease, Rachel wiped her eyes with her blanket. "It was my fault, I suppose," she began. "My mother's maid, Deborah—she convinced me that I should go to the springs of Arunah to bathe before the wedding. She said something about their waters making a bride-to-be fertile. I had heard the story. I didn't know if I believed it, but mother and Deborah convinced me to go."

"And?" Jacob interrupted, as Rachel paused to collect her thoughts.

"And on the way back Deborah lost the way. At least that's what she said. I see now that the whole thing was planned. It was never my father's intent to allow me to marry before Leah."

"I know," Jacob said grimly. He recounted his futile search for evidence to the contrary in the wedding contract.

"I am Jacob the Supplanter," he mused, clasping Rachel to his breast, "and another has supplanted my beloved." The two held each other in silence as the sun finally asserted itself over the eastern horizon and the compound came to life.

"What shall we do, my love?" Rachel asked.

"We—I—shall speak to your father," said Jacob. He stalked somewhat awkwardly from Rachel's room, embarrassed that he had allowed Laban to get the best of him. Again his pace grew stronger as he marched toward his uncle's quarters.

Laban, of course, was prepared for his nephew's outrage.

"Son, son," he cajoled. "Calm yourself. Did we not have a clear agreement? Shall I retrieve the contract so you can read it again?"

"I know what the agreement said," Jacob replied through lips tightened grimly. He did not go on to say that he had destroyed the document. "I come to you now as a man reasoning with a man, not as one seeking redress. I come to you as a man who loves your daughter Rachel."

Jacob's forthrightness disarmed Laban for a moment, but he soon recovered his usual cunning. "Ah, love," he said, looking upward and touching his fingertips together in front of his ample belly. "And do you not love my daughter Leah—or, as I should say, your *wife* Leah?"

"I am not seeking an annulment to the marriage," Jacob said, his directness again threatening to penetrate his uncle's cynical, conniving approach to the conversation. Laban liked this son-in-law. He would offer him another bargain.

"I clearly said that it is not our custom to have the younger daughter marry before the elder. And all is not lost, my son," he said soothingly.

"I will not consider all to be lost if you will fulfill the intent of our agreement," Jacob said sullenly.

"Well, now, perhaps I can adjust the terms, or add a supplement," Laban said, leading Jacob in the direction he knew he wanted to go. "You have served me well for one wife. Why not serve me for another?"

"For Rachel? I would serve the great Satan himself for her," Jacob said impulsively.

"No need, no need," Laban returned. "Simply serve me another seven years, and this my younger daughter whom you love is yours."

Jacob looked at the floor. Could he endure another seven years without Rachel? He made a counter offer: "Give her to me now," he said flatly, "and I will serve you another seven years."

Laban was very pleased with himself and with the bargain he was about to strike; but he would not show it. "Hmmm," he mused, pretending to reflect on the proposal. "Can I trust you to do so without dangling my Rachel before you as an incentive?"

"You know that you can trust me more than I can trust—." Jacob left the sentence unsaid.

"Hmmm," Laban said again. "Let us do this, then. Let us allow my eldest daughter Leah to enjoy this week of feasting in honor of her own wedding. Then, at the end of the week, we shall have another wedding! Think of that, my man! Two wives in the space of a week! Are we agreed?"

"We are agreed," Jacob muttered. Without discussing it, both men knew that this time there would be no additional bride-price—and no contract in clay.

Thus it was, my lord Philemon, that Jacob the deceiver came to be deceived. Thus it was also that he came to possess two wives in a single week. And thus it was also that the one wife, Leah, would become jealous and bitter toward her sister Rachel, because their husband loved Rachel above all loves.

Yet the God who loves the unloved, and favors those without favor, was to intervene and bring a joy to Leah over the joy of Rachel, blessing Leah with children while closing the womb of Rachel.

I have not answered the question, my lord, of why some such as Esau seem to suffer undeserved injustice; but at the least the stories show that we are bound also to ask why God elects an unloved woman such as Leah to receive undeserved grace.

CHAPTER 12

It was not an unhappy family, at first. As Rachel and Leah had learned to tolerate their differences growing up in their father's household, it required but small adjustments to make living with Jacob tolerable.

Of course Leah was never in doubt that Jacob favored Rachel. But she was a practical woman. She had wondered when her father would tire of her being unmarried and select a man for her. She could have done much worse than Jacob.

With typical frugality, Laban had given Jacob a dowry of only three rams and a dozen ewes—a quite conservative gesture for a man of his wealth. But he had indifferently assigned the task of selecting the animals to one of his foremen, who, as it happened, was a man Jacob had cultivated as a friend. So he had chosen for Jacob three exceptional rams that would provide excellent stud service for years to come, and the ewes were selected from a breeding line known for bearing twins and triplets—for two generations no ewe from the line had borne only single lambs. Hence, in addition to his wages from Laban, Jacob's private holdings grew in numbers and value at an unprecedented rate.

Rachel did not prove nearly so prolific a producer, and it was this factor that eventually bred strife in the family. If ever loving care from an attentive husband lent itself to a fertile womb, Rachel would have borne twins and triplets, too. Jacob's love for her grew with the unfolding of the months, then the years; yet she was barren. The two often spoke of children, and dreamed together of their future as a family—even a clan. But there was no fruit from Rachel's womb.

Meanwhile, Leah's status in the household gradually subsided to that of a well-regarded cousin. Although Jacob occasionally visited her bed, she knew it was more from a sense of doing his husbandly duties than from love. Further incentive arose when it became apparent that Leah was quick to conceive.

Broader in the hips than her sister, Leah seemed made for birthing. Healthy as an ox, she would pause only two or three hours in her daily household duties when her time for delivery came. It was, Jacob mused, much like unhitching an ox from the plow only long enough to calve.

Leah's first baby arrived barely long enough after the wedding to be respectable. Her time came when the family was camped in the fields to the north of the home compound, but she had thought to include a midwife in her entourage.

"See—a son!" exclaimed the midwife as she held up the bloody, screaming newborn for Leah to see. And so the boy was named exactly that—*Reu-ben*, "See, a son!"

As she rolled the name about on her tongue, Leah noted with a grim smile that it sounded very much like another phrase, which she went quickly to share with Rachel.

"Look, sister!" she exclaimed proudly, carrying the infant to Rachel's tent herself, on strong legs, only an hour after he had emerged from her womb. "It is a son! He is Reu-ben"—she said the word slowly, so that it sounded like the phrase meaning *He has seen my misery*. "God has seen how our husband favors you over me. But he will love me more when he sees that I can bring him sons!"

Her barbed remark had the desired effect, but Rachel forced herself to reply with civility instead of the angry envy she felt.

"Surely, God *has* smiled on you, sister," she said, smiling. "*Reuben*," she cooed, looking down at the barely-washed babe. He is a beautiful son." But she made the word sound only like a name instead of carrying the extra weight Leah had given it.

Over the next several years, Reuben was followed in quick succession by three other sons from Leah's fertile womb. She made naming them a game born partly of custom, partly of her continuing longing for Jacob's favor, and partly out of spite for her more highly favored sister. With her second son she announced, "God has heard my prayers! The boy will be called Simeon, 'He who hears!'" And generations later her descendants would lift one form of the name to the level of liturgy, as they recited the *Shemah*, "Hear O Israel!"

Only ten months later Leah delivered to Jacob the infant Levi, a name drawn from the word for "attached," as though to beg in less than subtle terms for her husband to attach himself to her emotionally as he now did physically on so regular a basis.

The game continued with the arrival of a fourth son. Even in the pain of birthing, when Leah saw that it was another boy she cried "Praise Yah!", and from the phrase drew the name Judah. It meant something less than conversion to the High God of whom Jacob spoke, but she was willing to give credit to whomever was responsible for her continued stellar performance.

With the birth of Leah's fourth son, Rachel reached the limit of her patience. She confronted Jacob angrily: "I see that my lord has not rationed his visits to my sister's bed!"

Jacob looked up from the bridle he was rubbing with rancid butter to make it supple. At first he did not understand.

"Rachel," he said calmly. "We have always had an understanding. You have not been jealous."

"I am not jealous," she retorted. "I am lonely. The more fruitful my sister is, the more you lie with her and the less you come in to me." Then, less angrily, "I wonder if I am losing your love. I wonder why you do not give me sons, too."

The source of her anger dawned on Jacob. "*Give you sons?*" he echoed. "You are angry with *me* because *you* do not bear children? It is not a matter of how often I lie with you. Who am I—God, that I can choose whether you conceive?"

Rachel opened her mouth to explain further, but Jacob was angry now, and he would not stop.

"Here is a wonder!" he said, his voice heavy with irony. "One might think that if I lie with Leah and she bears children, and I lie with you and you do not, that the difficulty might be with you.

But no—somehow you manage to blame me! I tell you, woman—give me something other than a barren womb to work with and I will give you a child!"

He had no sooner hurled this at Rachel than he wished he could take it back. But the words were said. Rachel bit her lip and looked down at the ground.

Then she looked up abruptly. "All right, you shall have it," she said defiantly.

"Have what? I meant nothing but—."

"No, no. You said what you meant. You asked for a better womb, and I shall give you one. Take my maidservant Bilhah. Perhaps she will give me a son."

Jacob was stunned. "Bilhah? I do not want your servant!"

"You shall have her anyway. I can bring the matter to the fathers."

Jacob was well aware of the custom. A man whose wife was barren could be pressured to give her children through her servant. It was his turn to look at the ground. Rachel was right. She deserved children, one way or another.

"It will not be necessary to bring the matter to the council," he said slowly, and then walked away.

Rachel hated herself for what she was doing, but her desperation to have at least a legal heir through her husband, if not one from her own body, overruled her regret. She went directly to Bilhah to inform her of her new and expanded role as servant.

For her part, Bilhah could not have been happier. "And when shall this be?" she asked demurely, trying not to appear too eager.

"Tonight!" Rachel snapped.

And so it was that, bathed and perfumed, the maidservant Bilhah went after dark to Jacob's tent to perform her pleasant duty. The union was not only enjoyable but fruitful. Nine months later, when a baby boy was born to Bilhah, Rachel immediately asserted her authority over her man and the child, claiming that it was in answer to her own prayer. She named him Dan, which is interpreted, "He has vindicated me," thus leaving no room for Bilhah to be more than a dam lent out to a sire.

Having found Bilhah to be a pleasant companion, Jacob soon decided he would use Dan for a precedent, and invited the maidservant to his tent again. Once more her womb proved as open as Rachel's was shut, and another boy was born. Rachel could not give up the sense of competition with her sister Leah, and named the infant Naphtali, "My struggle."

Neither would Rachel give up on the idea of having children of her own. This business of lending one's servants to one's husband had its limits. She even felt driven to discuss her barrenness with her aging mother, Ishtarah, even though she had never felt comfortable speaking to her about such things.

"What can I do, Mother?" she asked plaintively, as though reverting to the little girl her mother used to comfort years ago. "Why is my womb shut when my heart is so open for children?"

Sure enough, Ishtarah's round and wrinkled face broke into a frown and she turned away. She had never been one to discuss such things openly, even with her daughters. Without looking at Rachel, she did manage to ask about her health and whether the manner of women was regular with her.

"Yes, yes," Rachel replied impatiently. "I am well, and everything seems fine with me."

Ishtarah pursed her lips. Still busying herself with her cooking instead of looking directly at her daughter, she said, "Perhaps you should consult the seer."

Rachel was silent. She knew that her mother had always kept a spot in her heart for the goddess after whom she was named, and for the ancient pantheon she represented. The talk of one High God that Jacob had brought to this household had always made her mother uncomfortable. The seer of whom her mother spoke was supposed to be in touch with the old ways and the old gods. But would Jacob approve of her consulting him?

"What could the seer tell me?" she asked.

"If I knew that, I would be the seer, now, wouldn't I?" her mother returned sharply. She turned more vigorously than ever to her cooking, signalling that her part of this conversation was finished.

I would say here a word about the seers among the pagans, my lord Philemon. I tell the story as it was told to me, but without meaning to invest pagan seers with powers beyond those that the one God has given. I have known what they predict to come true, and I have seen healings at their hands; but I know also that our holy books condemn going in to them as though they give a true word from God. Perhaps their powers are merely the sleight of hand of a magician. Or perhaps they draw supernatural power from the Evil One. Or perhaps their skills are limited to the wisdom that the Holy One gives to all men, whether believers or not. Who am I to say? Yet I can do nothing other than to tell the story as it was told to me.

The story is that Rachel visited the pagan seer in his home high in the mountains to the west of the river Tigris, where generations had gone to seek wisdom and knowledge. What Rachel was told by the seer has not come down in the stories, only that she returned with the practice of arranging stones on the ground and of peering into a cup of some brewed potion, then drinking the potion itself. Such practices did not meet the approval of her husband Jacob, but I truly believe Rachel would have attempted anything at all for the greater approval she knew her husband would have of her if she could but bear him a child.

"What, may I ask, are you doing?" Leah asked. She approached her sister gingerly, not knowing where to step among the stones Rachel was laboriously moving here and there in a great circle on the ground.

"I am learning the will of God," Rachel said, not looking up from her task.

"In *stones?*" asked Leah.

"In the liver of goats, in the leaves of a tea cup, in stones on the ground—I will force Him by whatever means to reveal to me His will...why it is *you*, my sister, who is elected to bear my husband sons, and why it is I who am willing, but barren."

"Is it then necessary to know?" Leah asked.

"It is not necessary when your womb never lacks fruit," Rachel shot back quickly. "It is only when people such as I, those of us who long to do the will of God but receive no sign—we are the ones who are driven to discover whether the gods—or the God— have any use for us." She looked away to hide the anguish in her eyes, but she could not conceal the bitterness in her voice.

"I don't know...," Leah mused. "Just because it is my good fortune to bear fruit ..."

"*Fortune?*" Rachel echoed. "Is it then only chance that some are favored and others are not? Some nations, I have heard worship a god of fortune. The seer tells me that others worship Fate. I care not the name of the god who reveals himself to me. I care only whether he wills to will the good for me, and if so whether he then keeps his will a secret and tempts me to play clairvoyance with him."

"But must you think of everything as *planned*?" Leah persisted. "Don't some things just happen? I am not sure I could live so close to the guiding hand of El. I think I am more comfortable at a distance, taking what comes as it comes, and not having to decide who sent it or if it just…well, *happens*."

Rachel was slower to respond now. It was a large question. Was her anguish merely a reflection of her own need to be guided, instead of a legitimate request for God to reveal himself to her? Finally she said simply, "I only know God guides some, and smiles on some, and withholds his blessing from others."

"For me," Leah replied quietly, "it would be living too close to El, or whatever gods there be, to think to have the Presence every day."

"For me," Rachel said, "I think that I shall die if I do not have the Presence so near, so close, that it directs my every step."

Feeling there was no more to be said that would not further widen the distance between them, the two sisters lapsed into silence. Rachel finished arranging the stones, then stepped back to inspect the way their shadows intersected with each other. She followed an imaginary line from their intersection to the horizon, to see to what distant hill they might point. That would be the place where the stones advised that she should lie with Jacob in order to conceive. Surely, she prayed, something in the way their shadows responded to the sun would lead her to the light.

Meanwhile, Leah's body had protested the regularity of procreation and asked for relief. In response, taking a page from Rachel's book, Leah proposed to Jacob that he take her own servant, Zilpah, as a concubine.

"Why?" Jacob asked. "You have borne well. I have no lack of sons from your womb."

"Suffer it to be so, my lord," said Leah. "Your flocks and herds are increasing, and the greater our tribe the better we can manage them. Besides—" and here she gave her husband a coy look— "I am not ready to concede defeat."

"Concede?" Jacob asked. "And what warfare are you conducting behind my back?" He was willing to play the game for the moment.

"Not behind your back," Leah returned. "I have never hidden my intent to win a love from you like that you give to my sister. It may be that I am through bearing children. Giving you Zilpah my servant is my way to see that I do not lose ground. Please— take her, my lord."

As Jacob considered his answer, the memory of his union with Bilhah entered his mind to prompt assent. "Tomorrow night," he said with a smile. "I will see her in my tent tomorrow night."

So it was that, as two sons were born to Jacob of Rachel's handmaiden, so two were born of Leah's servant Zilpah. Their names, Gad and Asher, "What good fortune!" and "How happy!" spoke of Leah's joy.

Rachel's stones and entrails and tea leaves were not working. One evening, returning to camp weary from arranging her rocks, she spied four-year-old Reuben bringing his mother Leah the snacks he had found in a nearby field. Rachel started when she saw that they were mandrake plants.

"Fruit," the lad said simply, holding up the plants to show Leah as she emerged from her tent. He had already popped one of the yellow balls into his mouth.

"Mandrakes," his mother said, more precisely. "Fortunately, it's not something poisonous. But you can't just go around plucking every plant you find and eating it, Reuben."

"Sweet," the lad explained in his one-word style of conversation.

"I know, they're not bad. But next time ask me," said his mother. By then Rachel had approached. "May I see them, Reuben?" she asked sweetly.

The lad swiftly moved the plants behind him in protest. His mother put her hands on her lips and looked knowingly at Rachel. "Oh, yes. Your aunt Rachel would want some of your mandrakes, Reuben. Women in her condition always want them." She referred to the widespread belief that mandrake fruit was an aphrodisiac, and its root an effective treatment for infertility.

"Why, no, Reuben," Rachel persisted. "I don't want your nice 'apples.' I only wondered if you would like to share the *roots* with me." Reaching behind him, she gently brought the plants out where they could both look at them.

"See? You can keep these little yellow sweets. But you don't want the roots, do you? Could Aunt Rachel have them?"

Relieved that he could keep the sweet part of his treasure, Reuben nodded solemnly, then watched as Rachel plucked the few yellow fruits remaining. She lifted up the boy's skirt and made a basket for them.

"Good boy!" she said. "Thank you!" And she turned to go.

"A moment, sister," Leah said. Rachel stopped but did not turn around. "I believe my son was bringing his mandrakes to *me*," Leah said evenly.

"*You* hardly need them!" Rachel snapped, whirling around. "Apparently you have only to dine with a man and you are able—" She checked the loose accusation. "Look—I will buy them from you. How much?"

Leah allowed herself a slight smile, a cunning idea forming.

"Not how much, but *who*," she said.

"What do you mean?"

"Our husband, my dear. I believe he is to sleep in your tent tonight?"

"Why yes. It is what we all agreed on."

"That is my price, my dear. Give him to me instead, and the mandrakes are yours."

Rachel looked down at the plants in her hand. Somehow she felt cheapened by engaging in such bargaining. But the mandrakes were one cure she had not yet tried. "He is yours," she said, unsmiling and not looking up at her sister.

Ironically, although it did little to shake Rachel's belief in the myth of mandrake-fertility, it was *Leah's* womb that was opened after the incident with the roots. She bore Jacob a fifth son, Issachar, "My reward," and again a sixth, Zebulun, "Honor," saying, "Surely now my husband will honor me."

But it was not to be. While Jacob could not help but swell with pride at his growing quiver of male arrows, Leah next did him the injustice of bearing several *daughters*, esteemed among these desert people as neither rewarding nor a sign of God's honor.

As it turned out, it was finally Rachel's turn to bring honor to herself and her husband.

After all her longing, all her attempts to force the divine will to reveal itself to her, all her use of folk medicine—after all had failed, Yah chose to open Rachel's womb of His own will. She bore a son.

"He is called Joseph," Rachel said proudly—"'*May he add.*'" To this day, no one knows whether by this Rachel meant to praise God for adding to her womb out of the riches of His grace what she had been unable to produce; or whether "Joseph" was a prayer that now that her womb had been opened, God would see fit to add yet more children to her account.

CHAPTER 13

Life had been good to Laban. Now in his eighth decade, he had managed to expand his flocks and herds beyond all ordinary expectations, to amass a fortune in gold and precious vessels (which he kept in a cave near his headquarters, with guards posted night and day), and to marry off his two daughters to a responsible kinsman.

But few men could have been less secure in their good fortune. Laban worried incessantly about how low the price of wool always seemed to be at shearing time. He stayed in constant dispute with neighboring land-holders over boundary lines and water holes. And he constantly imagined that his health was failing.

Only one change in his declining years would have been thought positive by many. Laban became more religious. Of course, the faith that began to grow in his heart was as cramped and stunted as the space it occupied. It was also ambiguous: on the one hand Laban attributed his wealth to his own acumen, and on the other he blamed the gods for not smiling on him so he could have even more.

It was, he decided, high time that he visit the seer. He had many questions about the future, many business decisions to make. He would consult a diviner who could peer into the dim beyond and advise him about any plans the gods might have for him. Giving the *teraphim* in their niche a double caress as he passed, Laban set out to the west with three servants, to consult the same seer whom Rachel had visited.

Toward the end of the fourth day of their journey, the little party arrived at the mountain cave of Adullam the seer. The old shaman sat before a broad but shallow fire pit that threw his shadow in eerie, dancing contortions on the stone about the cave's entrance behind him. Oil lamps inside the entrance seemed to speak of mysteries so dark they could not venture outside.

An albino, Adullum's milky skin contrasted ghoulishly with his red and watery eyes. White, sparse hair extended to his waist. He sat motionless, unsmiling, inscrutable, each hand tucked up the sleeve of the opposite arm, and looked up at the visitors without rising in greeting.

He did motion for them to join him around the fire, but Laban, jealous of the seer's attention, waved his servants to the side. He alone sat down heavily before Adullam.

"I have come for *qesem*, the divination," Laban said.

"I know why you have come," replied Adullum.

"Of course," Laban said, chagrined at the lame beginning he had made. After all, the man was a seer.

Instead of the customary inquiry into his visitor's health, the seer said, "You are doing well, my lord."

"Well—in many ways, yes, I suppose."

"But you are troubled about many things," the seer went on, narrowing his eyes both against the smoke of the fire and in order to convey the appearance of sagacity.

Laban would have no more of the game of clairvoyance. He came straight to the point, in order to word it as he wished. "I have no way of knowing whether my estate will increase in the coming years, or—." Laban faltered after all. "I would have you divine how the future expansion of my holdings would be best served."

"You mean whether by expanding in the business of sheep, or in cattle, or in camel trading and the like." It was not a question, but a statement clarifying Laban's request for himself.

"Precisely," said Laban. He leaned forward, pursing his lips and touching them on the fingertips of his clasped hands.

The ancient seer took a quiver of arrows from the ground beside him. Shaking the shafts out of the case, he gathered them up as one, struck the ground with them three times, then stood them on end and let them fall willy-nilly in all directions. For long minutes he examined the pattern they made in their fall, and the direction in which they pointed.

"My lord's past and future fortune, in fact, does not depend on his business decisions," the seer said.

Laban's head rose abruptly. "Then what—how—?"

"You have had an addition to your household," the seer went on. "Your daughters have taken a husband who by the law of *erebu* is living with you and working in your employ."

Laban knew that Rachel had visited this guru. She could have told him about Jacob, so this was no sign that the arrows had divined information the seer did not already possess. But Laban decided not to press the point. "Yes," he replied simply. "My family is multiplying as is my fortune."

The seer's lips widened without tipping up at the corners in an ever-so-slight gallows smile as he said, "It is your son-in-law who has prospered you. He is the servant of the High God. Whether you prosper in the future depends not on my lord's skill in buying or selling or breeding, but on keeping this your daughters' husband in your service." Adullum obviously delighted in puncturing this rich man's pride, but, mindful of the fee he was about to receive, he spoke in a voice so low the servants standing nearby could not hear.

Laban scowled at the fire as the darkness insinuated itself over the scene. How much more satisfying it would be to hear that his fortunes depended on his own acumen. Still, perhaps it would be easier to continue to keep this Canaanite relative with him than to divine the future market for sheep. Jacob, eh? If he only had more daughters, he mused, and more Canaanite nephews.

There was more. The seer knew how far his customer had traveled, and he wanted him to return feeling that he had received his money's worth of *qesem*. As the night deepened, Adullum fingered a clay model of a sheep's liver that had magical cuneiform formulas engraved on it. He studied the secret words on the face-up sides of cubical stones that he threw to the ground. There were predictions of dry years and lean, of the settling of new disputes and the instigation of new ones.

But the primary word was about Jacob. Laban returned home with the uncomfortable certainty that his future depended on his son-in-law.

Jacob himself had other plans.

"It is time, my lord Laban," he said. He was helping to tend Laban's considerable flocks and herds a day's journey from the main house. Jacob had sought him out immediately after Laban returned from the seer.

"Ah, yes, my son," Laban replied, in his characteristic way of pretending to know all that was implied even in an ambiguous statement. But silently he wondered: *Time for what? For the ewes to deliver? Time to bring them closer to headquarters?* He would wait for Jacob to say more, thus maintaining the illusion of being in the position of totally managing the conversation.

"I have worked for you these fourteen years, and you have prospered at my hand."

"Yes, yes, that is true," Laban admitted, surprised at this immediate echo of the seer's words. "And it has been a good time for you, too, eh?" Actually, the years had brought several conflicts between the two over contracts and wages, with the miserly Laban constantly searching for ways to profit at Jacob's expense.

"Good years, my lord," Jacob admitted. Just *how* good he would not share with Laban, for despite the old man's attempts to take advantage of him, Jacob's good judgment and hard work had enabled him to gather herds of his own with the wages Laban paid him. But good years or not, Jacob had a point to make.

"But I am more numerous now," he went on. "I am engaged more in increasing my lord's estate than in caring for those whom God has given me—my sons and daughters, and my wives, your own daughters." However penurious the old man was, Jacob was trading on the fact that he doted on his daughters.

"It is time for higher wages, then?" Laban asked, searching even as he spoke for ways to make a proposal that would offer more than it delivered.

"No, my lord Laban. It is time for me to take my wives and my sons and my daughters and return to my homeland."

Laban looked up at Jacob in honest shock before he could shape a contrived response. "My daughters? You would take them away?"

"The *erebu* contract is fulfilled," Jacob said. "There is nothing holding me here now. Give me leave to return to my father Isaac before he reaches the end of his days."

Laban squinted shrewdly at his son-in-law. Unfamiliar ground though it was, he would try a straightforward approach. "Jacob, my son. It has been divined to me that your God has blessed me because of you. I pray you to reconsider. Stay in my service only a little longer. You can name your own wages!"

Jacob weighed the statement before answering. The old man seemed unusually guileless. His own wages? His mind wandered briefly back to his homeland, and to his brother Esau. He was sure that the years had not erased from Esau's memory the fateful incident over the birthright. Perhaps if he stayed in Haran longer, and built up a small empire to return with, he could overpower—or buy off—any lingering anger Esau might have.

Suddenly Jacob had an inspiration. He had taken up with some Aramean sheepherders of late, and they had shared the lore of the ancients of that area. He had particularly been fascinated with what they had told him of breeding experiments.

"My lord speaks kindly of my service to him through Yah. If it pleases my lord, let Yah determine my wages, and I shall yet stay awhile."

"Er, your wages would be set by the gods—that is, by Yah?" Laban was not sure how they would learn the amount Yah had in mind—or even whether he trusted His judgment.

"Let my lord not pay me in money but in animals. I have proved to manage your flocks and herds honestly and well. Let me now turn to breeding my own livestock."

"Well, now," Laban said thoughtfully. It was pleasant to consider an arrangement that did not involve money. "But how shall we tell stock from stock? How shall we keep our herds separate?"

"What about this?" said Jacob. "Let me cull from your flocks what few speckled or spotted sheep and dark lambs you have, and from your herds the few spotted kids and calves. These being not the most valuable, they will not be a great loss to my lord, yet they will be good enough to start my own herds. I will breed them, and every speckled and spotted and dark offspring shall be mine, while every white lamb and kid and calf shall be yours."

Laban considered the proposal only a moment before agreeing. It was often difficult to market spotted sheep's wool anyway. And if such an arrangement would keep Jacob, and Jacob's God, with him, it would be an excellent investment.

"Done!" he said. "We shall set the herdsmen to work on the culling immediately."

There were fewer than a hundred of the designated animals, so the dusty work took less than two hours. Laban ordered Jacob's new starter-stock taken to the farthest pasture of his domain to prevent any more of his own from joining them.

As in the case of the marriage contract, both men felt they had got the better of the other. It was the way they dealt best with each other.

Jacob was so excited about his breeding experiment that he barely noticed the months fading into years. Following the advice of the Aramean herdsmen, he arranged an elaborate and carefully contrived mating environment for his flocks and herds. It was designed to provide a slight shock to the females at the moment of their union with the males, in the belief that it would influence the formation of the seed planted within them. Of course the particular result Jacob sought was to produce spotted and speckled and dark offspring.

The scheme was to herd the best rams, bucks and bulls into a makeshift *kraal* or enclosure near an oasis where the herds regularly watered. Then those ewes and does and cows that were in heat would be driven to the waiting males. Low wing-fences of dull brown branches, forty feet wide at the farthest end, provided a narrowing lane leading to the inner enclosure. The sere coloring of the branches had a calming effect on the females as they made their way toward the males.

Suddenly, entering the enclosure itself, the females were confronted with a higher fence made of startling, multi-colored stakes. Jacob and his sons had partially peeled tall limbs from the poplar, almond, and plane trees that grew prolifically at the oasis, and arranged them in a wall that contrasted sharply with the rest of the setting in the hope that it would frighten the females just enough for them to be in a state of excitement when mounted by the males. According to the Arameans, the offspring from such unions stood a good chance of being as spotted as the peeled branches.

"It is done!" cried Jacob, when the first lambing time came. Sure enough, the spring hillsides were sprinkled with cavorting lambs and kids, and later with calves, all sporting spotted and speckled hides.

Jacob was on his way to becoming a very wealthy man.

My lord Philemon, it will not be necessary for me to elaborate on Jacob's foolishness or else his ignorance of the breeding of animals. Selective breeding is a science in my homeland, and there is no evidence that the excited state of a female influences the color of her offspring. As my lord will know very well, this is only another instance of Jacob's having been chosen for extraordinary blessing. The God who elevates the lowly and calls down the mighty—it is He who blessed the wombs of Jacob's animals, commanding them what colors to bear, just as His will was supreme in the filled and the barren wombs of Jacob's wives. But Jacob had not yet learned that the God who elected him from his mother's own womb does not need the assistance of plots and schemes.

I say this, my lord, even while acknowledging that I myself still struggle to learn this lesson.

CHAPTER 14

Six years after beginning to reap the fruits of his bargain with Laban, Jacob lay inside his tent, sleeping fitfully just before dawn. He dreamed of the matter that had been much on his mind of late: his overwhelming success in breeding animals that were marked as his from the womb.

In his dream, prize males and females were mating. With time collapsed, in the way of dreams, the gestation period was as nothing, and the females immediately bore yet more spotted and streaked and speckled young.

Suddenly the voice of God rose in Jacob's dreaming mind: "Jacob!" it said, from no place in particular but from every corner of the heavens.

"Is it—my Lord and my God!" Jacob heard himself reply.

"Do you see the way I have blessed you and made you great in the land?" the voice asked.

"I—yes, Lord." It was no time to bring up his supposed breeding skills.

"With every blessing I give to you, it is a curse to your father-in-law, Laban," the voice continued. "It is time for you to return to your homeland, to the fires of Isaac and Rebekah, for Laban's heart has turned against you."

Jacob awoke, and lay for a moment pondering the dream. It was as vivid as had been the vision of the ladder to heaven so many years ago. Was he to take it literally?

As he weighed the meaning of the dream, the voices of herdsmen drifted to him from outside the tent. Three of Laban's sons, herdsmen, were finishing their breakfast of goat's cheese and bread and talking around the morning's campfire. It was almost dawn, and since the men assumed that Jacob had already left for the fields, they talked rather freely.

"This duty is not to my liking," said one. "Why should we have to help our brother-in-law grow rich?"

"Agreed," a guttural voice returned. "And what's worse, I think he is prospering at our father's expense."

"I overheard our father say as much," said the third voice. "No breeder can be this lucky. You know that Jacob has some way of knowing what pairs of sheep and goats from our father's own herds will throw spotted offspring. Father thinks he simply steals their services and then steals their young. And since they're spotted, no one can tell."

By then, Jacob's heart was in his throat. The increase in his spotted and speckled property *had* been phenomenal, though honestly gained. Never had he seen more twins and triplets. But if his father-in-law and others thought he was stealing...

It was high time to flee. He would stay no longer in this foreign land. He would return with his wives and family and servants and flocks and herds to his home in Canaan.

Waiting until the men stamped out the fire and went off to the herds, Jacob sent his son Reuben for Rachel and Leah, who were at the main house with the younger children. "Hurry, my son!" he commanded. "Have my wives meet me at the spring of Jabaal, when the sun is overhead tomorrow."

Fortunately, Jacob's herds—of considerable numbers by now—were all grazing nearby. He sent Laban's sons home, saying that he and his own sons wanted to take the herds farther from the main camp to avoid the possibility of their mingling with Laban's.

Within half a day Jacob and his sons had gathered the stock, which by now included a herd of a hundred asses, and as many camels. Jacob was at Jabaal, supervising the packing of the last donkey when Rachel and Leah rode up breathlessly on their own camels.

"My lord!" gasped Rachel. "What is it? These pack animals, and the flocks—what is happening?"

Jacob recounted in even tones the conversation he had overheard. "It is time," he concluded simply. "Are you with me? Are you ready to truly show your loyalty to your husband, and to his God, and return with him to the land of his father, and to the land that Yah has promised to his seed?"

The two sisters looked at each other solemnly. Despite their frequent jealousy, they were united in this venture.

"We belong now to you, not to our father," said Rachel.

And Leah said, managing a half-smile, "Did not he sell me to you for a pregnant cow?" Actually, both women well knew that if they valued any estate or wealth, their loyalty had best lie with this man on whom Yah smiled.

Jacob smiled, too. "Go," he said. "Your father will be away at the shearing. Pack your things. Take Reuben with you. The rest of us will start with the herds through the way to the river. If you have not overtaken us, we will wait for you at the swamp of Agag. Go swiftly, my loves!"

Laban discovered they were gone three days later, when he returned from the shearing pens. He was enraged. Storming out of the house he swept a hand into the alcove to caress a blessing from the *teraphim*—and was left grasping thin air.

"What is this!" he roared. "It is not enough that this dog takes my daughters and the herds he has stolen from me—he has taken my gods as well! After them!" he shouted to his sons.

Mounted on swift camels, it was a week later, at sundown, when they spied the column of dust that signalled Jacob's party. They were in the hill country of Gilead, about to make camp for the night. Laban's small force decided to do the same, and to wait until morning when they were rested to make contact.

That night it was Laban's turn to be visited by God in a dream. Reflecting on it later, Laban realized that he heard no voice—perhaps because he was no particular devotee of Yah. But the experience left no doubt that the High God had communicated with him in some way. And the word was: *See that you do no harm to this my servant, Jacob.*

Nevertheless, Laban was up before dawn. He and his sons crept up to Jacob's camp and marched boldly upon the fugitives as they sat around the morning fires.

"You have wronged me, my son!" Laban said. His fleshy face was almost purple with anger. "Would not I have let you go in peace if you had said a word to me? Would it not be to your joy to be sent away with a feast and with tambourines and the blessings of the gods of my house? But as it is, you have stolen away like a thief without allowing me to bid my daughters farewell. Had not your God warned me in a dream only this night, I would have—." His voice trailed off. After all, these were his daughters and their husband. He did not know what he would have done.

"You would not have sent us away in peace," Jacob argued. "You have spent twenty years keeping me in your service by fair means or foul. Why would you do otherwise now that you believe I have been cheating you?"

Laban let the matter go, wanting to press a more urgent point. "And as if all this were not enough, you have stolen my gods. You would not receive their blessing at my home where they live, by asking my leave, and so you have taken them with you that they may bless you on the way to your homeland. In this, my son, you have wronged me grievously!"

Jacob's anger rose now. "I did not take your gods. I have Yah to bless me; if anyone in my company is found with them he shall not live! Here," he said, opening his arms wide, "my camp is yours—look for the *teraphim* where you will!"

Laban motioned to his sons to search the tents of Jacob's sons, while he himself stormed into Jacob's tent. He threw hide rugs and clothing and harness about in a less than thorough search for the *teraphim*. Nothing. Then he ransacked the tent behind Zilpah and Bilhah, the maidservants. Nothing. Next was Leah's, with the same negative results.

Only one tent was left. That would be Rachel's, Laban surmised, since she was the only one not standing outside with the rest. He threw back the goat-hide door and found himself staring at his younger daughter, seated over at the side on a stack of blankets lying across her camel saddle.

"Father! You startled me!" said Rachel.

Laban paused in his pell-mell search and drew himself up to

full height, arms folded across his ample belly, nose up. "You left without a word of parting," he said accusingly.

"And would you have gladly bid me farewell had I spoken to you?"

Laban did not answer. His eyes swiftly made the rounds of the tent. Nothing. Then his eyes came to rest on Rachel.

"My father will excuse me, I hope, if I do not get up," she said demurely. "It is with me after the manner of women." She lowered her eyes modestly.

"Yes, yes. It is enough," her father said grumpily, and turned on his heel.

"Well?" Jacob demanded. "You have ransacked my camp and what have you found? Set everything here before us so I may put to death the thieves!"

Laban thought it best to take the offensive. "It is you who have pillaged *my* camp. Everything I see here—your wives and their children, your goods and your flocks and your herds—could I not claim them all as my own? Yet you have taken them from me, and your God has warned me not to harm you..."

Pausing in his tirade, Laban had a second thought. Perhaps it would be more effective to appear pitiable. "But I am only an old man. What can I tell my daughters? What can I tell their husband, without whom I shall die in poverty—especially now that someone has stolen my gods, for with them goes the right of inheritance?"

"You can tell us farewell," said Jacob, unmoved. "You say I have kept you from poverty. I have also given you the best years of my life—twenty years, in which you must have changed my wages ten times and begrudged every shekel I have earned and every young born among my flocks."

Laban's mouth worked as though to shape a retort, but no words filled it. Finally, he said, half to himself, "Of what use is it all?" Then directly to Jacob: "Let us cease this wrangling. Take your wives and their children and your possessions and return to your homeland. Only let us make a covenant and a monument to mark our peace. You will not return to this my side of the marker, and I give my pledge not to go beyond it to your side, toward Canaan."

Jacob eyed his father-in-law aslant, wondering what this sudden change in attitude could mean. Finally he muttered, "Agreed."

Many of the hills of Gilead are topped with stone outcroppings, and it was in one of those natural quarries that Jacob spied a natural obelisk, a roughly cube-shaped pillar some four feet in length, lying on its side. He ordered three of his sons to loosen it from its moorings and send it tumbling halfway down the hill. There they set it on end, heaping smaller boulders around its base for support, thus fashioning it into a rude monument.

As the young men were finishing their impromptu work of stone masonry, old Laban began to intone a blessing: "May the Lord keep watch between you and me when we are away from each other. May you remember to treat these my daughters as beloved wives. And if not, may the Lord your God punish you in my stead."

Jacob was suddenly impressed by the intensity of his father-in-law's protective feelings for his daughters. His anger softened, and he added his own liturgical contribution to the solemn moment: "In the name of the Fear of Isaac my father, the God of his father Abraham, may God do so to me and more also if I harm your daughters or trespass this boundary or make light of this covenant."

His emotions fed by his own eloquence, Jacob went further. "My father Laban!" he burst out. "Let us sacrifice a goat from the flock on this stone, making of it an altar of witness and a table of feasting in witness of this our covenant!"

So it was that the prospect of their parting enabled these who had been both friends and enemies through the years to part as table companions. And so it was that the stones of witness that marked their peace came to be known also as *Mizpah*, or "watchtower," for Laban said, "May Yah keep watch between you and me when we are away from each other."

But in her tent, Rachel's heart was not one with the ceremonies outside. As her father Laban and his people settled down for the night, to prepare for their long trek back to Haran, Rachel took from their hiding place in the pockets of her camel saddle the *teraphim* she had stolen from her father. She smiled as she rubbed their worn surfaces. She had been unable to leave her homeland trusting only in Yah, the God of Jacob. Fondling the gods, she whispered softly to herself, "Thank you for protecting us from my father Laban's wrath. Be thou our strength and our stay in this wilderness."

Thus it was, my lord Philemon, that Jacob returned from his long sojourn in Haran in both the strength of Yah, in whom he trusted, and the weakness of the unbelief of his wife Rachel.

The hill on which Jacob and Laban raised the stone was called "Hill of Witness"—Galeed, *in the Hebrew tongue of Jacob, and* Jegar Sahadutha *in Laban's Aramean. It was a witness not only of their covenant together, but of the sad merging of faith and unfaith in Jacob's own family. The stone has long since been lost to all travelers, but in its time it was revered by the sons of Jacob as the stone that had been his help and protection on his long trek homeward.*

CHAPTER 15

"The messengers! Where are those messengers?" Jacob muttered under his breath. He squinted at the setting sun from atop his towering, lurching camel. It had been four days since he had sent his longtime servants Shinab and Sabteca south toward Edom, as emissaries to seek out his brother Esau and to sue for peace.

Jacob's party was approaching the brook Jabbok, to the west of the Jordan. The trek through the hills of Gilead had been uneventful, but Jacob's anxiety grew apace. Reverting to form, he found himself playing out a variety of schemes in his mind—ploys that might save him and his family from the wrath he had known to consume his brother Esau twenty years earlier.

Licking his parched lips nervously, Jacob tried to think of something—anything—that might have softened Esau's hatred. There was only his absence—perhaps simply not having to deal with him and his schemes for two decades was enough to make Esau's anger die from lack of fuel.

Not likely, Jacob reminded himself. Memories, like the mummies of the Egyptians, tended to be preserved indefinitely in the desert. All he could do was to offer gifts from his great possessions.

His darting eyes scanned the southern horizon nervously. There! Were the two camel riders bobbing toward the caravan friend or foe? Jacob pulled up and raised his hand to signal the rest of the caravan to halt. A cloud of dust that had been hanging at the rear caught up with the head of the band, enveloping all in a red cloak.

Jacob sent the captain of the caravan out to meet the approaching camel riders. Good! They raised their arms in friendly salute; they were his returning messengers. The captain escorted them back to Jacob. "Shalom," my lord, Sabteca said, saluting. The years that had seen Jacob grow in wealth had been accompanied by an increase in formalism between servant and master.

"Peace be with you, my brothers!" Jacob returned.

"Your brother Esau sends his greetings," Shinab began, "and—."

"You gave him my message?" Jacob interrupted. "You told him of our herds and our numbers?"

"We told him, lord," said Shinab, looking at Sabteca and wondering how to go on.

"And—and?" Jacob demanded, so nervous he did not know he was stammering.

"We can say little more," Sabteca offered. "My lord's brother said nothing about our numbers or our herds…only that he was coming to meet my lord."

"Coming—to us?" Jacob blurted out. "Why would he not wait for us to bring him gifts from our herds? Why—?"

"We cannot say," the first messenger said, shrugging. "My lord's brother said only that he comes—." He cleared his throat uncertainly. "That he comes to meet my lord with 400 men."

Jacob blanched under his dark skin. Esau was coming with a small army! Swallowing hard, Jacob waved the messengers away, and gave the captain orders to signal the caravan to resume its trek toward the Jabbok.

The long caravan with the flocks and herds clattered noisily down the rocky ravine that had been carved by the Jabbok on its meandering course to the Jordan. Jacob's left eye winked in uncontrollable spasms.

At the bottom of the hill a grassy plain spread out before them. They would camp here for the night. Weary camels loudly drank their fill from the brook, then groaned duets to their creaking bones as they sank to the ground. As night fell, lowing cattle and the tinkling bells on lead ewes spread their soft benediction over the camp.

But there was no calm in Jacob's soul. His restless mind continued to thrash about for a way to wrench a favorable outcome from the forthcoming encounter with Esau.

Dawn broke with a prematurely warm sun over the camp, and found Jacob having slept little. The only plan he could concoct was to shower Esau with his gifts in some impressive way that would send repeated and successive messages that Jacob sought a reconciliation.

He ordered his chief herdsmen to separate the gift animals from the rest—200 female goats and 20 bucks; 200 ewes and 20 rams; 30 camels, half of them with young offspring at their side; 40 cows and 10 bulls; and 20 she-asses and 10 male asses.

The animals were gathered by early afternoon. Jacob winced as he watched them mill in a great mass at the edge of the Jabbok. It was a costly offering; but there was nothing else to be done.

He ordered the animals sorted into three bands of roughly the same size. "You will take them across the Jabbok in three herds," he told the herdsmen. "Keep a good distance between each herd, so they will not intermingle. When you reach Esau's camp, tell whoever comes out to meet you that the animals are a gift to your lord Esau. Tell them also that the herd is only a part of Jacob's gift and sign of love for his brother. The entire herd, you will say, is too big to bring at once. And you who are with the second and the third herds—you will say the same, and that this token of your lord Jacob's regard for his brother will be followed by Jacob himself, who comes in peace."

So saying, Jacob sent the herdsmen and their charges on their peace-making mission. Then he busied himself organizing his family for the rest of the journey. He would send them across the river tonight. As for himself, he felt the need to spend a night alone, in prayer. If ever he needed the help of Yah, it was now. He helped Rachel and Leah, with their maidservants and his eleven sons, to cross the Jabbok with their belongings. Then he returned to bed down alone, in the open, on the north side of the stream.

For a second night he slept only fitfully.

It must have been a little after midnight when he felt the hand on his shoulder. It was not the clasp of a friend, but more like the iron grasp of a bandit or other ruffian who meant him anything but well.

"Who is it? Who's there?" Jacob asked startled and struggling unsusccessfully to release himself from the strong hand.

There was no response. Twisting up from the hide on which he had been trying to sleep, Jacob felt the man's form more than he saw it, in the darkness. Suddenly, his strange foe drew Jacob's arm behind his back swiftly, in a wrestling grip with which Jacob had been familiar as a boy. Once a troupe of Mycenaean wrestlers had passed through his father's camp and offered lessons in self-defense. Like them, this assailant was apparently not interested in robbing him or killing him; he wanted to wrestle!

Strange as it was, Jacob could do nothing but oblige. He tried valiantly but ineffectively to release himself. He certainly had no desire to kill the enigmatic figure before he knew more about him. Was he simply some wandering athlete who needed a workout? Or had he been driven mad by battling the wilderness and now sought human companionship, but on equally combative terms? No explanation seemed adequate, so there seemed to be nothing to do but try to hold his own.

They fought. Jacob's strange opponent even followed Mycenaean rules. Once, managing to throw Jacob over his shoulder onto the ground in a fair fall, the man sprang back to allow Jacob to recover—there was no attempt to pounce on him or to struggle on the ground. Instead, the match was conducted in full standing position, with wrist holds and leg thrusts and much spinning and twisting in an effort to elude a hold while gaining an advantage at the same time.

Back and forth the two combatants struggled, over an area not more than twelve or fourteen feet wide. Only their stamping and grunts and heavy breathing broke the silence of the night. Frequently they would reach an unspoken agreement to stand back from each other and catch their breath—it was obviously no blood sport for either man.

The pair seemed to be amazingly well-matched, with neither man able to get the better of the other. Under other conditions, Jacob might have considered the whole thing great sport. But the battle dragged on and on interminably. What was the man's aim?

Jacob decided that all he could do was to imagine that they were, indeed, at the games, and to fight on until his antagonist revealed some reason for the strange struggle.

The first light of dawn was beginning to streak across the eastern horizon, and Jacob's strength was ebbing. Although the stranger had not been able to best him, he apparently had greater endurance. Suddenly he gave Jacob a vicious shoulder thrust. Reeling backward, Jacob had his right leg a foot off the ground when the man curled a powerful right arm under Jacob's thigh and heaved upward with a mighty thrust.

A stabbing pain streaked from Jacob's hip up his lower back. In his pain he forgot all rules and clutched out at the stranger, his flailing arms landing around the man's neck and bringing his opponent down on himself as both fell heavily.

The sandy earth gave a resounding *whump*, and both men lay in a heap, panting. Jacob would not release his opponent, claiming the moment for a brief rest.

"Let me go!" the man spoke for the first time.

The voice! Jacob froze, his struggle suspended by a memory. There was no mistaking the supernatural quality of that voice. It was so similar, if not identical, to the voice he had heard in the dream, warning him to flee Haran.

Had he been wrestling with God? Or with His angel?

Jacob was desperate. "Who are you, my lord?" he gasped. I will let you go if you reveal yourself to me. Give me a blessing that I may know whether I wrestle with a man or with a god!"

Instead of giving Jacob an answer, the man asked a question of his own: "Who are *you*? What is your name?"

Jacob hesitated. Giving the man his name would be tantamount to surrendering the battle. The story of the Beginning flashed through his mind—the naming of the animals gave Adam authority over them. Then a bolt of pain through his hip reminded him that the battle was over in any case.

"I am Jacob, son of Isaac, grandson of Abraham, through whom the Promise came." Jacob found himself wondering why the man did not know his name, if he were indeed divine.

Slowly the stranger pulled himself up from Jacob. He extended his hand, and as Jacob seized it he pulled him to his feet. Jacob winced as he stood; the hip socket was either out of joint or the main nerve running up the back of his leg and his spine had been pinched.

The two stood staring at each other in the growing light. "Your name will no longer be Jacob," the strange wrestler said. "From henceforth you will be known as *Israel*, 'He who struggles with God,' for after your years of struggling with men, you have struggled with El—*and you have overcome!*"

Jacob was speechless for a moment. There could be no doubt that this was an angel of God, if not Yah Himself in the form of a man.

"My Lord," Jacob said gravely. "Please reveal your name to me. Surely I have not overcome my lord. But with whom have I dared to wrestle through this long night?"

"Why do you ask my name? Who else but God would have the authority to change the name of His chosen one?"

It also occurred to Jacob that the man might not want to reveal his own name, out of the same sense that this would be conceding the battle.

"Kneel, thou Israel of God!" the figure commanded.

The authority in the voice—could this be anyone but God? Painfully, Jacob dropped to one knee. As he bowed his head, the stranger placed a gentle hand upon it and said, "Blessed are you, chosen one of God! Know from this moment that you need not strive either with Him or with men for their favor. Know from your very name that God has chosen you for His blessing."

The moving words, coupled with his exhaustion, made Jacob's body tremble. He began to weep. After a moment, he stood, with some effort, to again address the stranger.

But he was gone.

"My Lord!" called Jacob, his eyes sweeping the area frantically. "Do not leave me!" But he knew he was alone.

"*Israel*," he repeated. "He who struggles with God." The enormity of the experience both lifted his soul and settled like a great weight on his very bones. "With *God*?" he repeated, incredulously. "I have wrestled with God!"

With the idea simply too vast to comprehend, Jacob could only project his wonder onto the place, giving it a name also. "This," he said solemnly, drawing himself up as straight as his injured hip would allow, "shall be known henceforth as Peniel, 'the face of God,' for I have seen the face of God, yet I live!"

With that, Jacob pulled himself up on the lone riding ass he had kept out of the herds for his own use. Shaking his long ears and snorting a vain protest, the animal splashed across the shallow stream to join the caravan up ahead.

CHAPTER 16

Jacob thought he was paralyzed when he awoke the first morning. Not only his hip but his entire body was immobilized from the wrestling match. His every muscle seemed to moan like a reluctant camel when asked to move. His head pounded, and for a moment he considered simply crawling to the nearest shade and passing the day sleeping—or dying.

The idea somehow took root, and set him to musing. His head often reeled like this from the heat of the Middle Eastern sun. Perhaps the condition would become so debilitating that he would simply be unable to function as a "chosen one." He could tell Yah to select someone else...that he was physically not up to the burden.

But as the sun warmed his aching muscles Jacob was able to require them to obey simple commands. Twice, as he stirred to prepare a meager meal, he found himself patiently lifting his leg with both hands to place it *here*, where it was needed. It made him admit, rather grumpily, that Yah could also place him where He willed, aches and pains or no.

Thankful at least to be riding instead of walking, Jacob was finally able to struggle on. Although he was anxious to overtake his wives and family, he welcomed the silence and the time to reflect on the strange experience with the wrestler El, or His angel, at the River Jabbok. Echoing in his mind were the wrestler's words, *You need not strive either with God or with men for their favor, for you have struggled with God, and have overcome.*

Gradually, he found his entire outlook being transformed as he mulled the saying over in his mind. If this were so, why would he ever again need to resort to his natural bent toward trickery and deceit? Even his anxiety about the attitude of his brother Esau was subsiding. As he walked, he allowed his mind to wander back over the devious paths his life had taken. Why had it taken so long for him to realize what the wrestler had said?

You need not strive—none of his machinations, none of his devious ways, manifested in so many forms, had added one whit to El's having selected him *before birth* to be the heir of the Promise. The idea echoed in Jacob's brain, shattering every small theory he had ever concocted about El's inscrutable will and ways. No wonder he had not arrived at it on his own; he would have dismissed it as self-contradictory had anything like that occurred to him.

Yet there was also the phrase, *You have struggled with God, and have overcome,* which seemed to imply *some* activity on Jacob's part. But overcome El? Jacob had no mental template against which to measure such an idea.

He forged on, south toward Seir, and Edom, the land of Esau. After seven days, he could catch glimpses of the Dead Sea, toward the west, as the road would top a ridge.

The pain in his hip and down his leg and up into his lower back was less severe now. He was relieved, for he must overtake his family and herdsmen before they made the offering of the flocks and herds to his brother Esau. God, not Jacob's gifts and attempts to appease his brother, would protect him, he was now convinced.

Meanwhile, thanks to the camel caravans that criss-crossed the land to the north and carried news with them as they snaked their way around dunes and across *wadis*, Jacob and his clan were the unlikely topic of conversation in the city of Shechem, in the hill country of northern Canaan. Named for the son of one Hamor, a Hivite, Shechem was comprised mostly of tents housing herdsmen in the nearby pastures. A few stone houses, belonging to the merchants of Shechem, formed the only permanent structures there.

Hamor was a heavy, white-bearded old man so squat and fat he almost lacked a neck; his great head seemed to be attached directly to his rounded shoulders. His son Shechem, muscular and swarthy, taller than his father, with greasy long curls, addressed his father.

"You have heard of the people called the Hebrews?" he asked.

"I know of them," the old man said. He shook his heavy head in distant admiration. "Wealthy clan, I am told. The patriarch Abraham sojourned in Canaan at one time. Now his son Isaac is an old man, a man of the fields, and his flocks range to the south, some say all the way to the Negev."

"It is true," Shechem said. "And they are now three clans. Isaac's sons, Esau and Jacob, have multiplied people and lands of their own—Esau in the land of Edom, to the southeast, and Jacob in Paddan-aram, beyond the River Euphrates.

"And word now is that Jacob is returning with great flocks and herds from Paddan-aram, and that there is nothing he cannot do, for the gods are with him." He paused, giving his father time to assimilate this piece of information before going on. Shechem owned a well nearby, whose water he provided—for a price—to caravans passing through, and he enjoyed nothing more than gleaning news as well as money from them.

"Returning? To his father? The land of the south will be hard pressed to support them both," Hamor mused.

"Exactly," said Shechem, his dark eyes flashing with the scheme toward which he was leading his father. "But why should they not settle here, instead? You could sell them that plot to the east, with the spring, and we could lease them their grazing lands, and make allies of them to strengthen our numbers against the raiders."

The hill country of northern Canaan had long been afflicted with marauders, soldiers of fortune dominated by Philistines, from the southwest, who lived by pillage and theft. A tribe like Jacob's, with several sons and dozens of herdsmen and servants, would go a long way toward stabilizing the entire area.

"Hmmm," old Hamor reflected.

Before he could comment, Shechem suggested, "Even now,

Jacob's caravan is reported to be across the Jordan, headed south from the Jabbok. You know," he exclaimed, as though the idea were just dawning on him, "I could perhaps visit them on their journey before they get to the country of Jacob's brother, Esau. I could make them a proposal about the land."

His father pursed his lips. Why not profit, if he could, from the blessings of this man's gods? "Go," he said. "Tell him about the good grazing here. And *don't* tell him about the nuisances we endure."

Shechem's long, jet-black curls bobbed up and down in agreement. Jacob's clan would need water, too...

Nine days from the Jabbok, Jacob was urging his donkey up and over a rounded peak, below which the caravan trail curved before him, providing a panoramic vista of the way ahead, and on south beyond the sea. Undulating, bare hills spread before him, with the road alternately dipping out of sight between them, then appearing again as it wound its way to Edom.

There below, not ten minutes ahead, and within earshot, were his wives and servants and children. And another quarter-hour beyond them, but around a point so they could not see each other, was a larger band of soldiers, with a colorfully-dressed figure on a camel out in front.

It could be none other than Esau.

He and his small army were on a little plain between two hills. Jacob could see that the herds and herdsmen he had sent ahead were spread out on the plain. Esau and his men had already met with them, and were now pressing on. In minutes they would round the bend in the road and come upon Jacob's family.

Jacob was surprised at the way his vantage point, placing him in visual control over the whole scene below, set his mind to puzzling again over the mystery of his new name, of the angel, even of his mother's story of his having seized Esau by the heel at birth.

He imagined himself as El, looking down at events that would inevitably occur. Esau and Jacob's family *would* meet, as sure as they were on the same road, even though the intervening hill prevented them from knowing it. Yet, Jacob felt a strange detachment from the scene—although he knew the two parties would meet, it occurred to him that he certainly had not arranged it thus.

Was this anything at all like the issue with which he had struggled these twenty years? Did Yah make plans for those whom His superior vantage point enabled Him to know would pass by certain places and stages throughout their lives, without *causing* them to do so?

The immediate demands of the occasion required that he put the idea out of his mind. He would come back to it later.

"Hail, the travelers below!" he called, as loudly as he could. His voice reverberated off the sere, brown hills. "Hail, the family of Jacob!" he called again.

The little band stopped. They had heard. They looked upwards and behind them, and saw Jacob.

"Raa-chel...Lee-ah!" Jacob called, pressing on even as he shouted. "Stop there! Wait, and I will join you!"

Although he had been too late to stop the herdsmen, he would at least overtake his family and confront Esau before they did. Soon he was at their side.

"My lord," Rachel and Leah said, almost together. "You are injured," Rachel added, noticing Jacob's limp. "What happened?"

"Later, later," he replied. "From up there, where I called you, I could see Esau just up ahead, around the bend in the road." He hurried to the front of the little band. "Let me go ahead of you, to be the first to greet him."

Jacob paused, looking over his family and servants. If Esau and his men planned to greet them with the sword, who among them should bear the first blows?

"Arrange yourselves in ranks," he said. "Bilhah and Zilpah— you will be first, with your children." The maidservants gathered their offspring and obeyed.

"Leah—you and yours are next. Then Rachel and her son Joseph, in the rear. Now—I shall go test my brother's temper. If there are blows, then all of you are to flee. Make your way back to Haran if I am killed or taken prisoner.

"But if you see that we are only speaking together, then approach us in ranks, as I have grouped you."

Rachel and Leah looked at each other apprehensively as they separated their children. It was unthinkable that they would have to return to their father, after the encounter a few days earlier. The parting had been too final.

Taking a deep breath, Jacob marched resolutely ahead. By the time he had gone fifty paces he could hear Esau and his band approaching around the bend in the broad pathway. Then the moment was upon him; his brother appeared.

Esau loomed large atop his camel, especially in relation to his brother Jacob, who was still on foot. Esau's rich garments were fit for a king. Perhaps he *was* a king, Jacob mused—king of Seir, perhaps even of all of Edom.

Then Jacob was on his face. In the eternal ritual of humility of the East, he bowed to the ground seven times.

"My lord, Esau," he said hoarsely. "My brother!"

High on the hump of the camel he had brought to a halt, Esau gaped at this, his long-lost brother, this deceiver, this supplanter, this thief of his birthright, lying prostrate before him. Esau had heard of Jacob's wealth, and he expected to find in his brother a haughty spirit, or at least a royal demeanor befitting the birthright he had stolen. Instead, here was a prince on his face before him!

Speechless at first, Esau finally rapped his camel to its knees and dismounted. Jacob had ceased his bowing and remained motionless, face to the ground, arms before him, palms alternately up in supplication, then down to show honor.

Esau paused for only a moment, as though to be sure the spectacle before him was real. Then he ran to his brother, grabbed him by an outstretched arm, and lifted him to his feet.

"Jacob, my brother!" he said.

Meeting his eyes, Jacob saw none of the wrath he expected, only the warmth of a man who had not seen his brother for twenty years.

The two embraced, kissing each other on each cheek, somewhat stiffly. Then they held each other at arm's length, each sizing up the other. Then they embraced again, this time with no tension, no pretense at protocol. It was the embrace of brothers who had been lost to each other, separated both emotionally and geographically, but now with both chasms bridged.

They wept.

Esau's eyes cleared while his head was still on Jacob's shoulder. He saw the ranks of women, children and servants approaching.

"Who are these, brother? What company is with you?"

"A true company, and faithful," Jacob replied. These are my wives and their handmaidens and our children."

Esau's ruddy face broke into a great grin as he released his brother and strode over to welcome the travelers. Keeping their ranks, the three groups marched up to him with some trepidation, but never faltering. They bowed low before him, as before a king.

"By the gods!" Esau roared. "I heard you had become a wealthy man. And for your wealth to be measured in wives and handmaidens and children—surely God has been good to you!"

Jacob noted that Esau's careless way of referring both to El and to "the gods" had not changed, but it was not a time to refine his theology.

"My lord measures aright. Yah has been with me." Then, looking at Esau's rich regalia, and over at the 400 men who flanked him, "I see that he has also blessed you!"

"Yes, yes—I rule all of Edom!" Esau said grandly. "But tell me— where do your herdsmen go with the stock we met earlier? Do you seek pasture for them?"

"They are my gift to you, brother. They are an offering of peace."

Esau would have none of it. In fact, as a king, he suspected he could better have afforded to give Jacob such a gift. "I have herds and flocks aplenty, my brother. You shall keep them for yourself. What need have brothers to make such offerings to brothers?"

"I beg you to take them, my lord Esau. They, and my bowing before you—will you not accept these as evidence that the matter of the birthright must no longer separate us one from the other?"

Esau's countenance grew grave. "Ah, yes," he said, more gently than Jacob would have thought possible. "The birthright. The chosen race, and all that." Then, his face brightening, "That is a thing of the past. Let us not dig up such bones, my brother. I have no need either for your gifts or for the birthright."

Jacob's mouth opened, but he could not speak at first. Was it possible? Were his fears that the years had not softened Esau's anger all in vain? Even further—could it be that the matter of the birthright meant so little to Esau?

"But I must speak of it, brother," Jacob persisted. "I have learned much...I have wrestled with God, and He has taught me—."

"Ho, then!" Esau roared, glad for a chance to change the subject with a jest. "You have wrestled with which god? And you are still alive? You have grown more powerful than I could have known!"

Jacob would not be deterred from a more serious tack. "I have learned that there is more to having the birthright than being in possession of our father's blessing..." Now that Esau was allowing him to continue, Jacob was suddenly unsure of how to word what he wished to say.

"More?" Esau echoed, condescending to encourage his brother to go on, if but for a moment.

"More, yes," Jacob continued. "It is also a matter of—that is—you and your descendants can also become God's elect!" The words were blurted out more forcefully than Jacob intended.

"Yes? And how might that be, brother?"

"By serving Him," Jacob said, finally discovering his tongue. "And by—I already sense in you a change, my brother. Your heart seems more tender. You have welcomed me more warmly than I deserved. It is this that El seeks in men. It is a way all peoples may become His elect—while I, in my striving both with you and with God—in so doing I put my own chosenness in jeopardy!" Jacob was surprised by his own words, not intending to reach this conclusion.

Esau looked at the ground, not sure he understood. Before he could reply, Jacob continued.

"And we have heard our mother's dictum from our birth"—'the elder shall serve the younger.' But by my bowing before you, and by these gifts, I mean to say that I have learned that the birthright is also a commandment to serve instead of merely being served. I beg you, brother. After all these years, after all that has happened—it would please me for you to accept this small token of my regard. Seeing you again is—it's as though I am looking on *peniel,* the face of God. And after the warmth of your welcome—shall I not be allowed in return to make this gesture of my love?"

It was an eloquent speech, and while Esau grasped little of it, he knew the code: to reject the gifts would be rude. But before he could speak he spied a cloud of dust arising from behind Jacob, on the caravan road they had just traversed. "Who follows you, my brother?"

Turning to follow Esau's gaze, Jacob replied, "It is the rest of

144

my flocks and herds." They made an impressive scene as they appeared on the ridges and wound their way down the road toward the brothers' conference, and Esau's reluctance to receive the smaller herd was removed.

"You could always drive a good bargain, brother!" The sly reference to the birthright incident was made without rancor. "It is good, then—I will accept your gift in the spirit in which you offer it...and with my thanks.

"But come, now! You have come from afar. We shall hasten to my home in Edom. You and all yours," he said, with a sweeping gesture that included the approaching livestock, "shall be my guests."

Jacob hesitated. This meeting with his brother had gone far better than he could have hoped for. But how deep did Esau's expressions of friendship and forgiveness go? Would it be wise to test it further?

"My lord is kind," he said, "but you will understand that we cannot go farther today. We have been traveling for more than two full moons, and the animals are leg-weary and foot-sore. Let my lord return to Edom at his own pace. We will camp here for the night, and on the morrow, for the sake of the animals, we shall follow more slowly."

"Let it be as you wish," Esau said. "Only do not linger on the way too long. We have much to talk about. You must meet my family, as I have greeted yours."

Bowing in assent, Jacob rejoined Rachel and Leah and the rest. They made their way to a small grassy area in a nearby valley, where a small spring seeped up from the dry ground with barely enough vigor to provide drink for the livestock. Esau and his mounted men clattered out of sight. Jacob's party would await the rest of the herd here, and spend the night.

"Shall we then follow my lord's brother?" Leah asked her husband. "Is it a trap?"

"Only God knows," Jacob said. "He seems sincere, but our herds are large, and Edom is not known for rich pastures. It may well put too much strain both on my brother and on the land for us to go with him."

The rest of the herds and flocks now came into view. As they did so, a strange rider detached himself from the band. Riding a small and weary brown donkey and accompanied by the faithful Sabteca, the stranger pulled up at the spring in a small cloud of dust. The grey dust coating his whole body could not conceal the inky blackness of his long, curly hair.

CHAPTER 17

"My lord Jacob," Sabteca said. "Here is one Shechem, son of Hamor of Canaan, who would speak to you."

"Shalom, my lord Jacob," the stranger said. Jacob had heard of the wealthy Hamor. Although this son's road-worn appearance hardly made him an impressive representative of a man of such repute, Jacob dismissed it since he had been so long on the dusty caravan road.

Saluting, the stranger continued. "I bring you greeting from my father Hamor, of the city of Shechem, after which he named me. I come from the hill country of Canaan"—repeating the last as though Sabteca had not already reported this bit of information.

Returning the greeting, Jacob said, "I have heard of your father, that he is a wealthy and important man. And I know of the city that bears your name, for my father's father, Abraham, once built an altar to his God there. What brings you to us?"

"My father has also heard of you and your pilgrimage from Haran, and sends you greeting. Such a company as yours does not travel far without news of it spreading abroad. He wishes to know, if my lord wills, of your destination; and if you will come through our hill country, he would discuss the sale of a piece of land on which you may settle near us."

Jacob looked at his wives. Was this an answer to the question of whether they should continue toward Edom and rejoin Esau?

While Jacob's attention was diverted, Shechem was appraising his wives and children. His eyes narrowed in admiration when he spied the comely Dinah, Leah's daughter. Even the dust of the journey could not hide her olive skin and comely shape, her luxuriant black hair and full lips. The corner of Shechem's mouth curled with the faintest suggestion of a lascivious leer. Only Dinah noticed.

Jacob turned back to the horseman. "As El lives, this may be the answer to our prayer to Him. This land your father would discuss—is it suitable for herds and flocks?"

"It is ideal," Shechem said. "That is why he thought of it. Perhaps you will go with me to see it, and to meet my father Hamor."

It was a sign, Jacob was convinced. He looked down the road so recently vacated by Esau. "It is well," he said quietly. "We have accomplished our mission here."

Turning to Rachel and Leah he continued, "To go farther would be to try the patience of both Esau and of Yah. Tomorrow we shall start back on the way we came, to the River Jabbok. Then we will see this land near Shechem."

The next morning Jacob dispatched a messenger to tell Esau of the change in plans. Of course, he mentioned nothing of his concern that dwelling longer with Esau might recreate the animosity between them. The messenger was instructed simply to say that the offer of a piece of land had made it necessary for Jacob to return to the north.

The return journey to the Jabbok, up the eastern side of the Dead Sea and the Great Rift, seemed shorter, without the anxious anticipation of meeting Esau. Along the way, Jacob recounted to Rachel and Leah the experience of the strange wrestling match. They were awed at the event, and especially at the renaming of Jacob as Israel.

Meanwhile, Shechem the Canaanite managed to walk much of the way near Dinah, leading his horse and taking every opportunity to speak to her. For her part, she was repelled by the man and tried always to walk with several other brothers and sisters.

After a week, Jacob's procession of sheep and goats, cattle and camels, wives and children and servants, crossed the Jabbok at the place where the wrestling match had occurred. They turned west, toward the Jordan, to search for a valley fed by springs and offering grazing and shelter for the animals. They camped there for three days, and Jacob called the place *Succoth*, or "shelters."

In the months ahead, the little clan would wish for more shelter than even this pleasant valley afforded.

From Succoth they traveled east, crossing the Jordan at a ford, the huge numbers of their flocks and herds churning up the mud and turning the river brown with silt.

The plot of ground that Hamor, Shechem's father, had singled out, hoping to sell to Jacob, proved to be a fair area, with great shade trees, and near grazing land that Jacob could lease for his livestock. Jacob stood on a little ridge overlooking a valley with a spring.

"It is good," Jacob said to Shechem. "Arrange for me to meet with your father."

"As you wish, sire." Shechem's swarthy face was tracked with the crinkles of his grin.

The meeting between Hamor and Jacob was duly arranged. Old Hamor could not risk baiting his son. "We will meet at the entrance to the city," he told Shechem. Then, his head turned aside and his eyes squinting shrewdly, he asked, "And what is in all this for my son?" It was as though he addressed the air. "Surely there is more here than wanting to sell them water rights."

Shechem did not look directly at his father, either, but first to one side, then the other. Directness was not their way. "My father," he said, continuing to use the third person, should have seen the fair Dinah, one of Jacob's daughters." The very remembrance of her made Shechem's lips part and eyelids droop in lustful fantasy.

"Ahh," was all that Hamor said. He well understood.

Jacob and Hamor sat at the city gates and haggled over the price of the land. They were a fair match, each protesting poverty and each, finally, parting with the feeling that he had bested the other.

As Jacob returned to his camp, he recalled the promise of Yah to give the land to Abraham and His seed. He breathed a deep sigh of satisfaction. Perhaps, after all these years, he himself was to realize that promise.

Gathering his growing clan about him, Jacob erected a stone for a marker and sacrificed a lamb in commemoration of the moment. He named the altar, and the camp, *El Elohe Israel*—God, the God of Israel. It was the first time he had used the new name the strange wrestler had given him at the Jabbok.

"Dinah, the daughter of Jacob, graces this land with her presence." It was the voice of Shechem, and it was his characteristic way of speaking to someone by speaking about them.

Dinah, who was filling a water jar at the spring, froze at the sound of his voice. Ever since Shechem first rode up to her family between the Jabbok and Seir, she had felt his designs upon her. Her pause in drawing the water was the only indication that she had heard; she chose not to reply. Perhaps he would go away if she ignored him.

But being ignored was something to which Shechem was not accustomed. Having found Dinah alone, he was not going to be easily put off. She arose from the spring, balanced the water jar expertly on her head and turned to go back to the camp, fifty furlongs away and around a bend so that it was out of sight.

Shechem sprang in front of her, blocking her way. With her right arm lifted to steady the water jar, and her left extended slightly for balance, he thought he had never seen such a graceful creature. Her long hair, as black as Shechem's, hung to her waist. He tried a smile that was as genuine and courteous as his lust would allow.

"Stay, I pray," he said. "Sit with me for a moment here in the cool of this shade tree. We are neighbors now. We should get better acqauinted."

Dinah tried to brush by him. "Thank you, no," she said coolly.

Again, *No* was not a word Shechem understood well. His smile turned to a leer as he repositioned himself firmly in Dinah's path, so close now that his chest was almost touching her breasts, which were by now rising and falling rapidly with fear.

"And is the daughter of Jacob, then, too good to sit with a neighbor, and to become friends?" He seized her by the wrist. As she tried to draw back, the water in the jar sloshed over the rim, dousing both of them. The effect of the water on the thin garment covering Dinah's bosom did nothing to deter her accoster.

"Let me go!" she cried, trying desperately to make her voice firm instead of fearfuly. "Let me pass! My father and my brothers—."

"Curses on your father and brothers!" Shechem interrupted. "I have already made sure that your brothers are in the fields. And your father cannot hear you; it will do you no good to cry for help."

Holding both wrists now in an iron grip, Shechem forced his face into Dinah's, his lips attempting to find hers. She reeled backward, and fell over and into a hedge of bushes—Shechem could have found no better cover for his rapacious intent.

It was not accomplished without a violent struggle; but when Shechem arose in only a few moments, his face bleeding only slightly from Dinah's fingernails, he had obviously been the victor. He stalked off toward home.

Plaiting a rope of goat's hair, Jacob looked up at his daughter when Dinah returned. Seeing her disheveled hair and rumpled garments askew, his mouth opened and worked a time or two, but he could muster no sound. He arose, his whole body forming a question mark.

"Shechem!" Dinah spit out the word with disgust as she faltered, and fell into Jacob's arms.

"Leah! Leah!" he cried. And as Dinah's mother came from running from her tent, Jacob handed Dinah over to be comforted by someone more capable than he.

A young servant, who had seen and heard Dinah's brief explanation to her father, stood ready for Jacob's bidding. He was dispatched to the fields, to tell Jacob's sons.

"Father!" Shechem shouted. He had found something that finally forced him to abandon his discursive style of conversation.

Old Hamor turned from the business he was discussing with a wool buyer. "Yes, yes? I am busy here."

Shechem seized the old man by the hand, still in the heat of passion from his encounter. Drawing him aside, Shechem announced imperiously, "You will get her for me!"

"What?" asked Hamor. "Who?"

"Dinah, of course! The daughter of Jacob."

Then Hamor remembered. Eyeing his son up and down, noting the scratches on Shechem's face, the old man knew immediately what had happened. "Get her, eh? You have already done that, I'll wager."

"Get me this woman for my wife!" Shechem said.

Hamor released his arm from his son's grip. Coolly appraising his son's disheveled appearance, he felt obligated at least to protest what he knew had been some mistreatment of his new neighbor's daughter. "Is this the way to get her to wife?"

"Still—," he added thoughtfully, his pragmatic sense taking over. "Intermarriage, eh? It could be a very profitable arrangement. Yes, yes, very well. I shall speak to Jacob about her in your behalf."

On the evening of the same day, Hamor and Shechem went to Jacob's tents to discuss the matter. The sons of Jacob had come in from the fields immediately upon hearing that their sister had been violated. They sat with their father under the shade of a great tree, discussing what to do in retaliation, when the two Hivites approached.

"Greetings, my lord Jacob," said Hamor, a trifle too loudly. He must not indicate that he knew what Shechem had done. His son only bowed. He hoped that Dinah had been too embarrassed to tell anyone what he had done. But little matter; it was a matter for his father and Jacob to work out; the sequence of his and Dinah's relations was of no great consequence.

"My lord Hamor," Jacob returned, stiffly.

"My son and I have come to discuss a matter of great import with you. Can we speak privately?"

Jacob did not trust the squatty old man. "My sons and I have no secrets," he said. "We will talk here."

Jacob motioned to the visitors to sit with them on the ground. The evening was still hot, and the little group crowded in toward the tree for its shade. Something in the firmness of Jacob's voice caused Hamor to pursue the issue at hand directly, without the usual formality of small talk.

"My son Shechem has set his heart on having your daughter—what is it—Dinah, isn't it?—on having your daughter Dinah to wife."

Jacob's sons glowered at each other.

"Is it not a very good idea?" Hamor continued. "The land here is as pleasant as I promised, is it not?"

"It is a pleasant land," Jacob said flatly.

"A pleasant land," Hamor repeated. "Then, my friend, consider staying here permanently. Let us intermarry our sons and daughters. There is room enough for all. Live in the land, and buy and sell. Let us become one family. Our enemies would be no match for us."

At this, Jacob's eldest son Reuben drew his brothers aside, amid much murmuring that Shechem and Hamor could not hear. Shechem pressed the point.

"Name your price, my lord Jacob," he said. "I will give whatever you ask as a bride-price."

Jacob began the usual parlaying by saying, "A bride-price? Well, now—."

"It is not done!" Reuben interrupted, rejoining the conversation with his brothers.

The eyes of Jacob, Hamor and Shechem snapped to Reuben in surprise as if on cue.

"Do you not recall, father?" Reuben continued, deep-set brown eyes flashing.

"Recall what, my son?"

"The covenant with Yah. The Promise is to be fulfilled among the family of the circumcised. We are to be a people set apart. How can we intermarry with *yam ha'aretz*, the people of the land?"

Jacob turned back to his guests. He was not sure whether Reuben's protest was sincere. Up to now, his sons had taken no remarkable interest in the promise. Perhaps it was only that the thought of marrying off his sister to a rapist was too repulsive to consider. Jacob needed to stall for time.

"Yes, of course," he said, as though having already thought of the matter.

Hamor and Shechem looked at each other. What kind of people were these Hebrews? They were familiar enough with the custom of circumcision, since it was practiced by other Canaanite tribes and as far south as Egypt. But what did it have to do with this "promise," and with intermarrying? They were not sure how to protest and to continue to argue their point. Perhaps this was a ruse to raise the bride-price.

Jacob's son Levi spoke next. "But of course there is a possibility…" he let his voice trail off.

"Yes?" said Shechem eagerly.

"Yes," Simeon went on. "Suppose the sons of Hamor would

also submit to circumcision. Then we would all be be as one tribe, would we not?"

"Of course, of course," returned Reuben, and the other brothers murmured their approval of the suggestion. By then, old Jacob knew that their earlier whisperings aside had been about some well-focused scheme. He, the schemer, would see where all this might lead.

"A fair part of the bride-price, is it not?" he asked the visitors. "We would then be marked as the members of one clan. We might even grow into a nation—one far too powerful to fear the raids of these hoodlums. Together, we could drive them from the land!"

The twin notions of nationhood and warfare brought excited murmurings of approval from the other brothers.

Shechem caught their excitement. "And why not! It is an acceptable part of the bride-price. Does not my father agree?"

Old Hamor was a little more reluctant. He sensed that there was something hidden in the suggested transaction. But unable to determine what it was, he nodded. "It is worth considering. We must return to the city and discuss it with the rest of the men among us."

After much embracing and excited talk about the possibilities opening up before them, Hamor and Shechem took their leave.

They were hardly out of sight when Jacob's sons began looking to their weapons.

The elders sat outside the gates of the city of Shechem discussing the plan with Hamor and his son.

"Consider," said Shechem, his voice loaded with persuasion, "we all know that the gods are with these Hebrews. And we all know how we long to rid ourselves of these raiders that keep our lives unsettled. Here is the perfect oportunity. We intermarry with these people and we gain their sons and daughters, the blessings of their gods—not to mention their land and herds and flocks—all in return for a little foreskin! Who can be opposed to such a bargain!"

To the man, the council was persuaded. After loud exclamations of "It is good!" "A bargain for us!" and "Why not?" they all trooped off to find the three pagan priests among them.

Although the priests were trained in the art of circumcision, having studied in Egypt, it was the first time they had practiced the craft in this city. They were kept very busy, and very bloody, for the better part of a day.

But it was nothing compared to the blood from the slaughter wreaked on the city of Shechem by the sons of Jacob.

It happened only three days after the Shechemites' operation, while they were still hobbling about in pain. Jacob was off tending to the flocks when Reuben, Simeon, and Levi led their brothers and their herdsmen and servants in a fierce attack that exposed the impromptu plan they had made when Shechem and his father asked for Dinah.

They had spent the rest of the day of Shechem's visit honing the gently-curved swords they had previously purchased from a band of Egyptians only weeks earlier. While they were more expert with shepherd's staves, they had heard tales of the havoc wrought with the short swords with the sharp inside edges. They could make as short work of an enemy as a sickle in dry grain, slicing and chopping them to shreds.

Quietly the family army crept up on a group of Shechemites lounging in the shade of the trees by a well. They moved as little as possible, the soreness of their recent circumcision rendering them easy targets.

"In the name of Yah!" screamed Reuben, as four ailing men fell under his sword.

"Slay the uncircumcised!" was Levi's battle-cry, "They have gone through the motions, but they could never be a part of *qahal Yah*, the people of God!"

The Hebrews attacked in waves, a second platoon providing a back-up force that hacked Shechemite strays who thought to escape the clusters of men who bore the brunt of the first wave of slaughterers.

Through tent after tent, shop after shop and house after house the angry swords of the sons of Jacob slashed their way. Ignoring the screams of infants and women, the Hebrews scooped them up on their horses and raced back to their camp with them to make of them servants and slaves.

By the end of the day, not an adult male survived. The wealth and possessions, the gold figurines and cult vessels of their worship—all was pillaged and confiscated by the raiding sons of Jacob. The tent city itself was set on fire.

Seeing the smoke from the burning city from afar, Jacob hastened back. Surveying the devastation from a little hilltop, he saw the carnage, heard the wails of the dying and the bereaved. Suddenly he felt very old and weary. He allowed his eyes to follow the smoke from the burning city to its highest point. Resting his eyes there, he prayed to the skies in a voice that trembled with shock:

"O God of Abraham and Isaac! Behold the violent work of the seed on whom the Promise rests! Is this, then, the way You will transfer to us the land of Canaan? Does the fact that You have Your mighty hand upon us carry with it such license?

"Great Yah…"

Jacob's voice trailed off, leaving the prayer unfinished. He had not enough words to express his horror, no way to give voice to the anguished questions that ravaged his heart. His greying head sank to his chest. Turning back to camp, he heard the continuing cries of the captives. He bridled a donkey and left to spend the night in the fields, alone.

CHAPTER 18

Burdened as never before with the weight of the Promise, Jacob pondered leaving the place he had named El Elohe Israel. He called his sons together, in part to rebuke them for the terrible vengeance they had wreaked on Shechem, and in part to see whether simply being together as a clan might enable some insight he had not seen to arise out of the group as a whole. Could the elect *family* see things together they could not see individually? He did not know.

"You have jeopardized our position here," he told his sons sternly. "You have taken the vengeance that belongs to God into your own hands, and now we shall face the wrath of the other Hivites, along with the Perrizites and every other tribe and nation in Canaan. If they band together, where shall we be?"

Most of the young men looked stolidly at their feet. But Reuben, Simeon and Levi, the chief instigators, were more defiant. "Dinah is our sister," Levi said sullenly. "We could not let her defilement go unanswered."

"There are ways to answer, and there are other ways," Jacob returned. "From this point on, I call Yah as witness that we will consult Him before going to war. If we are to be His people, we have a greater burden than all others to walk in His ways."

His voice, along with an inner conviction, grew stronger as he spoke. "Is there any among you who cannot accept this?"

Silence.

Finally, Dan, son of Rachel's maidservant Bilhah, spoke. "We have not all been convinced that Yah is the most High God. There *are* other gods, you know."

Jacob stood up taller. The reality of his own sense of Yah and His supremacy as the High God was so strong that he had been unaware that he had taken for granted that his sons shared his convictions. Yet, looking back over his life, he knew that his faith had grown only slowly, with many side-roads, many doubts. And as for his sons—he had not really schooled them to think of Yah alone as the Great God. Bilhah came from some unknown pagan background. It was only natural that her sons—and who knows how many others in his family—would cling to the gods of others—or to none.

"Are there, indeed, other gods?" he asked quietly. Then, in a low, firm voice: "No matter what other gods there may be, the sons of Israel will serve the Lord El, whose name is Yah. I will hear no more of other gods!"

And with that he dismissed the assembly.

That night, Jacob was restless and hardly slept. When he did drift off, it was only to be semi-awakened in that state in which he had heard the voice of God before. This time, it awakened him—there was no doubt that it was not a dream.

"Jacob, you whose name is Israel!" the voice said. Again, even though fully awake, Jacob could not have explained whether it was indeed a voice from heaven or one that welled up from some unknown depths within.

"Who is it, Lord?" he asked, in a hoarse whisper.

"I am the God of Abraham and Isaac, to whom I gave this land where you now dwell. And I will be your God as well, for you have spoken truly of me to your sons.

"Now, rise up and return to Bethel, to the south, where I appeared to you in the vision of the ladder, when you first fled your brother Esau. Build an altar there, and I will use it also to build faith in your sons. For they shall know that they are the sons of Israel, and that their lives are under judgment because they are devoted to me."

Suddenly Jacob shivered in the cold greyness of the dawn that was asserting itself over the eastern horizon. Back to Bethel! Of course. They would give the Hivites and Perizzites time to forget the loss of the tent village of Shechem.

Again Jacob called his sons together, this time with their wives and little ones and servants, along with Rachel and Leah.

"Many years ago, the Lord Yah appeared to me at Bethel, which is Luz, to the south. Now this God has told me to return to Bethel. Gather your possessions and bring the flocks and herds together, and release your Shechemite slaves."

His sons looked at each other nervously. Was their father about to become the type who spoke to his god, and who received replies?

"One more thing," Jacob said evenly. "Put away from yourselves every god and every sacred dish and ever relic from the gods of Canaan." His voice rose in authority as he went on. "Bring to me all the sacred jewelry, all the rings you took as booty from the Shechemites. Change even the very clothes that have been contaminated with the deeds of our sojourn here, and purify yourselves in the eyes of El. Follow me to Bethel and I will show you who is the true God!"

His sons were struck with the new intensity and power in their father's voice. With little grumbling they and their families went to their tents to retrieve the booty they had taken. For a whole afternoon there was a steady stream of penitents moving from the tents to the great oak outside the gates of what had been Shechem. Jacob's servants dug a deep pit there, and his clan threw in it all the jewelry and sacred objects and figurines of the gods they had plundered from the city.

As they worked, something of Jacob's own conviction began to overtake them—some even found themselves singing. The spirit pervaded the camp as they packed their belongings, and even as they wound their way out of the hills, down toward Shechem, a good three days' march.

A mile out of camp the spirit grew into a chant, and then into a caravan song:

At Yah's command, at our father's demand,
We buried the foreign gods.
With hearts aflame, we praised the Name,

And we buried the foreign gods.

Months later, they learned from a traveling seer that the chant had been heard by more than one band of robbers along the way. Awestruck at the oneness the singing implied, they had withdrawn; Israel and his beople moved unharmed to the south, back to Bethel.

My lord Philemon, I pause in the tale to comment on something I have seen in my own life, something that must have been apparent to Jacob as he journeyed back to Bethel with his whole company singing in their new-found faith. It is this: that often, a time when our hearts are lifted up is is followed by a time of sadness.

With Jacob, the sadness came when they arrived at Bethel and found there a strange thing from the past, a stone marked with the name of the one buried beneath it; the name was Deborah.

Now, Deborah was the nurse of Rebekah, Jacob's own mother, who had left Paddan-aram with her mistress many years earlier. She had lived more than a hundred years, and had died in Rebekah's own tent in Hebron. Rebekah attempted to nurse her nurse back to health, but she died.

How Deborah's body came to be at Bethel is a wonder. The tale of Jacob's encounter with Yah in the vision of the ladder had made its way back, as such tales do, to Isaac and Rebekah, after they had moved to Hebron. And wishing to place the body of her beloved nurse as near to heaven as possible, Rebekah insisted that she be taken north, to Bethel, to the spot where they had heard their son Jacob had raised a stone to Yah. And there they buried Deborah and erected her own stone to mark the grave.

But again a thing I have noticed, and that Jacob must also have seen: that even when sadness follows joy as night must follow the morning, those who trust in Yah can find a blessing. When Jacob saw the grave of Deborah, who had been to him like an aunt, amid his sadness came the thought that Yah is the God of the beginning and the end, and that as He had blessed even the servants of Isaac and Rebekah, He would also bless Jacob, son of the Promise.

So Jacob was comforted.

It was a bittersweet journey, with sorrow and joy tumbling in upon Jacob one after the other, keeping his feelings as undulating as the hill country of Canaan. Only two nights after he found the nurse Deborah's tomb at Bethel, El appeared to him again and called him to journey on to the south.

"Your father Isaac is old," the voice said. "Return to him in his infirmity." So the company, whose numbers were now swollen considerably with hangers-on and the additional servants required by the growth of the flocks and herds in Shechem, was on its way again.

Such continuous travel was becoming increasingly hard for Rachel, for she was again heavy with child. Even though Jacob had placed her gently atop the gentlest of his riding camels, the way was rough, and it was a poor way to prepare for a birthing.

Half a day's journey from Bethel, Rachel's shriek sliced through the hot Canaanite air.

"Jacob, my—" she cried. But the call died in her throat as she fell heavily to the ground.

Jacob kicked his own camel forward from their place several paces to the flank of the great caravan. Just as he slid to a stop near Rachel's riderless camel, he heard her scream. Birth-pangs, he knew. The maidservant Bilhah had dragged Rachel under a juniper tree, so Jacob dismounted to wait discreetly nearby, his hands anxiously twisting the reins of braided hair.

Rachel screamed again as she gave birth. "Do not fear, lady," Bilhah said, "for you have given your husband another son!"

Falling back on her pallet, there in the meager shade of the tree, Rachel formed a name for her newborn son with the last breath she was to draw. "*Ben-Oni*," she sighed.

"My lady?" queried Bilhah. "Is the name this, then—*My trouble's son?*"

Rachel did not answer. She was dead.

Bilhah ran with the child to Jacob, waiting nearby, almost in tears. The sad news and the good tumbled out together: "Your wife Rachel has breathed her last, and with her dying breath she has named for you yet another son—Ben-Oni."

Jacob was prepared for the worst. He hung his shaggy head, quite grey now, and wept.

Then, looking up at Bilhah, he took the child gently in his arms. "'My trouble's son'?" he said. "It shall not be. I will not have

Rachel, my beloved, remembered by a name of trouble. She has been my right hand; her last son will be called *Ben-yamin*, 'my right hand's son.'"

I briefly interrupt again, my lord Philemon, to note that Jacob's beloved wife Rachel was buried between Bethel and Hebron, near a place my lord knows and honors as the village of Bethlehem, "house of bread." Yes! On the same soil that accepted the wife of Israel, would later appear the seed of Israel, whom we know as the Christ, the Bread of the world. Thus it is that the God of Israel confounds the powers of death by wresting from them the life that now enlightens the world!

The siege of sadness was not soon to pass. As Jacob and his people plodded on toward Hebron, a dust-coated messenger met the caravan.

"Hail, the family of Jacob!" he called, wrenching his camel to a halt. News of the caravan's approach, and of the long-awaited return of the son of Isaac and Rebekah, had preceded the travelers by days.

Reuben, riding point, returned the greeting, his hand on his sword until he could determine the stranger's mission. "Hail to the stranger," he returned.

"I seek your master, Jacob, with news of his father," the swarthy man said, almost panting.

Calling his father, Reuben and several of his brothers gathered around the pair. Weary to the bone, both from the journey and from the loss of Rachel, Jacob approached slowly.

"You have news of my father?"

"Sad news, sire. He is not expected to live."

Jacob stiffened only slightly. His father was in his eighteenth decade, and Jacob had wondered more than once whether the old man would still be alive by the time Jacob returned from Paddan-aram.

"But sire," the messenger continued, "you are only a day's journey from the tent of your father near Hebron. He calls for you. If my lord hastens, you may arrive before your father is gathered to his people."

Jacob lifted his weary head to the south, toward Hebron.

"And what of my brother, Esau?" he asked. "Has he also been

summoned?"

"Yes, my lord," replied the servant. "He has been at his father's side for two days."

Of course, Jacob thought. The favored son Esau would have been called first.

"Let us go quickly," Jacob said, shaking off the dark mood that threatened to settle over him. "Simeon!" he commanded. "I will need your swift camel." Wordlessly, Jacob and Simeon exchanged mounts, and Jacob was soon out of sight.

Jacob was already weeping as he approached his father and mother's camp under the live oak trees of Hebron. His heart was flooded with memories of how close he had been to his mother, Rebekah, and how longingly he had yearned for his father's favor. Had the years and the distance since those days changed anything?

The question had no sooner formed in his mind than he saw a large, elderly woman emerge from the camp in his direction. He knew from the strength of her stride that it was Rebekah. He urged his weary camel on, over loud and indignant protests.

"Mother?" he called. "Is it you?" He sprang recklessly from his saddle, flinging himself down instead of commanding the animal to kneel.

"Jacob, my son, my son!" old Rebekah sobbed. Her hair was like spun silver now, and her face was as lined as the *wadi*-scarred terrain where she had spent her life. But her arms were still strong as she clasped her son close, ignoring the generous coat of dust and grime he wore.

"Mother—are you then as strong as ever?" Jacob asked, hoarsely, not knowing anything else to say.

"I am well, my son. It is your father who—"

"Is he, then—am I too late?" Jacob asked fearfully.

"You are not too late to bid him farewell," his mother replied. "But you must come quickly!"

Rebekah led the way to the largest tent in the encampment. Their eyes took a moment to adjust to the dimness as they entered. There, almost buried among his pillows, old Isaac lay, breathing in short gasps, his eyes closed.

Esau knelt at the edge of the skins on which his father was lying. He looked up as Jacob and Rebekah entered, but did not arise from his post. Immediately Jacob sensed a renewal of the tension between them, despite their cordial meeting a few months earlier. Even at death, Isaac's unspoken favoritism for Esau was a powerful barrier that Jacob knew he would have to overcome in order to properly mourn his father's passing.

"My brother," Jacob murmured softly. Esau, having turned back to his father, only nodded.

Moving to Isaac's other side, Jacob was again overwhelmed with emotion. The old man's once-craggy features were reduced to eroded plains now. Only a few wisps of hair remained around his ears. His toothless mouth drooled helplessly.

Jacob could not help wondering: Is this, then, how the Promise ends? Encouraged though he had been at the visitations that had assured him that God's promise of an empire would be continued through him, Jacob found himself lapsing into a mood of doubt. It was all very well for his father to hand along the birthright and the blessing to others. But where was the blessing for him? And what of the blessing to Isaac's father, Abraham? Was his long-dead flesh any less putrid because God had promised one day to bless his descendants?

Ashamed that he had allowed such thoughts to intrude, Jacob knelt by Isaac's pallet. "Father," he said softly. "Can you hear me? It is your son."

The ancient head turned ponderously toward the voice, and the heavy-lidded, blind eyes admitted a sliver of light. "Son?" Isaac echoed. "Is it my son Esau?"

Jacob bowed his head in bitterness. Swallowing his pride, he looked up. "It is your son Jacob, Father."

"Eh? Jacob? No—Jacob has gone to Haran," the old man said haltingly. "You would not trick me, my son Esau, as your brother did—" His voice trailed off, spent.

"It is truly Jacob, Father. I am home," Jacob said patiently. Despite the sharp reminder that the memory of his deception was still bright in the old man's mind, Jacob's heart melted at his father's decrepit state.

Esau interrupted. "Jacob has become a wealthy man, Father," he said. "He has returned with wives and concubines and sons and daughters." His graciousness surprised Jacob.

The few words he had spoken had exhausted the dying man.

He could only look up, in silence, his blind eyes guessing where to look. Was it his hopeful imagination, or did Jacob see a light of appreciation at Esau's words flicker for a moment in the blind eyes?

"Wealthy," Isaac whispered. "Ah, then. The Promise—" a wracking cough interrupted, and both Jacob and Esau reached to lift their father to help him get his breath.

"The Promise?" Jacob asked encouragingly when the coughs had subsided.

Suddenly, Isaac's breathing grew steady. Still held in a half-sitting position by his sons, the old man stared straight forward. Speaking with a vigor that belied his impending death, his voice as firm and clear as it had been forty years earlier, he intoned:

"The blessing of Yah is upon His chosen one, my son Jacob, who has returned from the land of our kinsmen in Haran a man of wealth, and with wives and sons and daughters through whom the Promise will be fulfilled. Blessed be the name of Yah!"

Thus it was, my lord Philemon, that although the patriarch Isaac was gathered to his people, his last words were spoken in the strength of a young man, so strong was he in faith that the God of Abraham would fulfill the Promise. Without requiring that he receive it in life, he rejoiced that he would receive it even through his seed.

And thus it was that Jacob and Esau at last found a venture in which they could agree: the ministration of burying their father and comforting their mother; for they together took the body of Isaac to the Cave of Machpelah in the field of Ephron the Hittite, where Father Abraham and Mother Sarah were buried.

And well it was that Jacob heard with his own ears Isaac's confession of faith. For the death of his father left his spirit lonely and oppressed by the very air of the land of Canaan, peopled as it was by the spirits of the power of the air, the great Satan, who was to put Jacob's faith in the Promise to the test.

And it was well that both Abraham and Isaac were now planted in the soil of the Land of Promise. For not long thereafter the people of the Promise would wander so far that they would doubt whether they would ever return.

CHAPTER 19

Raucous, drunken voices and the twang of tinny stringed instruments had kept the three of them awake half the night. Jacob and his old and faithful servants, Shinab and Sabteca, had spread their blankets in the soft sand of a *wadi* far to the northwest of Hebron, in the never-ending search for pasturage. The journey had recalled their first expedition together, the long pilgrimage to Haran. It had also renewed the friendship that had languished during the long years when Jacob was becoming a wealthy, if landless, owner of livestock.

They had camped at dusk, not realizing that they were within earshot of an isolated place sacred to one of the Canaanite ba'als.

"Enough!" Jacob finally muttered, sitting up abruptly on his blanket. "What is this madness in the distance? It seems to grow louder."

"It is the Ba'al worshipers, my lord," Shinab offered. The closer we get to the Great Sea, the more we enter the domain of the gods Ba'al and Dagan."

Sabteca stretched mightily and grumbled, "Can they not worship in the day? Or at least post notices of their rites, so passersby can avoid them?"

"Their rites are such as belong to the night, not the day, I am told," Jacob said. "Rekindle the fire; there will be no sleeping this night."

Little did he know how rightly he spoke. Just as Sabteca was forcing his stiff joints to obey, the three were set on by half a dozen shrieking madmen.

"Aieee!" their screams sliced through the cool night air. "Bind the Apiru! Take them to the sacrifice!"

Taken by surprise, the three could mount little resistance, and quickly found their hands bound behind their backs and standing in the middle of a circle of half-naked men.

"Apiru?" Jacob countered in a Hivite dialect. The name was often used for wandering bandits. "We are simple shepherds, from Hebron, seeking new pasture. We have no money. Release us!"

One of the attackers, apparently their leader since he wore an ostrich-plumed headdress, replied: "We do not need your money. We are not robbers, not Apiru. We are priests of Ba'al and his sister-consort Anat. And you have invaded the sacred grounds of our ritual!"

Jacob's blood ran cold. They were in the hands of the pagans whose revelry had kept them from sleep.

"Release us!" he demanded again. "We will retreat to another place. What do you want with us?"

"That remains to be seen," said the priest. "We have been unable to cast the proper lot for a sacrifice this night. The will of Ba'al has been obscure. Perhaps he was only waiting for you!"

"For us?" Jacob asked. "We are not worshipers of Ba'al." He had missed the point about the sacrifice.

The eerie lot of pagan priests erupted in raucous laughter. "Not worshipers of Ba'al!" mocked one, in vicious glee. "Then you will be perfect food for him—he will not be subtracting three worshipers from his cult!" More laughter.

Jacob and his two servants looked at each other soberly in the moonlight, the realization dawning on them that they were not only about to witness a Ba'al ritual first-hand; they were to have the dubious honor of being at its center.

The pagan priests shoved the three campers roughly down the *wadi* toward the temple area from which the sounds of music and revelry had come. "Would that we had scouted the place before making our camp," muttered Sabteca.

"Silence!" hissed the leader of the priests. His command was punctuated by a swift blow with the flat of his broad sword, striking Sabteca on his thick neck. The sword's edge nicked a roll of hide, and a thin trickle of blood coursed slowly down the captive's tunic.

The other priests put quick arm and body locks on Jacob and Shinab as they tried to shove their way between the swordsman and their friend. They could no nothing with their hands bound behind them.

They reached the ritual site in less than a quarter-hour's march. It was a rude circle of stones that served as an open-air temple constructed in a natural amphitheatre. The arena was crowded with half-naked worshipers who were shouting and writhing in some sort of dance—the loud devotees that had kept Jacob and his servants awake. Both men and women cavorted in drunken abandon to the accompaniment of loud flutes and throbbing drums. The unwilling guests could not believe their eyes, which they averted as pairs of the dancing figures would cease their gyrations long enough for sexual union, then fall spent to the ground.

Behind the revelers loomed a sight that was even more shocking to Jacob's religious sensibilities: a bronze statue of the god Ba'al, some ten feet tall, gleaming in the light of a fire that had been built in front of him. His heavy arms were bent at the elbow, causing the forearms to extend over the flames of the fire. A hollow core allowed the fire to creep up into the body itself. Holes forming the idol's eyes had been punched right through the metal, allowing them to flicker and gleam with an evil, red glare as the flames licked up through the brush that had been placed inside its body cavity.

Then Jacob looked more closely at the arms of the idol, and swallowed hard. The huge, flat upturned palms comprised a platform—no doubt for roasting a sacrifice in the roaring fire that licked hungrily upward.

The little party marched around the drunken revelers directly up to the gruesome statue. "My lord the high priest!" said the leader, addressing a tall and solemn man in a long, white robe—a strange touch amid the sea of flesh about them. "We found these spies encamped near our sacred grounds."

The high priest's eyes widened at the audacity. His eye sockets had been painted black, and the wide whites of his eyes made his gaze wild and staring.

"In the absence of a lot for a suitable sacrifice, would not these three intruders be useful?" the leader of the band of priests asked.

"We have a lot," the high priest said solemnly, folding his arms on his chest. "The child has just been selected."

A child! This was what Jacob had heard, but had not dared to believe.

Incredibly, Jacob's captors looked at each other with dark smiles of relief. "Good, good!" their leader gushed. "Then what shall we do with our guests?"

"Let them remain as our guests," his master replied. "Let them watch the sacrifice as a reminder that but for the will of Ba'al, it could be one of them—or all of them."

Jacob finally found his tongue.

"My lord—that is, if it please the priest. Surely you will not slay the child on this—this monster!"

The high priests sharp chin rose in silent and arrogant warning. "You are a captive, and you would question our ritual?" he said evenly.

"I mean no offense. But what god of justice would command that a child be slain? What has been done to offend him, that such an atonement is required?"

"There has been no offense—not that we should have to explain. The god Ba'al governs the fruit of our land. We give him the feast of the child in order that he will give us the fruit of the harvest. We join with each other, men and women, as the seed enters the womb of the earth, to ensure the fertility of the land.

"But enough! Let us proceed." The crowd of people that had assembled around the confrontation parted as a child some ten years of age was brought before the priest. The boy's eyes were glazed; no doubt he had been made to imbibe of the same libations that fueled the orgiastic dancing. Behind him came a woman, evidently his mother, alternately weeping and shouting with forced joy: "He is chosen! My son is the devoted one!"

"Sire, my—" Jacob stammered. "This cannot be! I could wish that you would hear your servant's word—take my life, not the life of this tender youth!"

The high priest drew himself up to his full height. His dark-ened eyes glared at Jacob from under heavy black brows. "Ba'al has chosen his own sacrifice. You are not worthy. Besides—by what justice would you rob this poor woman, the lad's mother, of the joy of having her son chosen?"

Jacob blinked away tears as he and his servants were rudely herded away from the worshipers. They were tied to low-grow-ing bushes to watch the grisly scene.

The wood piled before the idol was pulled away with long sticks in order for the flames to die down and allow the sacri-fice to be bound to the plate-like hands. Whatever potion the lad had been given was not enough to block the searing pain of the hot metal, and he screamed as he was bound into position. Then the branches of the fire were pulled back into position. As if to drown out the boy's cries, the crowd of worshipers broke into louder shouting and an even faster-paced whirl of leaping and dancing. What few bits of clothing remained were soon stripped away as the boiling, screaming cauldron of humanity celebrated the ritual from which the three guest-captives had to turn their heads.

"My lord Jacob?" The servant Shinab was first to regain his voice after the ordeal. The three were making their way back to the main camp at Hebron. Little had been said among them after they were released by the Ba'al worshipers. The scene had evoked such deep horror and disgust that to speak of it seemed to give it a dignity from which they recoiled. Finally, however, Shinab could no longer quell his anguished questions about the terrible night.

"My lord," he said again, determined to continue even though Jacob did not answer. "Are the Canaanites of the same race as—well, as other men?"

Jacob looked at him quizzically. "The same as men of what race? There are many, as you know. There are even many tribes among the Canaanites. Most, I suppose are Sem—"

"Yes, yes, I know," his servant said. "But I mean, are they—are they *men*? Are they a race of men at all, or are they beasts?"

Jacob then saw his point. He paused before answering. Illiter-ate though the diminutive Shinab was, he was asking a good ques-tion. "They are men," he said finally. "The Lord God made only one race. It is we who have divided into factions that war against each other, and—." He stopped, unable to put into polite words the scene they had witnessed.

Sabteca, indifferent though he was about talk of the gods, shuddered visibly as the spectacle was brought back to his mind.

"But if God made all men, how can some men behave so?" Shinab persisted.

Again Jacob had no immediate answer. Finally he replied, "They have become willing or unwilling servants of another god—the great Satan."

"There are *two* high gods? But you have always taught us to believe that there is only one God."

Trying to avoid being pressed to say more than he knew, Jacob fell silent for a while. Then he said simply: "The matter is hidden. I only know that there is only one true God. Whatever other gods or Ba'als or Satans there may be are enemies of the Creator God, Yah, El Shaddai—He has many names, but He is one God."

"And what will happen between these enemies? What will happen to those we saw commit such evil?"

Jacob reflected only for a moment. "They will be brought down to Sheol and their name removed from the land of the living!" he said angrily.

The three walked on silently for a long moment.

"Unless—" Jacob finally said, then paused again.

"Unless, my Lord?"

"Unless someone can cleanse their hearts." He was trying to connect the problem Shinab was raising with his sense of being chosen for a special mission and inheritance. "Perhaps Yah in His mercy may help such people to amend their ways. Perhaps He can use us, the people of the Promise, to somehow show them His way."

Shinab shook his head dubiously, recalling the orgiastic scene that had reeled so totally out of control, and the stubborn unwillingness of the priest of Ba'al to be questioned about his ritual. "And if they will not consider any other way?"

Again, Jacob was quiet for a moment. Then he said quietly, "If they will not allow Yah to cleanse their hearts, He may use His chosen to cleanse the land."

Jacob stood outside his tent at Hebron surveying the parched hillsides. An arid dawn sought to cloak the brown earth with a dusty haze of gold, but succeeded only in promising the emergence of a pitiless sun, and no moisture to break the long drought.

Two full cycles of the moon had passed since he and his servants had returned from the northwest and found the ritual of Ba'al instead of new pasturage. He had been forced to send his sons—all but his beloved Joseph—back to Shechem, in the north, with most of the livestock. It was time to attend to their success—or lack of it.

The long and widespread drought, coupled with the horror of the pagan ritual, weighed heavily on Jacob. When would the promise that Canaan would belong to the chosen people finally come true? He had to admit a hope that it would be under his own patriarchy over the clan. After all, some seers said that the affairs of men moved in three-part cycles after the pattern of nature—morning, noon and night; birth, growth and death. There would be something symmetrical about the full sun of the Promise dawning on the third generation after Abraham.

Yet, the long drought balanced Jacob's longing with questions about how long his flocks and herds could survive in the land. His mind bulged as he weighed possibilities and facts about how Yah might work it all out. He must try to put the matter aside and allow matters to take their own course—or was it the course set by Yah?

"Joseph!" he called, as the camp began to stir. His favorite son of his favorite wife, Rachel, had just emerged from his tent.

"Father?" Joseph replied. At the tender age of seventeen he was the most handsome of all the sons of Jacob. Standing two inches taller than his father, he had the same swarthy complexion and finely chiseled nose. His long brown hair fell in natural waves to his shoulders. And Jacob had further graced his favored son's appearance by having a handsome tunic woven especially for him—a garment that a nobleman or even a prince might wear, ornamented with tassels and having long sleeves and long folds that reached to his ankles, instead of the short, sleeveless tunics that most ordinary men wore. Joseph was rarely without the rare garment, and it did nothing for his acceptance among his brothers.

"You must prepare for a long journey, my son," Jacob said. "I would have you go to Shechem to see how the flocks and herds fare under the care of your brothers."

It was often thus—Joseph on the one hand and "your brothers" on the other. After all, several of his other sons took after the pagan ways of their mothers. It had come to Jacob that Dan and Naphtali, the sons of Rachel's maidservant Bilhah, made open references to their fascination with the worship of one or another of the ba'als of the Philistines. Gad and Asher, sons of Zilpah, scoffed at all forms of faith.

Jacob's favoritism for Joseph included long talks in the fields as they worked together. Somehow the young man was such a ready listener that Jacob found himself sharing his experiences, his wondering about the nature of Yah's Promise, the birthright, the choosing, and especially how it had all changed him through the years. He was eager for Joseph to learn the responsibility of living up to the Promise, for, in the light of the other brothers' lack of sensitivity to the promise of Yah, Jacob sensed that Joseph might be bearing much of the burden of the Abrahamic clan's destiny.

At the mention of his mission, Joseph's normally cheerful countenance clouded. "My brothers, Father? Surely you have servants who would know more about the flocks than I. Could you not send them?"

Something else was at stake here, Jacob knew. "What is it, my son? I thought the journey would be a welcome break from your duties here."

"Yes, it would, in a way. But—." Joseph looked at the ground. "I would not speak against my father's sons, sire, but—but there is always trouble when I am with them."

Jacob bristled. "Have they mistreated you?" he asked gruffly.

"No, not really," said Joseph. "It's just that they—they make sport of my faith in Yah," he finally blurted out.

Jacob folded his arms across his chest and rocked back on his heels. More difficulty from his sons' pagan ways, was it? He could not say that he was surprised.

"What do they say?"

"They say that there are many gods," Joseph went on, warming to his task. "They laugh when I speak of the promise of Yah to our fathers Abraham and Isaac, saying that anyone can claim to be favored by the gods.

"And they go in to foreign women, the prostitutes among the *goyim,*" he finished, almost triumphantly.

For the fact was that Joseph searched for such opportunities to portray his moral superiority over his brothers. There was an innocent enough reason behind this shoddy quest—Joseph had been visited with many dreams in which that very superiority was vividly depicted in surrealistic scenes more vivid than life. In one dream, he and his brothers were stacking sheaves of barley, when suddenly the sheaves of his brothers all bowed down and paid homage to his own stack as though he were their lord and master. In another, the sun and moon and eleven stars—representing his eleven brothers, of course—did obeisance before him.

Partly in the openness of youthful innocence and partly in sheer rivalry, Joseph made the mistake of sharing such dreams with his brothers. Once three of them set upon him and would have beaten him had not the others intervened. In self-defense, Joseph felt compelled to find ways to justify his dreaming.

In his fatherly wisdom, Jacob knew to discount at least part of his favorite son's rivalry with his brothers—although which part he did not know. At least, he thought, he should insist that Joseph go to Shechem. Perhaps being together away from the rest of the family would draw them closer together.

"The pagan ways of your brothers are a burden to me, as well, my son," he said gravely. Then more lightly: "But pagans can care for flocks and herds as well as followers of Yah. Go, and see how matters are with them—and see whether you can be brothers to each other, as well."

He would speak to Joseph's brothers later.

"Hah! The dreamer comes!" Simeon hissed bitterly. He and his brothers were tending a flock of sheep near Dothan, not far from the devastated city of Shechem.

"He is alone!" offered Levi, scrambling to his feet. He waved at the others to come. A hasty war council was formed, just out of sight of their approaching brother.

"Now is our chance!" Zebulon whispered loudly. "Let's rid ourselves of this thorn in the flesh, and his boastful dreams as well!"

"What!" Reuben rejoined. "You don't mean to kill him!"

"Just that," Zebulon returned. The others crowded around, smelling both blood and the excitement of a good plot to break the monotony of the shepherding.

By this time Joseph was nearing the crest of the little hill where the brothers crouched just out of sight. He had seen Zebulon and Levi lounging on a huge, flat boulder; and he approached them now.

"My brothers," said Joseph. "How goes the work, and the animals?"

"Well, brother," Zebulon returned. Then, without any further small talk he motioned for the rest of the gang crouched behind the rock. Like a tiny army they pounced on their younger brother. Vastly outnumbered, Joseph was beaten senseless and stripped of the hated tunic that symbolized his favored status.

As Joseph lapsed into unconsciousness, Reuben and Judah sprang into the midst of the attackers, throwing them off the youth one by one.

"Enough!" Reuben shouted. "We cannot do this thing. He is our brother!"

"You would have more of his dreams, then?" sneered Naphtali, wiping blood from his nose where Joseph had landed a lucky blow.

"No more dreams," Reuben returned, "but no killing, either." He looked about him, his mind in a whirl. He spied the rock wall of an unused cistern just off the brow of the little hill. The drought had long since caused it to go dry.

"There!" he said. "We will toss him in the well." Then, to appease their blood lust: "A lion will soon take care of him if he does not first die of hunger and thirst. Why do ourselves what we can have done for us?"

The brothers exchanged surly glares. "Why not?" Zebulon finally said gruffly. "And we can slaughter a kid from the herd and put its blood on this dreamer's coat. We will take the coat back to our father, who will assume the truth." The others agreed, and Joseph's limp body was placed in the dust of the shallow well.

"Back to work, all of us," said Reuben. He stalked off toward the band of sheep he had been tending in the little valley on the other side of the hill from the well. Later, after night fell, he would return to the well, tend to Joseph's wounds, and take him back to his father in Hebron where he belonged.

As night gathered, the other brothers built their evening fire near the well. Just as they were about to eat their simple meal, the tinkling of camel bells came softly through the dusk.

"Who goes?" demanded Judah.

"We are merchants, friend," came the reply. "We are from Midian and are bound for the Two Lands."

Egypt, the brothers knew.

Suddenly Judah had an idea. To avoid killing young Joseph, he would persuade his brothers to sell him to these traders, who would as soon traffic in slaves as in gold or silver or bolts of cloth.

"Pass by in peace," he called to the person on the lead camel as he emerged from the darkness that was fast falling. Then, to his brothers: "Quickly! We do not need to shed this dreamer's blood. Hasten! Retrieve him from the well and we will make a profit from him."

Before they thought to argue the point, Levi and Naphtali ran to the well while Judah began his bargaining.

"But stay a moment," he said to the caravan leader. "We have a small business matter that may interest merchants such as yourselves." The caravaner narrowed his eyes as Joseph, half-conscious and half-naked, was dragged into the cirlce of the campfire.

"We found this thief trying to take a sheep from our flock," Judah continued. "What would you give for him, to be your slave and to accompany you to Egypt?"

The trader was silent for a moment as he appraised the merchandise. "Are you sure he will live?" he asked.

"With certainty, my lord," Judah assured him. "He is not seriously harmed. He has just had a hard lesson. He is young and strong—you should have seen the fight he gave us!" Then, to his brothers, "Eh?" They mumbled their agreement.

"Fifteen shekels of silver," said the trader. If the thief was as strong as they said, he would bring fifty shekels in Egypt, he knew.

"Come, my friend," Judah bargained. "You would not take advantage of these poor shepherds. He is worth at least twenty-five shekels."

Knowing then that he had made a good bargain, the trader said, "Not at all, my friend," he said sweetly. "It is just that we have only limited food, and the way to the Two Lands is long.

Twenty shekels—my final offer."

"Done!" said Judah. Joseph was loaded atop a riderless ass, and the train disappeared into the night.

Late that night, when his brothers were deep in sleep and their fire had died down, Reuben wept when he came to the cistern and found it empty.

Seven days later Jacob stood holding the very tunic his beloved Joseph was wearing when he sent him north to visit his brothers. They stood before their father with bowed heads, having handed him the garment.

"What is this?" he asked in hoarse horror, gazing with unbelief on what could only be bloodstains.

"We found it in the field, near Shechem," Judah said convincingly. "Is it, then, your son's robe?"

"It is Joseph's robe," Jacob said heavily, tears beginning to streak his leathery face. He sat down wearily on a boulder. "I sent him to see how you fared with the stock. A lion or bear has fallen upon him! The fault is mine. I should have sent another. Oh, Joseph, my son!" The old man buried his face in the blood-stained tunic and wept bitterly.

Reuben glared reprovingly at his brothers, who in turn looked at the ground, then moved sheepishly away.

CHAPTER 20

Young and strong, Joseph soon recovered from his wounds. He was not treated unkindly by the caravaners; it was to their advantage to have a reasonably well-fed and contented piece of merchandise to sell in Egypt. The only untoward incident came as the party entered a little valley that Joseph knew to be near Hebron, and camped for the night. Joseph slipped his loose bonds and was about to steal away from the camp and take flight for home when a guard intercepted him.

"Thwack!"—a sharp clout to the cheek was enough to cause him to revise his plans.

From there, the party veered to the southwest, then west, keeping to the coastal plain that skirted the inhospitable desert wilderness of Shur. By the time they crossed the *Wadi* of Egypt, Joseph was able to treat the whole experience as an adventure.

The caravan wound its way toward the lower end of the famed River Nile. Paying dearly for a primitive ferry, which had to make seven trips, they crossed one of the tributaries that helped form the great delta land of Goshen, known throughout the world for its rich produce. Their passage, accompanied by great groans and belches and fearful snorting from their camels, brought them to a flat land of luxuriant crops growing from the nourishing delta soil, brought down from the Upper Land year after year at the annual flooding of the Nile.

The Midianite caravaners made their way to the city of Avaris, where one of the "Shepherd Kings" so hated by traditional Egyptians had transformed an ancient village into a modern new capital. "We will stable the beasts here," the caravan leader announced, as they entered the city's outskirts. He would escort his merchandise, Joseph, across the city without the encumbrance of the rest of the caravan.

Plodding through the strange place, the shepherd's son was awed at the marvels of the gleaming, urban civilization, the likes of which did not exist in Palestine. The upstart Pharaoh, uniting several Semitic tribes that had taken up residence on the delta 200 years earlier, had driven the traditional ruling parties to the south, in the Upper Lands.

At the city center, the pair skirted the marketplace. "Sacrifices for Seth!" cried a vendor, selling doves and lambs in behalf of the chief god of the Lower Lands. Another man was hawking baby alligators—a sight that brought both grins and grimaces to the face of the youth from the desert. Fortune tellers and seers offered bargains to anyone who would have the gods' plan for their lives sketched out before them.

Never had Joseph seen such grandeur. Two-story homes with sun porches atop them lined their way. The city's main thoroughfares were paved with limestone, and the public buildings veneered with marble facades, the likes of which Joseph had never dreamed. Reflection pools brought a sense of calm that contrasted with the frenetic bustle of the small metropolis. Joseph's Midianite interim master told him of the great pyramids, which were already ancient history by then; but they lay out of view, to the south.

But for all the polished urban grandeur so impressive to the rustic shepherd Joseph, the land was gripped by political chaos. More Semitic Hyksos peoples, who included the Shepherd Kings, filtered in from Canaan weekly. The traditional rulers had lacked the will or the power to resist these intruders. Their influence now was largely limited to the ancient capital of Thebes; and Egypt's long-standing suzerainty over the lands to the northeast, from which Joseph came, was weakening. Traders such as the

Midianite caravaners gladly exploited the open trade afforded by the flux and flow of peoples.

The trader who had bought Joseph had too many contacts to make it necessary to take his captive to the public auction. Instead, he went directly to the garrison buildings housing the king's guard. Its captain, one Potiphar, would be a likely prospect. An hour later the trader had proved the soundness of his estimate, for he emerged from Potiphar's fine quarters fifty shekels richer and with one less mouth to feed.

My lord Philemon, I interrupt to note how one Manetho, an ancient Egyptian historian, describes the Canaanitish Hyksos kings under whose reign Joseph entered Egypt:

"There was a king of ours whose name was Timaios, in whose reign it came to pass, I know not why, that God was displeased with us, and there came unexpectedly men of ignoble birth out of the eastern parts, who had boldness enough to make an expedition into our country, and easily subdued it by force without a battle.

"And when they had got our rulers under their power, they afterwards savagely burnt down our cities and demolished the temples of the gods, and used all the inhabitants in a most hostile manner...At length they made one of themselves king...who rebuilt [the city of Avaris] and made it very strong by the walls he built around it and by a numerous garrison of 240,000 men."

And I cannot but note the mysterious and sovereign providence of God, who used these very Canaanites through whom to bless Joseph and his family! Had the Abrahamic clan stayed in Canaan during these days, the vigor of the Canaanite culture may well have overwhelmed them. But although the Canaanite Hyksos also vigorously entrenched themselves in Egypt, they sought other Canaanites to accompany them and strengthen their hands. They gladly welcomed a strong, young slave like Joseph, since he came from their own background.

If this was what a slave's life was like, Joseph jokingly told himself, he was not sure he would choose freedom. He had been a servant in Potiphar's house for two years. His memory of the days of pain and sorrow that had begun with his beating in Shechem had long since dimmed under the Egyptian sun.

Joseph's indomitable disposition spared him from cursing his lot as a slave. His optimistic outlook, his willingness to work and his cheerful disposition quickly earned him his master's favor. As the months grew into years, Joseph so proved himself that Potifar conferred on him the position of chief of the household's servants. Although he lived in the servants' quarters, he had his own room separate from the large area where the other servants bunked together.

He also enjoyed free access to the main house, coming and going as freely as a member of Potiphar's family. It was on one such entry, in the fifth year of his service, that Joseph came upon his mistress dressed in a filmy net garment far too revealing to be ordinary house wear. She gave a little gasp as though he had surprised her, and scurried around the corner into another room and out of sight. Joseph pretended he had not seen her and marched on to the rear of the house to direct the cleaning of some heavy-scaled carp his under-servants were preparing for the evening meal.

He had forgotten the incident, until the next day the same thing occurred. This time, his mistress was less discreet.

"And has Joseph, my husband's trusted overseer, returned to catch another glimpse of his master's wife?" she asked coyly.

"Please—" Joseph began. "That is—I meant no indiscretion, my lady. Please excuse me." He tried to back out of the entrance, but the woman abandoned all pretense and grabbed him by the arm, her negligible clothing falling teasingly open.

"It is all right," she said, her voice liquid and low. "You may glimpse what you wish. Come! My husband is away!"

With that, Joseph freed his arm and fled.

But Potiphar's wife was not so easily rejected. Day after day she managed to appear to Joseph in dress that should have been reserved for the bedroom, and day after day her invitations grew more brazen.

As for Joseph, he had to admit to himself that his normal young manhood ached for the woman. He awoke more than once, deep in the night, tortured with passion. Yet he was beset also with echoes from conversations with his father on the moralizing effect of being chosen for the Promise. He recalled the story Jacob had told him of the gambling game in the tavern of Damascus. But could he be as strong? Did he even *wish* to be as strong? What a burden was this business of being a chosen family!

Finally Joseph knew what he must do: he would confront the temptress directly and make clear both his determination to remain chaste, and why.

One evening when Potiphar was at the garrison drilling his troops, Joseph marched resolutely into the main house. He found his master's wife in her private quarters. None of the rooms had doors, and he could see a maidservant with her mistress behind an ornate, carved screen, adorning her mistress's finely sculpted head with the finishing touches of an extravagant coiffure. Joseph stood awkwardly at the doorway for a moment, then gave a little cough to announce his presence.

Potiphar's wife stood up immediately at the sound. "Leave us, my dear," she said to the maidservant. Her glistening ebony tresses, piled high, flashed ice-blue highlights. Regal, painted eyebrows arched high above a nose that was slightly too long for her face. She wore a loose robe over a filmy gown, and smiled a little as she realized her appearance was as a magnet to Joseph's eyes. She transfixed him with lowered eyelids, heavily laden with Egypt's finest cosmetics, until the maidservant was well out of hearing.

"Ah, it is the handsome young overseer," she said. "Come in, my dear."

Joseph steeled himself against the seductive tone of her voice. He moved cautiously forward when she motioned him to a sumptuously cushioned boudoir chair, but did not sit.

"I am here only for a moment," he began. "You must know that I cannot serve my master and his mistress well when there is this—." He hesitated, not knowing precisely the terms in which to couch his complaint, and flustered by the tempting woman before him and the heavy smell of perfume that hung in the air.

"Yes?" Potiphar's wife encouraged, enjoying Joseph's discomfort.

"My lady knows—," Joseph began again. But before he could continue he gasped in horror as the woman seized his outer garment and tried to pull him to her richly tapestried bed.

"Enough talk, my love!" she whispered. "Let us allow love to speak for us!"

Joseph pulled back, trying to release himself from her clutches, but found her grip surprisingly strong.

"My lady!" he said hoarsely. "You cannot do this to me and to my master. He has entrusted me with everything in his household, and it would—."

"Am I not a part of his household?" his mistress interrupted. "Then he has entrusted *me* to you, as well!"

Seeing that no amount of reasoning could stifle the woman's advances, Joseph did the only thing he knew to do. He shrugged off his garment, leaving it in her hands, and literally raced from the room, clad only in his light undershirt and loin cloth.

His hasty exit was accompanied by shrieks from the mistress's quarters—calls that he knew would be quickly answered by another servant. Soon, he realized, his tormentor would be claiming he had attacked her—and holding his garment as the indicting evidence.

CHAPTER 21

Joseph's trial was predictable. A slave had no rights in court; the mere accusation brought by a man in Potiphar's position was enough for Joseph to be summarily cast into the crude jail.

Prison tested Joseph's sunny disposition, but did not subdue it. Thoughts of his father and home did not make him depressed with longing, but rather sustained him. If being a son of the Promise must curb his passions, he would also call on it as a source of hope. If Yah had gained for him a victory over the wiles of a woman, what were mere prison bars before Him?

With such a spirit, the young Hebrew began a second ascent to favor in the eyes of his superiors. The chief jailer made him his first assistant, and Joseph found himself in charge of the daily welfare of the other prisoners. Surely, he thought, Yah is with me. Could I ask for a surer sign?

One day as Joseph was completing the supervision of the light noon-day meal, a loud clamor rang from the entrance to the prison. He raced forward to see if perhaps an attempted escape was in progress. But instead of prisoners leaving the jail, he found two well-dressed men being thrust roughly inside, against their loud and violent protests.

"What have we here?" Joseph demanded.

"Two very royal prisoners," said the guard. "But prisoners they are, even though they are from the king's own service!" He clanged the heavy iron gate shut behind the reluctant new prisoners.

Joseph sized up his new charges thoughtfully. One was a black man, a Nubian by the looks of him. The other was of lighter skin, but bore himself proudly. Joseph was startled to find welling up within him a surge of premonitions. *This Nubian is surely innocent,* he found himself asserting inwardly, while the other is nothing but a traitor! He brushed aside the strange forebodings to complete the process of admitting the new prisoners.

He learned that the black man whose innocence struck him was named Amun-ptah, the Pharaoh's personal butler. The other was one Zoser, the royal baker. Both had been implicated in a plot to poison the king. Both loudly protested their innocence.

A week after the new prisoners had been admitted, Jacob lay on his blankets one night pondering again the strange, omen-like sensations he had about them. Since he had been in Egypt he had been impressed with the great emphasis on divining the will of their gods, on seeking omens, and on predictions of the future. Every village had its seers and prophets—some of whom were such obvious charlatans that wags were fond of caricaturing them on the walls of the taverns and stables. This seer was portrayed as a cat, beguiling its mistress; that one as a bull raping a cow, to symbolize the advantage some prophets took of their gullible clients.

All this had made Joseph recall his own dreams—especially those he had been foolish enough to share with his brothers. He remembered dream interpreters in his boyhood home of Haran, and the dreams his father Jacob had confided in him. He wondered long about Jacob's vision of the stairway to heaven, and especially about the strangely exciting wrestling match, which Joseph supposed was a kind of wakeful dream—at least something had happened to injure his father's hip.

Of course, his father Jacob believed strongly that Yah was behind his own dreaming. But was He also the maker of dreams among these *goyim?*

As the years went by, Joseph tried to be open to more dreaming himself. He was surprised to find that a little practice seemed to put him into a state receptive to dreams. From there he went on to trying to interpret them. He discussed his experiments with his fellow prisoners and learned that the art of interpreting dreams had been developed into a system that put the charlatan seers he knew about to shame with its safeguards and sophisticated schemes that assigned certain meanings to certain animals and objects that frequently recurred in dreams.

One morning Joseph was tending to his records with a reed pen on papyrus sheets in the little office the chief jailer had given him. He looked up as Amun-ptah, Pharaoh's former butler, and his companion Zoser, the baker, approached. They looked haggard and worn.

"You have not slept," Joseph diagnosed.

"It is the truth," said Zoser, looking at the butler knowingly.

"We have spent most of the night dreaming," said Amun-ptah.

"Both of you? That is strange," said Joseph.

"It is even stranger," said the baker. The dreams were remarkably similar. But we have no idea what to make of them."

"Ah, yes," said Joseph. "That is the hard part. There is no shortage of seers on the outside to interpret them for us. But here, in this place—. Ah, well, the interpretation of dreams is in the hands of the Great God, in my view. It is He who gives their interpretation, not men."

Zoser and Amun-ptah exchanged glances. "That is why we come to you," Zoser said. "It is whispered throughout the prison that you are a servant of a high god, and that—."

"I am a servant of *the* High God," Joseph corrected. "I serve Yah, the God of my fathers Abraham, Isaac and Jacob."

"Yes, well—," Zoser acknowledged noncommittally. A theological argument on the number of gods in the universe was the last thing he wanted. "At any rate—you say this Yah whom you serve gives the interpretation of dreams?"

Joseph put down the pen, eagerness rising within as he sensed a fine opportunity to put his theory and practice to test.

"It is true, as I said. Whether He will give the interpretation to *me* is in His hands. But come—tell me the dreams and let us see." The three settled themselves in a corner of the entrance to the jail. "Amun-ptah," Joseph said invitingly. "What did you dream?"

The butler breathed deeply and a little deliciously as he began. It was good to be at the center of such an analysis.

"I saw a vine before me, growing in size before my very eyes—."

"Collapsed time," Joseph interrupted. "It is common in many dreams."

"Yes," said Amun-ptah, anxious to continue. "The vine grew into three branches, and each one immediately put on blossoms, and then grapes—delicious bunches that were immediately ripe for the squeezing, then immediately fermented as in good wine.

"Then somehow my lord Pharaoh's cup was in my hand, and I felt called to resume my duties by offering him drink. So I pressed the grapes into his cup, and gave it to him.

"You know of the rumors that I was plotting to kill the king. This made me fear, in my dream, that somehow the wine was poisoned, and I watched anxiously to see what effect the drink might have on the Pharaoh. But as it turned out, it was pure wine, and the king was pleased.

"That is the dream. Does it mean anything to you?"

Joseph leaned back and scratched the side of his head thoughtfully. He closed his eyes and breathed a silent prayer that Yah would give him the interpretation.

He was almost startled at the words that came to him.

"Thus says the Great God, Yah," Joseph intoned. "The meaning of the dream is this. The three branches are three days. And within three days the king will exonerate his butler of all guilt and suspicion and will restore him to his position as butler and cupbearer, with honor."

Amun-ptah's mouth opened and closed before the tears of joy and relief began to roll down his cheeks.

"My lord!" he said to Joseph in hoarse admiration. "Can I believe in this interpretation? You would not say this just to please me?"

Joseph was irritated. "I would not say anything that Yah did not give me to say."

He looked away to give himself time to reflect on the words that had come from his mouth. In a way, Amun-ptah was right; they *had* been his words. But they seemed to well up from within with no prompting or effort. It was as though they had taken on a personality of their own—*Yah's* personality, dare he to think? His mind raced back to the interpretations he had given his brothers of his own dreams, the dreams of superiority. Somehow, he knew, they had a ring of truth beyond the boyish rivalry he had felt toward his brothers.

Joseph wrenched his thoughts back to the scene at hand. Turning to Zoser the baker, he said, "And what of your dream, my friend?"

Excited by hearing the favorable interpretation of the Nubian's dream, Zoser plunged enthusiastically into the account of his own vision.

"Mine was a dream with the symbol of three as well," he began. "I was carrying three baskets of cakes on my head, as was my custom, bearing it to the king's table from the royal kitchen rooms outside the palace.

"But on my way across the courtyard, I was attacked by birds. They plucked most of the cakes out of the basket, so that it was almost empty by the time I reached the king's table. What can this mean? Will I, too, be restored to my position, as you predict of this cupbearer?" Zoser leaned eagerly forward for confirmation.

In an equal but opposite motion, Joseph again leaned back against the wall of the entry room. He visualized his mind as an open scroll, completely blank, open to any message Yah might have. Suddenly his brows came together in a scowl that made the baker draw back in fearful anticipation.

"My lord Joseph!" he said, knowingly using the term of honor. "What is it? What do you see . . . or hear?"

Joseph was reluctant to respond. He shut his eyes tight against the Voice in his mind, as though to shut his ears to it as well. But he had come this far, almost boasting of the power of Yah to give the interpretation of dreams. To remain silent would be not only embarrassing but disloyal.

"It is an interpretation of sadness," he said slowly. "The three baskets are also three days. But their meaning is that in three days the king will bring you out from this prison only to have your head!" Then, before he could open his eyes, Joseph's voice rushed on angrily.

"Traitor!" he exclaimed, his eyes now open and fixing themselves on the baker, whose countenance turned from fear to guilt. "You are guilty!" Joseph charged. "You tried to poison your master, the king!"

"No, no!" Zoser protested. "You lie! You did not receive this from your god. You——." But knowing how unconvincing his voice was, the baker arose and stormed back to his cell.

The banquet three days later, at which Amun-ptah served, was followed by Zoser's execution, along with three co-conspirators.

Joseph's fame as a seer spread.

The dreaming in the Lower Land was far from over. Years later, Amun-ptah was summoned one morning to the presence of the Pharaoh. The king's bedraggled visage brought back to the Nubian that day in the prison when he had come to Joseph with similar evidence of a sleepless night.

"My lord?"

"Butler," the king said, half-groaning. "I am not well. I am afflicted with dreams that disturb my sleep. I have laid out the dreams to the seers in my court. Half of them have no idea what to say. The other half give such wildly different interpretations that it is obvious they are lying.

"But you—I have heard that you know of some servant in my household who claims to receive interpretations of dreams from a high god. Is this true? Can you find him?"

Amun-ptah hung his head. The king's plight had reminded him of a forgotten promise.

"It is as my lord says," he said. "I remember my faults this day—that I have forgotten to tell my lord earlier of this man of whom you speak."

"Well—tell me now!" the king said impatiently.

"He is not actually a servant in your house," the Nubian continued. "He is a prisoner, but a man of honor, and he has been made the chief servant of the king's chief jailer. He indeed does have the gods' ear, for he correctly interpreted the vision when I myself dreamed I would be restored to the king's favor some years ago."

"Well, get him, then!" Pharaoh roared, coming to his feet. "And pray that this prisoner does not fail to tell me my dream as he told yours—else. . . ." He did not need to finish the threat; nor could the Nubian have heard it, for before the king had finished speaking Amun-ptah had fled to the prison.

Joseph marveled at the rich appointments in the throne room. Columns of polished black marble from islands in the Great Sea arose in contrast to gleaming white marble floor tiles, inlaid with chalcedony. The whole palace smelled sweetly of roof joists made from cedar from the land of Lebanon to the northeast, and of ever-burning incense arising to the Egyptian gods. Behind the Pharaoh's throne hung a huge bronze disk symbolizing the high sun god, Ra. Yet, for all the grand elegance of the place, Joseph felt remarkably calm as he approached the throne. Instead of trembling in awe at these pagan appointments, he found himself wondering whether there were some relationship between Ra and Yah.

Pharaoh's authoritative voice interrupted Joseph's musings.

"You are a guest in my prison?" the king began.

"Unjustly accused, my lord."

"Yes, aren't they all? But you are not here to debate your innocence. You are a seer—an interpreter of dreams?"

"My God, Yah, the God of my fathers, Abraham, Isaac and Jacob, gives me the interpretation."

"The distinction is without a difference," said Pharaoh, indifferently. "You are Semite, as I understand it."

"I am from the land of the Semites, a Hebrew, of the tribe of Abraham."

"Whoever," Pharaoh said impatiently. He had no interest in following this prisoner's family tree, but, being a Hyksos king, it was reassuring to know that the young man was at least not Egyptian born.

"I would tell you my dreams," he continued, "which none of my own magicians and wise men can interpret. You will put the dreams before your god to see if he can do any better."

Joseph merely nodded. A twinge of anxiety swept over him. What if Yah decided to withhold the interpretation? Joseph could lose his head. But there was no time to allow his anxiety to intensify, for Pharaoh was plunging into the story of the dreams.

"I was standing by the Great River when seven sleek and fat cows came up out of the water. I was about to summon my servant to slay one for my table when seven other cows—as poor and sickly as the first ones had been healthy—followed them up out of the river. To my horror these seven ugly kine set upon the healthy cows as though they were lions and devoured them!"

Joseph had been listening with bowed head, the better to concentrate. As Pharaoh paused, Joseph lifted his head and opened his mouth to speak—using what words, he knew not.

"Silence!" the king commanded. "There is more." He arose from the throne and began to pace nervously.

Joseph meekly lowered his head again, grateful for the reprieve.

"I awoke in a cold sweat, in some kind of dread at what the attack on the fat cattle might mean. Then I fell asleep again, and again I dreamed." Pharaoh was walking faster now, his arms waving wildly to punctuate the sense of disaster communicated by his dreams.

"Again, the dream was in sevens. This time I was standing in the rich wheat fields near the Great River. My eyes were directed to the seven-headed grain that was growing there, and then to a single stalk on which the seven heads were the fattest and richest ever seen.

"But as I marveled at the harvest such a field would produce, a second branch of seven heads suddenly appeared on the first stalk. This bunch of grain was as poor and sickly as the first bunch was healthy; and to my horror, the ugly, blighted sprouts set upon the healthy heads of grain and devoured them—just as the fat kine had been eaten up."

Pharaoh slumped back onto his throne, exhausted by the very telling of the torturous dreams. "Now," he said tiredly. "Go away and commune with your god and ask him the interpretation." It was as much a threat as a command.

Again, Joseph raised his head. This time, all anxiety was gone, for he felt welling up within him a message so urgent he could hardly get the words out clearly, so fast did they tumble over each other.

"I do not need to go away, my lord, for Yah has already placed the interpretation within me. And let not the king be anxious, for Yah has given you a sign of what is about to happen—a gift rarely seen in the throne rooms of men."

Pharaoh stared, strangely calmed by this prisoner who seemed to know both the mind of his god and what goes on in the chambers of government. "Go on, my son," he said.

"They are not two dreams," Joseph continued, "but one and the same. The seven fat kine and the seven good ears of grain represent seven good and plentiful years of harvest."

"Good, good!" exclaimed Pharaoh. He sat up straight on his throne, attracted to the young prisoner before him not only because of the optimistic prediction but because of the unwavering certainty of his voice and the absence of any of the magicians' sycophantic fawnings.

"But there is more, my lord," said Joseph, "and it is not all good."

"Go on, go on," he said quickly. "Better to know the whole of it than the good alone."

"The seven lean and poor kine and the seven blighted ears of grain are also of one interpretation. They are seven poor and lean and blighted years, which will follow the seven good years. Famine and hunger will threaten to devour the effects of the years of abundance. My Lord God, Yah, has given my lord the king a preview of the cycle of the rain and the land for the next fourteen years."

Pharaoh's mouth hung open for a moment, so amazed was he at the panorama of the future so deftly sketched by this Hebrew prisoner. Of course, he could not know whether it was the truth. But the young man before him did not hesitate to give him the unfavorable interpretation along with the good, and his manner held no sign of currying favor.

A test, the king decided, would be to press Joseph to go beyond the interpretation of dreams and suggest a plan of action to deal with what he had predicted.

"I am impressed," he admitted with just a touch of sarcasm. "But can you do nothing more than mouth the words given you by your god, Ka—."

"*Yah,*" Joseph corrected.

"Whoever," said the king. "Can you not give me some idea about what to do about the things you foresee?"

Joseph's expression did not change, for again he felt the same sensation of words welling up within from some unknown depths—or were they being infused from above? With the same direct gaze and steady voice he said:

"Yah not only gives the king a word about what is to come, but also the measures my lord can take to transform the evil years into good. Let my lord—."

It was Pharaoh's turn to interrupt. "Wait, wait," he said, turning his head aside in a gesture of skepticism but never taking his eyes off Joseph. "Is not the future fixed and unchangeable? If your god gives a dream of what is to come, will it not happen thus? How could what the gods foresee be changed?"

"I—." Joseph hesitated for the first time since he began to feel the messages build up inside. It was a fair question, and he lacked the philosophical tools to deal with it. There was nothing to do but admit it. "I know not how, my lord. I only know that Yah, the Creator-God, El Shaddai, whom I serve, is not only mighty to create the future, but is also strong enough to give us, His creatures, strength. He does not begrudge us some hand in shaping His future."

"Hmmm," Pharaoh mumbled. "A novel idea . . . one that I should like to debate with our priests, and perhaps with you—but at another time. You were saying . . . ."

"I was saying—*Yah* was saying—that my lord should let his vice-regents store up grain and goods during the seven good years, for distribution during the seven poor years. Let the people be rationed in the amount of grain they consume during the years when the rains come, so they may eat during the times of drought and famine."

Pharaoh sat silent, staring at Joseph as though trying to assimilate the momentous things he had heard—or, Joseph wondered, was he only comparing the sweeping if grim panorama of the dreams with the simplicity of the plan to dull the effect of the years of famine? Perhaps the strategy was so obvious that the king would dismiss it in scorn.

He was not to know the answer to the question on that day, for Pharaoh arose abruptly and dismissed him.

The next day, a servant of the pharaoh came the prison and announced to the chief jailer that his chief assistant was free.

"Make way, make way!" the steward riding in the front of the chariot called.

The command was met by cries of "He who comes in the name of Pharaoh!" and "Zaphenath-paneah!"—the Egyptian name Joseph now wore. Riding in state behind the steward, Joseph gestured gravely to the crowds. Even in the hubbub of riding through the city streets on the way to examine the grain fields of Goshen, he could not help but contrast the acclaim he received from the

Egyptians with the harsh treatment he remembered at the hands of his brothers. The power of Yah had never seemed more real, with his pilgrimage from slave to second-in-command in all of the Two Lands.

Pharaoh had summoned his nobles the very night Joseph had interpreted his dreams and outlined the plan to save Egypt from the coming drought and famine. As the nobles trooped in, they took note of the king's changed countenance. He was more relaxed than they had seen him in days.

Elaborating for them in great detail his dreams, and the young Hebrew's commanding presentation of their meaning, Pharaoh then asked, "Is it not an omen that a Semite such as we has been given such power from the gods?"

An incoherent rumbling of voices indicated general approval amid great nodding of heads. But one council member had a question: "How do we know his voice is indeed the voice of the gods? Any charlatan can predict weather patterns, but who can know if he tells the truth?" A lesser level of crowd noise supported the question.

"A good question, my friend," said the king. "But what have we to lose if we were to put this man who seems to have the ear of his god in charge of doing what he advises—buying up surplus grain and storing it for the future? The salary and supporting funds for one additional minister—it is nothing! If he succeeds, our rule here is strengthened. If he turns out to be wrong, it will not be difficult to dispose of him."

The voices of approval were louder now. If nothing else, it would be worth it to have the Pharaoh in such a fine spirit; if fewer heads would roll with another minister in the cabinet, so be it. As for the king, he could create an office for Joseph by fiat; but his court would function more smoothly if he first obtained the approval of the rest of his cabinet.

"Then it is done!" he had said. "He is to be appointed Grand Vizier over all Egypt, second only to me, with particular responsibility for the Ministry of Agriculture. Let it be written in the annals of the Pharaoh that this Joseph is set over all the agricultural affairs of Egypt."

The ceremony at the palace the next day was brief, but heavy with the air of invested authority. The king solemnly presented

Joseph with his signet ring, a robe with the royal insignia emblazoned upon it, and a gold pendant from which hung the sun disk of Ra.

At first Joseph felt uneasy about the distance he had traveled overnight from prison to palace, and especially about wearing the symbol of a foreign god. But somehow he sensed Yah's hand on the whole matter so strongly that he determined to follow events wherever they led.

Who knows? he found himself thinking. Perhaps Yah would use his new position to further His scheme to bless the family of Jacob.

CHAPTER 22

The squalls of a newborn in Joseph's household brought only smiles to his servants.

"And what will my lady call this one, the brother of Manasseh?" asked the chief maidservant of Asenath, Joseph's wife. As the years had gone by, Joseph so earned Pharaoh's favor that he had given him his own daughter in marriage.

"He is Ephraim," the proud mother replied. "It is from the language of my husband Zaphenath-paneah's clan. It means 'To bear double fruit,' he says." She looked down at the infant's dark curls and smiled as only those can smile who have brought a child into the world. "Surely he has doubled my joy!"

Joseph, summoned from his office in the palace, entered the bed chamber. For five years now he had been second in command only to Pharaoh over the produce of the land of Egypt. It was good to be chosen for such a position. But as he saw Asenath smiling dotingly at the newborn Ephraim, he could not suppress a frown.

"What is it, dear?" his wife asked innocently.

"Nothing, nothing—are you all right? And the little one—is he healthy?"

"Neither of us could be any better. But the frown I spied—what is this about?"

Joseph embraced his wife affectionately. "I was just thinking of our other son. I cannot ever recall your looking at him with such—that is, so lovingly."

Asenath sought to reassure him. "Why, Joseph. You know I love Manasseh. But he has always been—well, *your* son. You yourself called him after the words from the tongue of your house— 'Causing me to forget,' wasn't it? It was a sign that all your troubles were forgotten. And somehow, just as they were your troubles, and not mine, Manasseh has always seemed closer to you. And now, cannot I have a son for myself? Should his birth bring again a troubled look to my lord?"

"I am very happy. But Manasseh, after all, is our firstborn. If we are to favor any of our children, it should be he. As I have told you, I myself was my father's favorite, though not the firstborn— and little good came of it. I would not want our home to have the jealousy and strife that was in my own. But come—enough of this. Let me hold my new son."

Joseph cradled the baby, darker skinned like his mother, in his gentle arms.

"Doubly fruitful," he repeated in Hebrew, approximating the name Ephraim. He smiled; but he could not shake the vague apprehensiveness that Manasseh, his firstborn, might find it more difficult to smile if Asenath did not curb her favoritism. Being chosen as a favorite, he thought bitterly, could sometimes seem very close to being cursed.

Joseph had occasion almost to wish that his interpretation of the second part of the king's dream had not been so literally accurate. He stood on the parched and cracked river bottom that ordinarily would have been flooded by now from the overflowing waters of the Nile. Although it rarely rained in the lower stretches of the Two Lands, the seasonal rains far upstream above the Upper Kingdom usually sent the great river high over its banks, bringing both water and rich silt to the narrow but fertile crop lands on either side, and spreading the fecund mixture out broadly over the delta before it emptied into the Great Sea.

But it had been nearly two years since the Nile had spilled its treasure over its banks. The carcasses of cattle dotted the land that had not been plowed for twenty full phases of the moon.

Egypt was dying.

But Joseph's strategy had proved to be life-saving, at least up to now. The people were alive only because they could buy grain from the storehouses he had established. Word that there was grain in Egypt spread all over the then-known world, which was also experiencing drought and famine.

So both the famine and the word about grain in Egypt found their way also to Canaan—even to the house of Jacob and there to Joseph's brothers.

"There is grain in Egypt, Father." It was Reuben, Jacob's first-born, who was counseling old Jacob. The years of drought had seemed to double the normal aging process. Jacob's stringy white hair was as sparse as the grass on the parched hillsides.

Benjamin, the youngest, brightened. "I want to go! May I go? Please Father!"

Jacob's dry lips cracked painfully into a wry smile. "Benjamin, son of my old age, what would I do if you left me to go on such a long journey?" He tousled the youth's ruddy hair affectionately.

"And will not the Lord our God provide us with what we need here?" Jacob asked, turning to Reuben. "Is this not the land of the Promise, not Egypt?"

Reuben dug a toe in the dust outside his father's tent. The last thing he wanted to do just now was to argue about the Promise. Real or imagined it may be—but about the famine there was no question. Still, he would get nowhere arguing about Yah with his father.

"It may well be that Yah is testing us," he said slyly. "Perhaps this is the land of the Promise, but its fruitfulness will come only in His good time. Until then, perhaps we are to find grain wherever grain is to be found."

The circular logic was lost on Jacob, but he knew something must be done. He looked across the clearing at a flock of gaunt and dirty sheep. They lay in the heat, tongues out, panting heavily. A child playing in the meager shade of a bush began to cry. Its belly was already distended from long hunger.

"Egypt, eh? I suppose so." Then, squinting up at Reuben, "Go, then. Take your brothers and buy grain in Egypt." And as young

Benjamin opened his mouth to resume his clamor: "No. You will stay here with your father. It is not a trip for a boy."

Zaphenath-paneah, who is Joseph, sat behind his table in the Ministry of Agriculture as the ten journey-spent pilgrims trailed in to appear before him. The steady stream of buyers from famine-starved lands was increasing daily, it seemed.

"Yes?" he said, not looking up from the papyrus inventory sheets before him. His brown beard, cut square in the manner of Egyptian royalty, was buried in the cup of one hand.

"Canaanites, my lord," said Joseph's steward. "Ten brothers, who say they represent some three-score more in their clan. They would buy grain," he added uselessly.

"Of course," said Joseph. "The whole world would buy grain." He looked up briefly, then down again to scan the sheets to decide which granary to draw from next.

Then a strange, small flame seemed to flicker in his brain. *Canaanites ...brothers...ten of them.* His head snapped up again so abruptly that the two strangers closest to the table started. Slowly, Joseph's eyes took them in, one by one. Surely it could not be...

"Canaan?" he asked. "And you are brothers from the same household?"

The steward, also a native Canaanite, translated Joseph's Egyptian into Hebrew. At the sound of his native tongue, Jacob arose slowly from his stool.

"Yes, my lord," said a spokesman from among the ten. "We are but a small clan—Hebrews, from Beer-sheba and Hebron, in the land of Canaan."

Joseph had to force his mouth closed as he heard his rarely-used tongue spoken in tones that were unmistakably familiar. He placed both hands on the table. Leaning over as far as it would allow, he stared full into the spokesman's face.

"Ask them if their father is still alive," he instructed the steward hoarsely, in Egyptian, not willing to reveal that he knew the strangers' language. Then, swiftly counting the men before him again, he added, "And also another brother—ask them if they have a younger brother."

Through the steward, the spokesman replied: "We do, my lord!

We are twelve—that is eleven—sons, and our youngest brother and our father awaits our return with grain and provisions."

There could be no mistake. This spokesman, Joseph thought—this would be Reuben. Yes—there was no mistaking the scar above the left eye! The very men standing before him and failing to recognize him were the brothers who had sold him into Egypt. The irony of his present position and theirs was overwhelming. For a moment his boyhood dreams of superiority flashed through his mind. Joseph felt faint.

But even more staggering was simply the fact that they were standing there facing each other after being separated by so many years and so many events. Hot tears welled up in Joseph's eyes, and he turned away. How could he handle this impossible situation? Should he simply reveal himself to them? No, that would not do—he was in a position now that would call for them to say anything to appease him, and to make lavish apologies for their crimes against him so many years ago—anything to obtain the grain—and probably, they would think, to save their necks.

Well, let them think the worst, Joseph decided. It would be a good test of whether their character had changed through these intervening years. Restoring his composure, he whirled around to face the visitors.

"You lie!" he hissed.

The steward blanched, and was able to translate the charge only in a stutter.

"My lord?" asked Reuben. He turned to his brothers helplessly, then appealed to the steward. "What is he saying?"

The steward had the same question, but Joseph continued before his meaning could be queried.

"Yes!" he continued, allowing his voice to rise. "You are spies, no doubt sent here by some Canaanite chieftan to see if the famine has weakened Egypt so he can mount an attack."

The translator framed all this carefully, seeing that his master might well have a point.

"But my lord!" Reuben protested. "This is not so. We are the poor sons of our father Jacob. We have no army. We represent no king. Please—."

"Enough!" Joseph roared. "Take them away!" Immediately the guards at the door sprang forward, lances menacing. Roughly they herded Joseph's brothers out of the room and off to the prison—the very prison that had been Joseph's home only a few years earlier.

Three days later, Joseph had decided on a plan. He had his brothers brought before him, and spoke less harshly. "There is a way for me to test the truth of your story," he said.

"Anything," the brothers responded as one man. "Tell him, please," they said to the translator. "We are not spies! And we will do anything to prove it."

"You will bring this supposed youngest brother to me to show that you have not lied," said Joseph evenly. "And one of you— *you*," he said, suddenly recognizing the second eldest brother, Simeon, and pointing to him—"will remain here in custody as surety to guarantee that the rest return."

The ten looked at each other in despair, and nervously discussed the proposition. It was Judah who then spoke:

"My lord, I implore you," he began.

"There will be no imploring," Joseph said crisply, his brothers failing to notice that he did not wait for the translator. "Guard!" he ordered, pointing to Simeon. "Seize this one. And the rest of you—begone! I will sell you your grain, and you will return home to your father, if he in fact exists. And if you want to see this one alive, you will return again with the one you say is your younger brother."

With that, Joseph turned on his heel and stormed from the room. Turning after he rounded the doorway that hid him from his brothers' view, he signalled the steward to follow.

"My lord?"

"Their money," Joseph said. "Secretly return their money to the sack of each man."

"But my lord," the steward protested. "Surely you don't mean to *give* them the grain!"

Joseph drew himself up to his full height and stared down at his subordinate. He needed to say nothing to elicit the reply, "As you say, my lord."

"Welcome to the Two Lands, father of Zaphentah-paneah!" Pharaoh was expansive, glad for the opportunity to reward his favorite minister by urging him to bring his old father and his rediscovered clan out of Canaan to make a new home in Egypt.

It had not been accomplished easily, for Joseph had not been too quick to forgive his brothers' betrayal. It had taken them more than one trip across the burning desert, and more than one ruse in which Joseph exacted mental torture in revenge, before he had shown them who he was, and an uneasy reconciliation had been effected.

"I am honored to be in your presence," Jacob returned.

Joseph beamed with pride. In his mind it was as though he had brought two kings together. His own reunion with old Israel had been so emotional that Joseph had commanded his attendants to leave him alone with his family. Now it was like bringing a priceless heirloom out of its case to display it before the world.

"And how many are the years of your life?" Pharaoh asked Jacob.

"My years are few, compared with those of my father and his father. They are only a hundred and thirty, and have been filled these last years with woe, as I cling to the promise of our God Yah, who has chosen my clan for His special people."

Special people. The truth is that old Jacob's faith in the Promise had wavered when his sons told him that Joseph was alive, and that they must emigrate to Egypt to join him. On the one hand, of course, the joy was almost more than he could endure. "He is alive!" he had said to young Benjamin, who could barely remember Joseph. "I must go and see him before I die!"

On the other hand, Jacob had no idea how the promise that Canaan would belong to him and his seed would be fulfilled if in fact they were in Egypt when he died. But arriving in Egypt, the reception given him by Pharaoh, and finally being reunited with Joseph had put a new spring in his step and a new light in his eyes. Yah could fulfill the Promise when and if and how He wished; Jacob was happy to be reunited with his son Joseph, whether in Egypt or the lands beyond the Great Sea.

"A special people?" Pharaoh had singled out the phrase. He had been intrigued from his first encounter with Joseph by this sense of Yah's special presence. Intrigued, but hardly convinced.

Pharoah looked keenly at Jacob, his royal head turned slightly aside but his piercing eyes drilling themselves into the old man's face, taking in every detail. This, too, was royalty, he decided—desert royalty, on hard times, but kingly nonetheless.

"Chosen, are you? Yes. We also know of the idea. In earlier days in our own land, the pharaohs of the Upper Land conceived themselves to be such. But times have changed now…" His voice trailed off. He had no need to boast of the Hyksos domination of the land, and his own role in it.

"Changed," my lord?" Jacob responded. "Or postponed?"

An unanswerable question, Pharaoh knew. "Whatever," he replied, dismissing the argument with a wave of his hand. "We only know now that it is one thing to agree that the gods—or a god, or *the* God—may have it in their power to choose one man or one people or another. But it is another thing for a particular person to believe that *he* in fact is that choice. I believe you will find that in our land such a notion is considered arrogant."

Joseph was surprised at the king's directness. No matter; his hospitality was genuine.

"I can assure my lord the king that we will not live arrogantly in a land which my lord has been so kind to give us," Joseph said. He had not served in his position this long without learning diplomacy.

"Live in the land, the rich land of Goshen," the king said grandly. "May that land, which has received the gift of the Nile through the centuries, now give to you rich produce in return."

And so it was, my lord Philemon, that Israel descended into Egypt. It was Joseph's firm belief that God had brought them there to spare a remnant of the Chosen People from certain death from the famine in Canaan. In any case, Jacob's last years were spent in peace and plenty instead of in want. And his people grew and made alliances with other immigrants who had fled to Egypt for its grain and other produce, little knowing that their numbers would one day become a threat to the very rulers who welcomed them under the sponsorship of Joseph.

CHAPTER 23

"Your father is ill. He sends for you, my lord." Joseph detected anxiety in the messenger's voice. As he arose from his table the steward added, "He asks that you bring your sons."

It was more serious than he thought. Joseph startled the guards at the door by breaking into a trot. He ran to his nearby quarters to get Mannasseh and Ephraim. They were teenagers now. It was time for the blessing. Joseph had heard the story of Isaac blessing his father Jacob and his uncle Esau. The mere change of geography had not lessened these Semites' strong belief in the formative power of the word of the blessing as a patriarch was about to breathe his last. It was as though their final sighs had the power to project themselves into the ether and remain as a kind of ethereal womb that served to nourished and shape those they blessed throughout their lives.

The boys were impatient. They were awed by the sheer age of their grandfather and were especially reluctant to be in his presence when he was ill. They hung back as Joseph ushered them into his father's well-appointed rooms across the courtyard from Joseph's own home.

Indeed, his father was very ill. He lay motionless on the low bed. For a moment Joseph wondered if he were too late. Then the old man half-opened his heavy-lidded eyes. Seeing Joseph and his sons, however, roused him. He sat up more suddenly than Joseph would have supposed was possible.

"Ah," said Israel, "I am glad you have come, my sons." Brushing strands of wispy white hair to each side of his leathery face, Israel motioned for his visitors to come closer.

"Father," Joseph began, "I was told you are ill."

"I am only ill with age. Bring your sons closer to me. I would give them each a blessing before I go the way of all flesh. I have also called your brothers to me. The time is not long. But there will be no wailing and excessive lamentations, I trust? I am full of years, and have gone wherever Yah has led me. What is it to me to follow Him again into Sheol? But enough of such talk. Come, my sons."

The old man stretched out his arms to Mannaseh and Ephraim. More comfortable now, seeing that their grandfather could sit up, the two lads approached. Careful to observe the protocol of the firstborn at the right hand of the one giving the blessing, Joseph stepped forward and saw to it that Mannaseh approached on Jacob's right and Ephraim on his left.

Old Jacob raised his hands, lifted his head and closed his eyes, in the age-old Eastern posture of the blessing.

"Sons of Joseph, son of Israel," he began. "I thought I would never see my son Joseph again, but now He who blesses all mankind has allowed me even to see his sons." As he spoke, Israel crossed his hands and laid them on the boys' heads, his right hand on Ephraim instead of Mannaseh as Joseph had planned.

"Not so, father," Joseph interrupted. "Mannaseh is the firstborn and receives the right-hand blessing." He gently uncrossed his father's gnarled hands; but the old man's arms were as springs, and returned themselves to their crossed position. Seeing his firmness Joseph's thoughts flashed back to Ephraim's birthing bed, when his wife Asenath had made no secret of favoring him over her firstborn. That scene triggered then the memory of the story he had often heard from his father, how even though second born, he seemed destined to seize the blessing of the firstborn even from birth.

Joseph's brow was furrowed in a sudden moment of anguish. How could human affairs be just, when the ways of God apparently plunged on, divinely heedless of human conventions?

His thoughts were interrupted by old Israel's intonations:

"Blessed be my son Joseph, and these his sons . . . ."

"Mannaseh and Ephraim," Joseph supplied.

"Yes, Mannaseh and Ephraim. In them let the name of Abraham, Isaac, and Israel be perpetuated forever. And let them receive each a half-portion among the sons of Israel."

Embarrassed, the two boys murmured their thanks and backed away. A portion among the sons of Israel? Joseph thought. The fact was that his brothers had no portion to share, being only guests and sojourners in the land. The boys would be much better off as his own heirs. Little matter. The old man must have his say.

Joseph and his sons were taking their leave when his brothers—all eleven of them—rounded the corner of their house on their way into Israel's quarters. They nodded gravely at this brother, who seemed more Egyptian than Hebrew. The tension between them had not totally dissipated despite Joseph's best efforts.

"Stay a moment, Joseph," his father called, seeing his other sons come trooping in. "Gather round, I pray, brothers all."

The moment took on the air of a royal court and the solemnity of a burial rite. Instinctively some of the men dropped to one knee and others to both, in the presence of their dying father. The two boys shrank nervously behind their uncles, to be near the door.

Now Israel rose slowly to his feet. His heart seemed strangely light in view of the solemn atmosphere in the room.

"Assemble, my sons, and hear the word of Yah as it is given through your father Israel concerning things to come." Each brother bowed his head—but not so much that they could not keep an upturned eye on the old man who had been to them a father and a taskmaster and a teacher. Benjamin began to weep softly; others nervously cleared their throats.

"The word of the Lord concerning Reuben, my firstborn," Jacob intoned:

"First-fruits though he be, he was not true to me.
For he went up into his father's bed,
From henceforth, therefore, he shall be wed
To trouble."

Benjamin's sniffles stopped abruptly, and the room grew as silent as a tomb. Reuben looked up at his father, then at his brothers. Indeed he had seduced his father's concubine, Bilhah, shortly after the clan had returned from Paddan-aram; but he had no idea the deed was known.

The old man resumed his sing-song blessing—which by now began to sound like a curse to his assembled sons.

> *"Simeon and Levi, two of them,*
> *Preserve me from their wrath,*
> *For they have slain a thousand men,*
> *And hamstrung oxen in their path."*

The two brothers looked at each other, recalling how they had led the ruthless raid against Shechem in the avenging of the rape of their sister Dinah.

"Judah," Israel contined, causing Leah's fourth son to look up abruptly. What bit of doggerel would his father hurl at him? he wondered.

> *"Judah is a lion's whelp,*
> *Whose ruling staff shall not depart*
> *From him and those whom he will help*
> *To bring in him within whose heart*
> *Yah does dwell."*

Whatever this might mean was completely beyond both Judah and his brothers, but he was relieved at its tone when compared with the previous spiels issuing from Jacob.

> *"And as for Zebulon, Leah's son,*
> *No wasteland his; instead, he comes*
> *To settle at the sea's fair shore,*
> *And dwell at Canaan's northern door."*

By now the men's joints were aching and their knees called for relief from kneeling on the hard stone floor. One by one they shifted positions. Then Reuben, still stung by his father's disclosure of his escapade with Bilhah, arose and abruptly left. As if given permission, Levi, Simeon, Judah and Zebulon all walked out quietly as well. The others stayed, whether out of courtesy for their father or curiosity as to what he would predict for them.

Israel went on, his breath laboring now.

"Issachar's a stalwart ass,
Who wastes his strength in idle sloth,
He settles in a place of grass,
But to another pledges troth."

"Hmph!" Issachar grunted aloud. Never one to seek work, he nonetheless resented the implication that he, an heir to this highly-touted Promise, would become a slave to another. He followed his brothers out of the room and away from the strange ceremony.

"A serpent there beside the road
Is Dan, whose sly ways are a goad
To all who go up toward the north,
By foot or camel or by horse."

Shaking his head, Dan arose and left. He recalled having a hopeful eye on the land to the north, a place at the foot of Mt. Hermon, while the clan was living at Shechem. But was anyone able to make sense of this doddering old man's strangely veiled prophecies?

Jacob's son Gad was next.

"Gad, the raider, by the Jabbok,
Shall raided be, by hound and havoc.
And only by his warlike ways
Will ever win his brothers' praise.
"And Asher, growing fruits so rare,
Will on the coastlands find his place
And by travels wide and fair
Will perpetuate his race."

Looking at each other and shrugging, Gad and Asher left together. The old man went on:

"Upon the mountains, Naphtali,
In the northland hills to fly
Like a fleet and lovely doe
Will bear fawns whose feet shall go
Nowhere."

Naphtali managed a wry smile, and left the room leaving only Joseph and his sons, and the youngest, Benjamin. Joseph was more comfortable now that all his brothers but Benjamin were gone. He waited.

"Joseph, who was set apart,
Whose branches spread to Egypt's heart.
Blessings of the sea so deep,
Blessings of the breast so sweet,
Are Joseph's evermore."

Smiling almost grimly, Joseph arose. His sons were anxious to leave, but he motioned them still while he waited for his younger brother Benjamin. Since he had become Jacob's favorite after Joseph disappeared, the pronouncement the old man sent his way would be especially sweet, Joseph suspected. He was therefore surprised to hear:

"In the morning devour the prey,
In the evening divide the spoil,
Benjamin shall have his day,
In the midlands soil,
A wolf!"

Both Benjamin and Joseph looked up startled. It was a saying that seemed out of character with Benjamin's gentle spirit. But it was not a time to discuss the details of prophecy. From his own experience years ago, when Yah spoke to him about the dreams, Joseph knew that when the words came, one simply gave them. They were not arguable.

The long session had exhausted old Israel. With the last word about Benjamin he slumped back on his bed. Joseph and Benjamin went to him, straightened his legs, and covered him with a light linen spread. As they turned to leave, the old man spoke weakly.

"My sons."

"Yes, father." Joseph and Benjamin were solicitous despite the questions raised by the old man's prophetic blessings or curses.

"It is time." Jacob's breath was rasping now. "Listen to me carefully. I would instruct you about my burial."

"Father, please—," Joseph objected.

"No—I must say this. I am ready to be gathered to my people. And it is with my people that I would have you lay my bones to rest. Promise me that you will take them back to the land the Lord our God has promised us. In that way I shall inherit it by claiming it as my resting place."

The two brothers looked at each other solemnly. Alive or dead, their father would never cease claiming the inheritance, the Promise.

"Bury me in the field of Ephron the Hittite, in the cave I purchased from him. For it is there that my people lie—not in this land."

Again Joseph and Benjamin exchanged glances. They knew well the story of the field of Ephron; and it was not Jacob, but his grandfather Abraham who had bought it. Suddenly they realized as never before the oneness their father felt with his ancestors. By now he had so identified himself with Abraham that they were as one; since Jacob was, as it were, in the loins of Abraham when the transaction was made, it was as though Jacob had bought the field himself.

The dying man went on. "It was at Machpelah that they buried father Abraham and his wife Sarah." Joseph was relieved that his father could at least distinguish his separateness to some extent. "And there we buried my father Isaac," Jacob went on, "and my mother Rebekah, and there I buried Leah. And it is there—."

The old man's voice broke and his shoulders heaved with a wracking cough.

"Run, Mannaseh!" Joseph commanded. "Bring the priest of Pharaoh." Benjamin looked at him wonderingly. "Not for the priesting," Joseph explained, "Here, our priests are also physicians."

But when he looked back at his father, Joseph knew that it was too late for either priest or physician.

His father Jacob was dead.

A band of Canaanite marauders drew up sharply when they saw the Egyptians in procession near the Jordan. They were accustomed to seeing Pharaoh's troops on expeditions this far north of Egypt, but this was hardly a military procession. Chariots draped in rich black brocade were accompanied by a wagon bearing an Egyptian-style sarcophagus. After the forty-day embalming period, Joseph had led a party of servants and attendants, with several guards, on this solemn pilgrimage. A group of mourners threw dust in the air and upon themselves as they made their way toward the field of Ephron the Hittite, and the Cave of Machpelah.

The band of opportunists retreated. There would be no booty in this company worth risking the retaliation of Egypt in return for desecrating the dead. And dead bodies they could have aplenty; they did not need this one.

Back in Egypt, Reuben called his brothers into council. "We must be careful now," he said. "With our father dead, who knows what this our Egyptian brother will do? He has not forgotten what you did to him when—."

"Better, what we did for him," said Simeon, still reluctant to face fully the heinousness of having sold his brother into slavery. "Look at the man's position here—he has hardly suffered."

"No," said Judah. "Reuben is right. With the power our brother enjoys here, he could easily have us put to death."

"Let us speak to him," offered Dan. "Better to deal with this directly than to wonder how he stands."

"Dan is right," Reuben agreed, and the others nodded their assent.

Seven days after returning from burying their father, the brothers arranged to meet Joseph. He was again at his table in the Ministry of Agriculture. As they trooped in, all were reminded of the day, so long ago, they had stood before Joseph without recognizing him, asking for grain.

"I am glad you came," said Joseph, coming around from behind the table to greet them.

"My lord," began Reuben, again the spokesman, "we—."

"Not 'my lord,'" Joseph interrupted. "Please—are we not brothers?"

The eleven brothers looked at each other with some relief. This might go better than they could have hoped.

"Very well," Reuben said. "It is good that we can discuss this as brothers. The fact is, our father Jacob asked of us a brotherly thing before he died."

"Yes?" Joseph responded, somewhat surprised, for he had been with Jacob more than anyone in the days immediately preceding his death.

"Yes," Judah said. "He asked that all of us live in peace after his death—especially that you, brother Joseph—that is, if you would..." His voice trailed off as he lost the words.

"He asked that you forgive us," Reuben blurted out—"that you look upon us with mercy and pardon us of the crime we committed against you so many years ago."

Joseph looked intently into his brothers' eyes. They had been so devious so often. Could he believe them now? Would not his father have approached him directly with such a request?

But as Joseph looked from brother to brother, the need to know their hearts, and whether old Israel had actually made such a request, seemed to fade. He leaned against his table, relaxing in the awareness that at last he and his brothers were standing together as a family in the same room. With their father dead, they had become Israel. They were not only brothers, but children of the Promise. Indeed, as Jacob had been one with Abraham, they were now Israel.

"Am I in the place of God?" he finally asked. "Is it mine to avenge myself, or to pursue you as the guilty? Look at what Yah has done with us, and for us! Whatever harm you had in mind when you set upon me, Yah has transformed it into good!"

His brothers looked at each other in amazement and relief. At first they felt guilty for concocting the story of old Jacob's deathbed request. Then, as Joseph's tone of acceptance and forgiveness permeated the room, they grew more relaxed, too.

"We would be your slaves," Reuben said, a new note of sincerity in his voice.

"I would be your brother, not your master," Joseph replied. In a spontaneous surge, the brothers surrounded him, pressing his shoulders, kissing him on both cheeks.

"We are sons of the Promise," Joseph said, voicing some of the thoughts that had just coursed through his mind. "Perhaps this is what it means to be elect—to extend to each other grace, just as we have been graced."

A rush of emotion interrupted. The Egyptian stewards left the room, neither understanding nor approving of the family of strong men huddling together anointing each other with tears.

Here ends, my lord, the story of Jacob, whom God loved, chosen with his sons to embody the grace with which they were chosen. Mysteriously, the story ends in Egypt, not in the land of the Promise—and my lord knows that after Joseph himself was gathered to his people, a pharaoh arose who knew him not, and that God's people grew mightily in number but were enslaved in Egypt for four hundred years before being led by our God's mighty arm through the Sea of Reeds and the wilderness, and back to Canaan.

Yet, we know even better that the story really has no end, but will continue to be told in the eternally recurring events in the lives of the elect. For while the Hebrews view the passing of the years as though they were in a line of succession, my own heritage can view it also as a sphere, or like the rings on a tree. We serve Him who sees the end from the beginning, and who chooses what we cannot see from the vantage point of His position above all the books of days and years that men devise.

So in the end I must confess that it is in serving, rather than understanding, that I am enabled to believe both the story I have recounted and the others that were to arise from the sons of Israel, as they followed the God who would say, "Out of Egypt have I called my Son."